The killing never stops!

The Russian pilot looked around wildly, fearful he had been duped.

Then he saw it—rearing up against the clifftops. The game was over. It was time for the kill.

The Soviet ace watched that horrible silhouette swing into his sights. He had flown in her, sweated in her and exulted in her power and agility. He had put that helicopter through her paces. The Dragonfire was his ship.

The only thing Strakhov had never done was attack her. Now he was going to blast her out of the sky.

As he reached for the button, the last thing Strakhov saw was a blazing stream of liquid fire streaking toward him . . . .

MACK BOLAN

The Executioner

MACK BOLAN

TERMINAL VELOCITY

A GOLD EAGLE BOOK FROM

W🌐RLDWIDE

TORONTO · NEW YORK · LONDON · PARIS
AMSTERDAM · STOCKHOLM · HAMBURG
ATHENS · MILAN · TOKYO · SYDNEY

First edition April 1984

ISBN 0-373-61402-0

Special thanks and acknowledgment to
Alan Bomack for his contributions to this work.

Printed in Canada

"No, the Cold War is not over.
But let us henceforth call it
the Third World War, for that
is what it really is."
                                    —Brian Crozier
                                    Strategy for Survival

"Don't tell me that I can't. I can,
and I will, because I must.
For every action there is a reaction,
for every evil a good, for every weakness
a strength—and for every injustice
there is somewhere a final justice."
                                    —*Mack Bolan*

AFTERMATH

"They'll pay for it.... I'm going to get every-one responsible." Bolan forced out the words as he stroked April Rose's hair.

Hal Brognola stepped forward. His square beefy hands fluttered open in a gesture of com-passion. Bolan rocked on his knees, the body of April Rose still supported in the crook of his arm. "Everyone, Hal! I'm going to get them all."

The two medics stood there uncertainly, then there was a soft rustle as they straightened out the plastic body bag. The dry rasp of the nylon zipper dragged across Bolan's raw nerves like a distant burst of machine-gun fire.

His mind was clouded with bitter, roiling smoke, his vision red with flames.

This war never ended.

The battle raged on.

His ears pounded with a rushing, roaring sound as strong as a gunship's rotorwash.

From somewhere behind him came an an-guished bellow of pain. Bolan did not turn—for him the sound came out of the past. He did not see the second medic team lifting the wounded Aaron Kurtzman onto a stretcher. Bolan just heard that universal cry of agony and felt its echo within his own heart.

He would never forget the screams. The sounds were etched in his soul.

Mack Bolan.

Sergeant Mercy.

The Executioner.

Colonel John Phoenix.

The same man. . . fighting the same ceaseless war.

Or was he? Could he ever be the same again?

So many good people had been lost. Their faces haunted him still. Familiar features drifted in that crimson haze, forever beyond his reach: the family he loved; the comrades he fought with; and April Rose, the woman who had meant so much. Her face hovered before him now. Those smiling, loving eyes. An image to be fixed imperishably in his mind's eye.

He must hold fast to that living memory. But already it seemed she was encircled by a garland of flames. Brazen leaves of fire. Bolan reached out as if to brush them away. If only he could reach far enough and touch once more, he'd hold her safe forever.

Their fingertips brushed lightly. And then he clasped her hand.

Her pale, cold hand.

One of the medics tried as gently as possible to disengage his grip.

"Don't...you...touch...her!" Bolan grated between tightly clenched teeth. Eyes still closed, he lifted his head. "I'll kill you. I'll kill you all!"

"Steady, Striker, steady!" said Brognola, his brow furrowed in compassion. He touched the big man's shoulder, nodding to the two stretcher bearers to back off for a moment.

Bolan's lips brushed across April Rose's forehead as he eased the ring from her finger. The ring he had given her.

He turned the ring over between his fingers, as if mesmerized by the myriad twinkling reflections in the fiery stone.

Stony Man...the Phoenix program...it had all turned to ashes in his mouth.

It could never be the same. What a hollow victory they had won here this night.

April Rose had been his right arm. The loss was immeasurable.

Mercy was a name he'd earned. Sergeant Mercy they had called him. But that was in another land, another hellground, another story...almost another man. This time there would be no mercy. No more than he had shown the Vietcong. No more than he had ever shown the Mafia. Bolan would grant no quarter. His lips moved in a silent vow: they are going to pay dearly for this! Whoever is responsible, wherever in the world they hide, I will track them down. . . .

Brognola watched him for a moment longer, then signaled for the medics to proceed. Wearily he turned and walked toward Dr. Ogilvy.

"Looks bad, Hal."

"Hmm?" Brognola said absently, still keeping half an eye on Bolan.

"That man, Aaron Kurtzman. It doesn't look too good for him," said the doctor. "There's a bullet lodged close to the spinal column. It's going to be a tricky operation. With no guarantee he'll ever be able to walk again."

"The Bear, paralyzed?"

"It's a definite possibility," replied the physician, nodding.

Elliot Ogilvy's reputation was well-known: he had once saved the President's life, but he couldn't work miracles. Brognola stared bleakly at the carnage on the Stony Man grounds as Dr. Ogilvy assured him, "We'll do everything possible for Kurtzman. I just felt I should warn you. How about the colonel over there? I have a sedative that . . . ."

Brognola shook his head stiffly. "No, he won't take it."

"Then get him out of here. Away from this mess."

The head Fed stuck a cigar in the corner of his mouth and chomped on it hard. Sure, he could find some excuse to move Mack away, find him someplace to rest up. But he could do nothing about the memories of what had happened here—they would scar Mack's soul forever.

THE MEDICS HAD TAKEN AWAY April's body. Following Dr. Ogilvy's advice, Brognola had gently coaxed Bolan away from the scene of death on the estate's rainy grounds for the dry warmth of the Stony Man War Room.

The red phone rang. Brognola picked it up.

The outside world knew nothing of the terrible battle fought in this isolated arena of the Blue Ridge Mountains. Even as the Stony warriors were touched by the cold shadow of death and destruction, life in the everyday world went on as usual. Brognola stood straighter, taller, when he heard the familiar voice.

"Yes, sir . . . uh-huh . . . immediately? I understand." He took the cigar out of his mouth and threw it away. "Yes, sir, I shall ask him. I know that, sir. Thank you."

Brognola carefully replaced the receiver.

Mack Bolan looked up as Brognola approached him.

"Mack, you're needed. . . ."

PART ONE

A HAWK FOR THE KILLING

1

Tiny dust devils whirled in the shimmering haze over the distant dunes that ringed Fullerton Air Force Base.

Bolan stared, unseeing, at the horizon between the hangars as the driver showed the necessary passes to the sentry at the main gate. But the Stony warrior was not lost to grief.

His whole being had been shattered into fragments by the terrible price of April Rose's sacrifice. But each distinct facet of the man was functioning methodically, now fueled by a white-hot anger as great as the rage he had felt in Pittsfield a lifetime ago.

Once again the nearest and dearest to him had been snatched away. Bolan felt an eerie glow. A total connection with the man he once was, and would have to be again. It was a tremor in the spine. A physical manifestation of the psychic force behind his vow: *I will track down every last person in the conspiracy against Stony Man—for they must face their Executioner.*

He would make it simple once more.

Identification.

Location.

Confirmation.

Destruction!

Lurking behind that uniform he wore, behind that plastic lapel badge that identified him as Colonel John Phoenix, was another man. A man who had stalked the city jungles to annihilate the predatory packs of the Mob. A man whose own personal motivation had been transformed into a crusade for justice.

A killing machine, some thought him, but with a living heart. And now, regardless of orders, the Executioner was ready to walk the night streets and concrete clearings once more.

Even now, behind that blank stare, every sense was alert.

His guard was up. The hellfire rained on Stony Man Farm was intended to take out one target: Phoenix. And the men who organized the attempt on his life would not give up until they could deliver his head to whoever was paying the price.

All of his being was on red alert. The sensory perception, the memories of what had gone before, the will to do what must be done—they were fused together by the hot breath of anger.

"Looks like there's a gentleman here to meet you, sir," said the driver, as he pulled up short of the main entrance to the administrative complex.

David McCarter was standing by the curb. He wore a denim shirt with epaulets and a pair of crisp bush pants. The Englishman was not in uniform, yet he managed to preserve a casual military air carried as much in his bearing as in his choice of attire.

"Hello, Mack." McCarter offered his hand as soon as Bolan had climbed out of the car. "I'm broke up about what happened."

"Don't break," Bolan grunted. "Is everything ready?"

"I got here a couple of hours ago," said McCarter, gesturing for the American to take the glass door to their right.

The tough, cocky Briton was a professional fighting man through and through. He lived hard, loved hard and fought hard. Once an officer with the elite Special Air Service, he was now a key member of Mack Bolan's Phoenix Force. He had waged war alongside the colonel in the Congo, but never had he seen Bolan in so dark and brittle a temper.

He felt it was taking all of the other man's effort to contain the simmering rage beneath that exterior of icy calm. As Bolan brushed past him through the doorway, McCarter could sense a kind of heat radiating from the tense muscular frame of The Executioner, as if the blood boiling in his veins was lava waiting to vent.

Mack Bolan was a human volcano. And McCarter wasn't sure he wanted to be there when it exploded.

"This way, sirs," said a sergeant, who hovered nearby. His manner was as sharply creased as his knife-edged pants. "Hurford, take the colonel's bag to his quarters."

They were escorted by a small patrol to a conference room adjoining the base command center. Four men waited for them.

All signs of rigid military protocol departed with the guard detail.

"Colonel Phoenix, Mr. McCarter, I'm Dan Ford." He left a thin, dark cheroot smoldering in the ashtray as he rose to greet them. Bolan noted he carried enough gold braid to make him a major general, but he couldn't tell if Ford was stationed at Fullerton or if, like them, he had flown in for this training phase of the mission.

"I'd like you to meet Glen Knopfler," Ford said, indicating the expensively tailored civilian seated at his left. "Glen is an intelligence analyst and a presidential adviser on, uh, such delicate matters as this."

"Good to meet you at last, Colonel," Knopfler said.

"And this is Andrew Webb, who has just transferred over to the ISA."

Bolan stiffened at the mention of the rival agency. He had not forgotten how they slowed him down when he was tracking the KGB assassin, Fyodor Zossimov.

Ford sensed trouble and wished to avert it. He qualified Webb's attendance. "It was the ISA boys who got hold of the footage you're about to see." He jabbed a button on the console in front of him and a portion of the wall slid apart to reveal a projection screen.

"Mr. McCarter, I'd like you to meet a countryman of yours. This is Geoffrey Miles." Ford waved his hand to indicate the balding pipe smoker seated next to Knopfler. "Mr. Miles works for a well-known aviation almanac. He's here to provide us with a narration. And he's been a big help to the technicians in Hangar G."

"Should be ready for you two sometime tomorrow," Miles said, smiling at the major general's compliments.

"We got this reel of film from a contact in a laboratory in West Germany," explained Webb. "It was being developed for a free-lance filmmaker who had smuggled himself into Afghanistan as a peasant."

"It's our first look at the Russians' latest war machine in action." Ford pressed the intercom switch. "Roll it as soon as you're ready, Jim."

Along the far wall the array of television screens displaying data, graphics and straight visuals shut down or flipped to silent test patterns. The illumination of the back-lit map of the world faded away. A squiggled string of writing and numerals flickered on the large screen in front of them.

The darkened room was momentarily dazzled by the bleached-out image of the noonday sun arched high above the hard-baked rocks of the Afghanistan wilderness. The camera tilted downward to show a panoramic view of a wild and desolate valley.

The rock-strewn slopes on either side rose sharply into steep bare cliffs. A single track wound through the cleft, following the edge of a dry watercourse. The only sign of life was a solitary eagle floating high on the thermals generated within the oppressive heat of the canyon.

"This view is looking down the length of the Khazani Valley to the Devil's Gateway," said the aviation expert. "The *mujahedeen* are located behind that ridge on the left of the screen. Now, watch, at the far end. See, the first Russian vehicle is coming through the gap."

For an instant, Bolan thought of the *mujahedeen*—the beleaguered Afghan warriors who believed they had a divine dispensation to resist Soviet efforts to annex their ancient land.

Then Bolan's eyes refocussed on the screen as the first armored car came through, kicking up a trail of dust from the beaten earth roadway. As the vehicle disappeared behind a squat column of rock around which the road detoured, a troop carrier sped through the constricted opening.

The towering valley walls could not have been much more than eighty feet apart. The Russian convoy was squeezing through at a fast pace, fearful of an ambush.

"This is an ammunition convoy traveling west, probably to the garrison that mans the new Soviet airstrip outside Sharuf."

Having reached a less claustrophobic stretch of highway where the valley floor widened, the lead vehicle slowed, giving the other drivers the chance to take up station again at their proper distances.

That was when the first rocket was fired.

The armor-piercing projectile punctured the BRDM-2 command car. The scout vehicle slewed down the graveled embankment, exposing the next troop carrier. Most of the soldiers had leaped clear before the second missile struck home.

Plumes of smoke streaked from the rocks as a fusillade was fired from the guerrillas' position overlooking the hapless Russians and Afghan militia below.

"Two rockets, gentlemen. That's all these freedom fighters have to stop a Russian convoy. Now they must rely on their rifles. Lee-Enfields, mostly. World War I vintage." Miles shook his head wearily as he recited the sorry details.

The camera zoomed in to catch sight of a Soviet trooper scrambling for better cover. He didn't make it. A *mujahedeen* marksman hit him between the shoulders and sent him sprawling in the rust-colored grit. Then the filmmaker panned across for a medium close-up of a radio operator shouting frantically into his microphone.

"He's calling for help." The screen went blank for a moment. "Schroder reloaded his camera at this point, then started filming again. As you can see, the situation doesn't seem to have changed a great deal."

Another truck was smoldering in the background; perhaps a lucky shot from one of the ancient rifles had set off some of the ammunition. Suddenly the whole picture blurred as the camera swung up to the right. The German filmmaker must have reacted instantly on first hearing the sound of the helicopter's approach.

It came soaring over the contours of the surrounding mountainside like some prehistoric flying reptile. The side-painted red star stood out against the olive and sand markings. The pilot was good, Bolan silently conceded, to hug that close to the cliff face. The camera followed as the machine rushed headlong down the valley, its rocket pods belching three waves of air-to-ground missiles.

They straddled the *mujahedeen* position.

Geysers of dirt, rock and roiling fireballs erupted in eerie silence, obscuring the left side of the picture in a dusty pall.

"We estimate the speed of its attack run at well over two hundred miles per hour!"

"That's even faster than a Hind!" exclaimed McCarter.

"This machine can outperform anything the Soviets have ever built before." Miles sucked on his pipe before he added, "Or anything that we've got on our side for that matter. The Russians have taken all the best features of Western-built choppers to come up with this one."

Bolan's eyes were riveted to the screen. For a moment the camouflage-painted gunship hovered in midair like some loathsome slug as the pilot inspected his handiwork. Then it twisted away in a sharp climbing turn.

It appeared surprisingly maneuverable within the dangerous confines of the Khazani Valley. It was coming back on the reciprocal of its approach course. This time the camera panned smoothly with it.

The film shuddered into slow motion, then froze. And the central portion of the image was zoomed up into greater enlargement. When it stopped, a grainy portrait of the new Russian helicopter filled the screen.

"That's better than any of the satellite shots

we got when they were trying out the test model in the Urals," confessed Webb.

"It's designated the M-36 PD. *Plamya Drakona*. We call it the Dragonfire," Miles told them. "I'll give you all the technical specifications—at least, as far as we can deduce them—when we work in the cockpit simulator. To put it simply, the Dragonfire can outmaneuver, outdistance, outshoot and outperform any other helicopter in the world."

"But the main thing we've discovered," added Knopfler, "is that the M-36 is equipped with the new Nevski missile-deflection system."

"What exactly is that?" asked McCarter.

"That's what we've got to find out. And fast," replied the intelligence analyst. "Today this machine is being combat tested in the Afghan mountains. Once in production, it could alter the whole balance of power along the European front.

"Your job, gentlemen, is to get inside Afghanistan and steal that Russian chopper."

2

"Is this guy for real?" whispered McCarter, affecting an American nasality. No one had warned them about Captain Hillaby, other than that he was sharp, tough and very competent at his job.

Frank Hillaby had never been to Vietnam. It was over before he graduated. But he remained more acutely aware of missing out on the real action than any of his colleagues. And now he proved his dedication to the service by a rigid adherence to the rules. He played everything by the book. Even if it didn't fit.

"'Fraid so," said Bolan, as Hillaby strutted toward them. They resigned themselves to humoring this gung-ho youngster. There was no time for personality conflicts.

Hillaby, in helmet and flak jacket, packed a survival kit and a personal firearm holstered low on his hip. The early-afternoon sun was making him sweat under that padded vest, but he was looking forward to having a retired colonel and a Briton under his command. This pleasurable anticipation began to falter when he got his first look at them.

They had been instructed not to shave, in preparation for their cover. The Englishman's mustache was already spreading out into a growth of thick stubble, and Bolan's chin was darkly shadowed. It was an affront to Hillaby's sense of military crispness.

He eyed the two men warily, turning his introduction into an informal preflight inspection. Bolan let him play at this pointless ritual. They were going to be cooped up with him in a cramped cockpit for several uncomfortable hours to come.

"Follow me, gentlemen. And we'll see how much you remember," said Hillaby, disguising his instinctive dislike for the two cowboys. "We'll also find out how much you've got to learn."

A jeep ferried them out to the chopper pad on the far side of the field. They rode in silence.

The whole mission was structured on a strictly need-to-know basis. Hillaby was not aware that his two charges had spent all morning in a mock-up of the Dragonfire's cockpit that had been hastily constructed, using the shell of a Hughes AH-64, inside Hangar G.

Geoffrey Miles had drilled them in the use of everything—from the all-weather sensors to the missile pods, from the laser trackers to use of the integrated sighting helmets. Bolan and McCarter had twice swapped places as pilot and weapons' operator, although it was believed the M-36's controls were fully interchangeable.

All the switches and instruments had been marked in Russian, and Bolan was thankful for the immersion course he had taken in San Diego the previous fall. McCarter had caught on almost as quickly; he had a natural aptitude for anything that flew.

Hillaby pulled up fifty yards from a painted circle. Standing at its center was an olive-drab machine, with the graffiti Death Coming Down! only partially scoured from its blunt nose. It was a standard-issue Huey—Nam style.

"A Hog?" McCarter sounded dismayed.

"What did you expect? Do you think they'd risk your wrecking a brand-new aircraft on a training course?"

"A refresher course," Bolan corrected him sharply.

"Yes, well, I expect they figured this was what you'd be most familiar with."

"Yeah," said Bolan. "Been for a few rides in this one."

Hillaby kept a close watch on their every movement in the cockpit.

"You should leave the mixture on full-rich for a second longer," he instructed, trying to find some fault with their start-up procedure.

Bolan purposely exaggerated his look at the instrument panel as he flipped the fuel boost to On and checked the oil pressure.

He increased the collective and corrected right as the chopper became light on the skids. They rose smoothly to hover. Bolan adjusted the throttle and moved forward on a straight take-off path.

Hillaby was torn between being rattled by these two hard-eyed strangers and a reluctant respect for the skill with which they handled the machine.

Bolan flew a wide sweep over the desert basin practicing running approaches, autorotation and quick stops. Hillaby had some comment to make each time, whether it was fully justified or not. McCarter began to fiddle with the radio to keep his own temper in check.

The fuel gauge was dipping low. Bolan tapped the glass. Hillaby checked his watch and signaled they should return to base.

Bolan began to turn left around a huge broken butte. At one end of the flat-topped monolith stood a separate spire about eighty feet out from the main block. He aimed the Hog straight for the gap.

It was Hillaby's startled gasp that made McCarter look up from the radio set. The dappled cliff face loomed large through the windscreen.

Bolan's lips were compressed in concentration as he touched the left pedal, lined up with the narrow notch and roared through. The racket of the engine bounced off the rock wall and redoubled the reverberations in the cockpit. They had little more than fifteen feet of clearance on either side of the rotor sweep.

"You—you're...." Hillaby clenched his teeth and his knuckles and his guts as the Hog bounced on an updraft then settled on course for the base. "That was a crazy stunt to pull, Colonel!"

Bolan glanced across with a completely straight face. Behind the instructor's shoulder McCarter gave Mack a broad wink.

"I THINK YOU'LL PASS at a distance," said Webb, as he went over the cover plan for the fourth time. Bolan and McCarter now sported disheveled growths of beard.

A conference call was arranged with a CBS cameraman who had been on an undercover assignment in the war zone. A costume designer from a Hollywood studio was flown in to put together two outfits, from woolen caps and long vests to rough-woven cotton pants, all carefully presoiled. All Bolan and McCarter were waiting for was contact to be established with the right guide to take them over the Pakistan border. They would be posing as a film unit for the television newsmagazine *The World This Week*.

Webb and Knopfler double-teamed for intensive briefings on the current situation in Afghanistan. Parallels were drawn with America's involvement in Southeast Asia, but several careful distinctions were made, too. Bolan had to admit the ISA man knew his material. Webb was as thorough as Knopfler was perceptive.

"The Soviets cannot force a decisive military resolution," explained the presidential adviser, "so the main thrust of their strategy now is to make war on the civilian population. It's a policy of indiscriminate destruction, making it impossible for ordinary villagers to live out their lives as they have always done."

"Population estimates were around the fifteen million mark prior to the Soviet invasion," said Webb. "So far hundreds of thousands of Afghans have been killed and three and a half million have been forced to flee to refugee camps in Pakistan and Iran, anywhere that will have them."

"The Dragonfire has been developed specifically as a terror weapon for this strategy." Knopfler checked his watch. "Geoff Miles will be waiting for you in Hangar G. He wants to go over the refueling procedure. And when you're finished there, these briefing books will be in your quarters. Study them thoroughly. They'll give you background on Tarik Khan. He's the man you'll have to contact. He's the guerrilla leader who might help you break into the Sharuf air base.''

"TARGET PRACTICE, GENTLEMEN! The range we'll be using is thirty miles due west.'' Hillaby tried to sound sprightly. He knew this would be the last training run, but he was tired after a night-flying exercise in the Cobra. Colonel Phoenix and his English comrade should have felt equally exhausted, but if they were, it didn't show. ''Okay, let's go!''

The Hog carried four fixed 7.62mm machine guns, with two more on flex mounts in the doorways, pods filled with 2.75 HVAR rockets and the deadly M-5 that could spit out a stream of 40mm grenades.

Bolan shook off the weight of lethargy as the chopper rose from the concrete pad. The hours of briefing, map and aerial photograph inspection, cover preparation and flying with Hillaby had left the midnight warrior with little time for conscious brooding.

And yet below that threshold of instinct and reaction, beneath tactical decisions and strategic considerations, a deeper part of him was still formulating the most effective response to the terrible events in Virginia.

Hedgehopping across the dusty scrub Bolan

appeared preoccupied with the controls, but foremost in his thoughts was what had happened at Stony Man Farm.

"Use that highway down there as a reference line and make an S-turn," ordered Hillaby. "Gain more altitude and correct for wind drift, Colonel."

The instructor still wanted to get in a few last licks at his unorthodox trainees. McCarter turned his attention to the radio: terse instructions from the Fullerton control tower were followed by more traffic from the civilian airfield at the south end of the city limits.

"Okay, Tango Delta One-Niner...clear for takeoff...."

McCarter flipped through the channels. Hillaby looked annoyed that their foreign visitor was not giving him his undivided attention.

"Oh, geez...two officers down...Christ, it's a mess! They got everyone...." The voice of the cop on the police channel was tinged with panic. "The guys in the armored car are all dead...yeah, a bright red Charger...three men, they're heading west...."

"We're nearly at the range," snapped Hillaby.

"There's a robbery in progress," McCarter replied evenly.

"Switch that back to the proper channel! And, Colonel, you turn fifteen degrees west and watch for the markers."

Bolan ignored the captain. "Did he just say a red Charger? Looks like that's the car down there!" Three hundred feet below them Bolan saw a Dodge careering down the black ribbon of asphalt. The driver was in the left lane, overtaking a U-Haul trailer and two riders on motorbikes. Bolan estimated its speed at well over a hundred miles per hour.

"Geez, I can't believe it...they just blew the sucker apart...yeah, everyone's dead...." The youthful-sounding voice choked back a sob. Bolan wondered how long he would last on the job.

"They're turning off," McCarter called out from the doorway.

The car cornered at high speed, spewing out a curling wave of sand before the driver fishtailed onto the secondary dirt road. The chopper had already overshot their position.

"They must be making for the old Consolidated Mining airstrip," guessed Hillaby, as absorbed in the chase now as the other two.

Bolan banked steeply in a tight turn. "Let's go down and take a look," he said with cold determination.

He reduced the collective pitch, increased pressure on the right rudder pedal and adjusted the throttle. The Hog came skimming down low alongside the getaway car.

"I count three men inside," McCarter called from the open doorway.

The guy crouching in the rear seat rolled down the window and whipped off three shots. One of the bullets clanged off the skid. Hillaby looked ashen as Bolan rose even more sharply than he'd descended.

From their increased altitude they could see the mining company's abandoned airfield about six miles dead ahead. Hillaby peered through his field glasses. There was a Lear jet standing at the end of the badly cracked runway. This was crime with all the corporate trimmings.

"We've got to radio this in," shouted Hillaby.

"We've got to do something about it ourselves or let them get away," said McCarter, moving back behind the flex-mounted machine gun. He had no doubt of the colonel's decision.

The Lear jet pilot was standing beside the open door of his aircraft waving frantically at the billowing dust plume of the approaching car.

Bolan saw red.

He swooped in over the paddies again, streaking toward the hoochline.

"Let's do it!" he snapped. "Now!"

The loaded Hog was a powder keg and Bolan's anger the spark.

McCarter swung the muzzle back to hose the road. The close confines of the chopper cabin were rocked with the concussive crescendo of gunfire. Bolan lined up the small jet in the illuminated target sight and unleashed two of the HVARs. Tongues of brilliant orange-yellow flame flashed from the rocket pods.

The pilot ran for his life as the first missile plunged straight through the open hatch and exploded inside the jet. The fuselage ruptured with the roaring blast.

Bolan swung round for a second pass. The pilot was now racing for the scant cover provided by a nearby clump of mesquite. The searing hail of machine-gun fire made the desert sand jump in a pattern of endless eruptions. Bolan ejected a string of grenades: desert scrub, dirt and the man disappeared in a whirling cloud of grit and gore.

The car was approaching the last rise in the road before the airfield. As the Charger leaped over the bump, Bolan unleashed another wave of rockets.

The punk in the passenger seat was the only one to leap clear before the 2.75 HVAR projectile vanished through the grille and the car became a raging fireball. But the guy who escaped had only bought himself seconds to live. McCarter's machine gun spat out a stream of death.... The last crook was instantly shredded into a crowd.

Bolan circled over the scene. The smoldering wreckage of the car lay scattered on the sandy track. The plane lay broken-backed and still smoking. Some bloody rags dangled from the upper branches of a mesquite bush.

"My God!" Hillaby muttered, shaking his head. He looked pasty white.

"Don't worry," said McCarter, giving him a reassuring pat on the shoulder. "It only gets hairy when everyone's firing back at you!"

Hillaby opened his mouth to reply but nothing came out. He swallowed dryly. For the first time the captain suddenly felt very glad he hadn't been in Vietnam. He would stick to training other pilots. He'd leave real combat to cowboys like these two roughnecks.

3

The gears failed to mesh properly as the Moskvich saloon turned into Marx Prospekt and tackled the short hill up to Dzerzhinsky Square. The driver glanced nervously at the mirror. The second-rate black vehicle was a replacement car, and he was not used to it. But his passenger continued to stare soullessly through the side window.

Colonel Vichinsky did not notice the old woman on the corner pull her gray shawl tighter against the bitter chill, although he looked right at her.

This morning his mind was concentrated on one thing: *glavni protivnik*. The principal target. Not as Soviet officials most often thought of it—the United States in general—but how it was symbolized in the work of one dangerous man, John Phoenix.

He was the *glavni protivnik*.

The main enemy.

Phoenix!

It was only when the colonel found himself

staring out at the statue of Felix Dzerzhinsky, the founding director of the secret police that Lenin so desperately needed to consolidate his power, that he realized they had already arrived at headquarters. The car sped past the imposing facade of Moscow Center, turned the corner and pulled up by the side entrance. Only department heads were permitted to enter 2 Dzerzhinsky Square through the main doors. Vichinsky had not achieved that rank. Not yet. But he had every intention of doing so.

Breath steaming on the early-morning air, Vichinsky waited at the doorway for the guard to demand his identification. The sentry—who knew Vichinsky well by sight—asked to see the colonel's pass, then made a show of checking the narrow, pockmarked face in the photograph against the features of the man who held out the card. Junior Sergeant Teplov saluted crisply.

Vichinsky decided to walk up to his office on the third floor. Sentries were posted at intervals of sixty to eighty feet throughout the building. This half of the KGB headquarters, the slightly higher right-hand side of the baroque complex, was constructed by German POWs still held captive after World World II had ended.

The older part of the building, which had once been the head office for the All-Russian Insurance Company, before being taken over by the infant Cheka—predecessor of the

KGB—housed the quarters for the chairman and his senior deputies.

As their global work load increased—and they were spending well over three billion dollars a year on propaganda, terrorism, covert action and corruption—it had been necessary to move the bulk of the administration to Machovaya Ulitza.

And the swollen first chief directorate, which ran the KGB's foreign intrigues, had been transferred into a modern, crescent-shaped office block on a forested estate beyond the twelve-lane expressway that ringed Moscow.

Colonel Vichinsky said nothing to the guard standing outside his office. There was no lettering to indicate what department worked behind the door. But this anonymous green-painted office suite was the nerve center of the deadliest ultrasecret group within the vast KGB organization. From here its tentacles spread out around the world.

At the very beginning, Felix Dzerzhinsky had demanded a special police force for "the revolutionary settlement of accounts" and so was born the Cheka. And they generally exacted their payment in blood. As the initials of the organization changed over the decades: OGPU, NKVD, NKGB, MGB and now the KGB—that abbreviated litany of endless terror—so, too, had the official title for its most important department, the one that specialized in assassination, sabotage, kidnapping and extortion. These operations were designated *Mokrie dela*: the so-called "wet affairs," for they were wet with blood.

Line F.

The Thirteenth Department.

Otdel 9.

The Secret Division.

Department *V*. As in Victory.

And now it was known as the Department for Executive Action.

Vichinsky, who had been seconded from the GRU—military intelligence—four years before, and his chief, Greb Strakhov, stood even deeper in the shadows behind the KGB's international murder squad. They headed the invisible Thirteenth Section, which specialized in only the most sensitive operations. And they were nearly always "wet."

Strakhov was a stolid secretive man who had left Vichinsky free to extend their uneasily shared empire. And there was power for the taking. Especially since Executive Action had botched the big job in Rome by using an unreliable Turk.

The colonel stamped his boots on the parquet floor and hung up his coat. Crossing to the table behind his desk he picked up the first of the three phones. "No calls. I do not want to be disturbed for the next hour. No, wait. Admit only Mozhenko.''

It would be Mozhenko who would be bringing written confirmation of the news that they had awakened him with at home that morning.

Their American mole had finally gotten an assessment through to Moscow Center. It seemed that he had taken it upon himself to launch an all-out assault on Stony Man Farm, the Virginia headquarters of John Phoenix. The attack had failed. Phoenix had survived.

The Russian cursed under his breath. He was surrounded by bunglers.

Madness! Vichinsky clenched his fists. From the first time Phoenix had been identified, he had insisted that they lure the American into their own territory and take care of him themselves.

Vichinsky crossed to the filing cabinet. He opened the second drawer and pulled out the file on Phoenix.

Vichinsky knew there was still much work to be done before his plan could be put into motion—not the least problem being to find the American's present whereabouts. The colonel was glad that Strakhov was away from the office.

Strakhov was spending the morning at the administration's computer center. Together with Lev Zalozny of Records and Archives, he was

ostensibly checking through the newly central-
ized files on the KGB's foreign operations. Even
Zalozny was not aware that Strakhov was pre-
paring a digest of the organization's current position for the general secretary himself.

Vichinsky knew there was a good chance that
his boss would stay there for most of the afternoon, too, probably trying to find out if the
data-processing center had turned up any more
files or cross-indexed Chekist information on
the Romanovs.

From the previous head of his department,
Strakhov had inherited the musty brief on the
fate of the last czar and his family.

In recent years Vichinsky's chief had been responsible for little more than investigating the
claims of an East German pretender to the imperial bloodline and diverting Western interest
in the Soviet Union's ultimate act of regicide.

But for Strakhov, over the years, this histori-
cal curiosity had become a private obsession. He
was fascinated by what had happened so long
ago and still pondered the true fate of the czar's
youngest daughter, the pretty teenager, Anastasia.

Vichinsky would use this time by himself to
further his own plan to neutralize the meddle-
some Colonel Phoenix.

He opened the file and stared at the photograph that had first been brought to their attention by Operations Analysis.

Phoenix's name, his description, had begun to crop up in case after case, from San Francisco to South America, from Tuscany to Toronto. Then at last, a photograph. A grainy blowup of the American agent taken in Spain.

More photographs had been obtained, now that they knew whom they were looking for. But hard information on the man's past had been impossible to acquire; even the American connection, with all his influence, was unable to come up with anything more than a sketchy outline for the past two or three years.

Strakhov had been the man who found a double for Brezhnev in his final days. Then he had called Vichinsky in on the search for another official impostor, this time for their former boss, Andropov, when he first became ill in office.

Ivan Trichin, one of the casting directors of Mosfilm Studios, had helped them "cast" the needed double. Vichinsky had turned up at the meeting with the Phoenix photograph supplied by Operations Analysis. Trichin had caught a glimpse of the face beneath the thatch of dark hair. "Stefan Boldin? I thought he'd been...."

"Who did you say?"

"Boldin. The poet. A Pole...a troublemaker."

"Yes, of course," said Vichinsky quickly, remembering the dissident's trial. He even had a good idea where Boldin was now—being reeducated in the Gulag.

He had said nothing more to Trichin, but it was at that moment he conceived of the Janus Plan. . . .

"GIVE OLEG A HAND unloading that cement," said Roykov. Stefan Boldin looked bleakly at his foreman. Roykov pulled one hand from its mitt and exhaled into his clenched fist. He stared across the snow at the half-laden truck. "Move! Or we'll never finish on time."

Two weeks earlier, work had stopped because of the storm. Then they'd had a few days of watery sunshine, giving just enough warmth to start melting the first snowfall. But now the temperature was dropping again. Boldin moved unsteadily as his feet cracked the thin crust of ice, and the softer snow beneath sucked at his worn felt boots.

He trudged up the low incline toward the cement truck the only way he knew how—one step at a time. It was the way he had learned to live his life.

One day at a time.

One crust of bread at a time.

One cigarette butt at a time.

Sometimes it seemed that Roykov asked the

impossible, and yet Boldin willingly complied. He knew the foreman's one concern was that they fulfill their work quota for the day.

Roykov wanted to make sure that all the men got their full ration that evening—nine hundred grams of bread and a bowl of salted fish soup. Besides, thought Boldin, this just might be his lucky day. He might be able to get hold of some paper from the cement sacks to wrap around himself under his coat.

There was a single black bird perched atop an unfinished wall of the pumping station they had been ordered to build. Boldin hoped he could acquire the materials to build a slingshot to take advantage of the occasional feast that flew by.

Pumping Station 27B was being built close to the western border of Siberia. The men were housed in the bare wooden barracks at Karashevo. It was but one of the hundreds of "corrective" labor camps inside the USSR.

Since the Soviet Union occupies almost one-sixth of the world's land surface, it can be classed as the largest prison camp on earth. Its thousands of miles of borders are guarded by nearly 400,000 men under the control of the Chief Border Guards Directorate, one of the largest organs within the KGB empire.

These guards face inward. The Russian people live out their whole lives within a cage of barbed wire and searchlights, mine fields and machine guns, informers and watchdogs.

The party faithful have their ZIL limousines, their private shops stocked with Western consumer goods unavailable to the masses, and the dachas, the holiday homes on the Black Sea coast or in the Caucasus. They are the ruling class. But in order to ensure their continued hold on power, they have to rely completely on the ruthlessness and terror of the KGB.

The KGB *is* the Soviet state. Its decisions are often arbitrary, but always final; its motivations unquestioned, and its authority unchallenged. The Russian secret police hold a power unparalleled in political history.

As for the ruled, they are like people anywhere. The more opportunistic among them try to ingratiate themselves with their superiors in order to climb another rung of the party hierarchy. But most of the ordinary people simply struggle to survive under the numbing weight of totalitarian rule.

Hidden within the vast body of Russia and its satellite socialist republics, riddling them like a cancer, lies that terrible network of imprisonment known as the Gulag.

Pain and suffering are linked in an endless chain of interrogation chambers and forced labor camps, psychiatric hospitals and the frozen death mines of the Arctic. Uncounted

millions have died in the Gulag, and today perhaps two million or more still slave for the hollow dream of communism.

Stefan Boldin had only completed three long
years of his twenty-year sentence.

They had not broken the Polish dissident
when they arrested him. He did not betray his
friends under interrogation in the Lubyanka
prison. He had somehow remained defiant at
his trial. He had not succumbed, even on the
freezing cattle train that brought him to Siberia.
But it was here, at Karashevo, that he had finally broken.

The authorities had discarded him, consign-
ing the outspoken poet to a numbered fate like
so many others before him. They did not even
know that he was beaten.

Here in the camps there was a harsh code of
honor and loyalty, but those fine abstractions
were subservient to survival. In Karashevo—
from one day to the next—survival was all that
really counted.

"Boldin!"

The once controversial writer put down the
cement sack he carried and looked back down
the slope to where Roykov, the foreman, was
trying to attract Boldin's attention. The commandant's car waited for him on the track of
packed snow.

Neither the driver nor the guard said anything

to prisoner #220143 as they drove back to the camp. Boldin assumed that either the Politburo had finally relented and granted him an exit visa, or that he was being summoned for another and perhaps even more publicized trial. One he dared not hope for, the other he dared not contemplate. Boldin simply stared at the desolate snowscape and blanked out his mind.

It was not until he was sitting in the warmth of the commandant's office and was introduced to the high-ranking visitor from Moscow who offered him a cigarette, that Boldin felt this really might be his lucky day.

Colonel Vichinsky scrutinized the prisoner's face as he held out his lighter. Boldin looked down at the floor. He did not want to give the appearance of staring back. Vichinsky, sitting on the front edge of the old wooden desk, shifted his position so that he could inspect the prisoner from another angle.

Several times the colonel glanced at the black-and-white photograph he had set down on the commandant's desk, comparing Boldin's features with those of the man pictured there. Boldin thought it was his own portrait until he caught a long enough glimpse to see that there was a definite difference in the eyes.

"This is not a comfortable place to be," Vichinsky said candidly, looking out of the window at a column of prisoners being marched across the compound. "But you need not remain here. There is something you can do to get out."

Boldin remained silent. He would not give them the names of the printers who had circulated his poems. He'd held out before and, if that was what they wanted now, he hoped he could hold out again. In truth, Boldin was not certain that he could, but he'd try to play out this interview long enough to finish the welcome cigarette.

"You bear a very close resemblance to a man we are interested in." The colonel observed Boldin's malnourished frame and pinched features. "At least, you did, and you can soon do so again. You will be fed well. You'll have better clothes. It won't be long before you are back to your old self again."

Such honesty went against the very grain of his personality, but Vichinsky knew that if the Janus Plan was to work he must have this prisoner's willing cooperation.

Still Boldin said nothing. He wondered what it was that they really wanted. Did they intend to take compromising photographs using him as a model? It had been so long since he had been with a woman that he doubted he could perform in such a role.

Boldin stubbed out the cigarette and slipped the butt into his pocket. "When do I leave?"

His decision was a reflex response. This was the best opportunity for survival that had been granted him since his arrival at Karashevo.

"Immediately." Vichinsky permitted himself a thin smile of satisfaction. He had guessed right.

IT HAD TAKEN FOUR MONTHS to effect the physical transformation that was necessary. Boldin was fed three square meals a day and all the snacks he wanted in between. An operation on his nose and careful grooming by a skilled hairstylist produced the results that Vichinsky was trying to achieve.

Now the colonel stared down at the open file on his desk and compared the latest photo of the Polish convict with that of Colonel John Phoenix. He was well pleased with the progress that had been made, doubly so that it had been achieved entirely on his own initiative and without Strakhov's knowledge.

Strakhov was hard at work drawing up a detailed master list of current KGB activities throughout the world for the leader of the Soviet Union. Vichinsky envied his boss the power represented by such knowledge, but not the tedious task of compiling it.

The colonel lit another cigarette even though one was still smoldering in the ashtray. He would wait to find Strakhov's fatal weakness.

His boss's passion for Anastasia was not enough of a lever to depose him; there must be something else. And Vichinsky was confident that he could put his finger on it.

But today he would concern himself with Janus.

The plan to trap Phoenix.

Vichinsky had been staring at the two photographs for some time. He realized he could not tell the difference between the American and his counterfeit double.

The Janus Plan was going to work.

4

Dawn approached as a blush of lemon above the dark, jagged line of the horizon behind them. Then the molten disk of the sun rose to burn away the sandy haze. To the untrained eye there appeared to be no movement at all in that jumbled spectrum of ochers, rusts and strangely velvet mauves. But from the snipers' vantage point, a single shaft of sunlight spearing down over the broken lip of the escarpment trapped a faint dancing cloud, just a lighter smudge against a background of deep brown.

Bolan tipped his head toward the approaching convoy. He did not have to point it out. McCarter had already picked up the far-off rumble of the Russian vehicles.

A six-wheeled armored car was riding point.

The Englishman shifted the strap of the power pack dangling from his shoulder and wished he held a good rifle instead of a camera.

To the left of their position, concealed behind a spine of bare rock, lay the main force of Abdur Jahan's ragged band. Jahan himself crouched

beside the two Western "news correspondents."
Bolan scanned the faces of these men who
served Tarik Khan: weather-beaten skin, dark
brows over hawk noses, they waited, proud and
defiant.

They were used to such waiting. They had
outlasted the ambitions of other empires: the
Persian hordes of Darius the Great; Alexander
and his Macedonian army; Genghis Khan; the
Arab cavalry and the British with all their pomp
and ceremony and scarlet tunics.

Now the Russian bear was astride their land,
seeking out its age-old goal to reach India and
the warm-water ports that ringed the Arabian
Sea. But as the Soviet Union sought to expand
its slave empire it had run into the *mujahedeen*,
the soldiers of God, the holy warriors of Afghanistan.

For four years the holy warriors had fought
the Red Army colossus to a standstill. They
would not be crushed. They would not submit
meekly to the northern invaders.

Despite crippling losses, lack of financial support from abroad and inadequate arms, they
had stalled the Soviet thrust, tied up more than
one hundred thousand troops, killed at least five
thousand and inflicted another ten thousand ca-
sualties.

They would wait, strike, run and wait again.
Even if the West would not aid them, the

mujahedeen believed they had two things on their side. Time. And God.

"Here." Jahan handed the tall American the ancient brass telescope. His English was thickly accented. "The Russians are foolish to set off so early. The sun will be in their eyes by the time they reach the top."

Bolan accepted the telescope. He scanned the length of the valley. It was a lot wider than the Khazani rift, which lay thirty miles southwest of their present position. The road hugged the rumpled slope of the barren escarpment. On the other side was a rock-strewn riverbed, carrying a trickle of icy water. Bright emerald tufts of grass and purple flowers sprouted amid the boulders.

The road wound perilously through a series of switchbacks. During the night the *mujahedeen* had used a long bullock team to tow the wreckage of a Russian tank into position at the top of the longest incline, where it would create a dangerous bottleneck for the approaching column.

"Mostly Afghan regulars," said Bolan, inspecting the truckloads of soldiers interspersed with the supply carriers.

Jahan spat in the dust. Their quarrel with the successive regimes in Kabul had started long before the present puppet-ruler had invited Moscow to send in their troops.

"Fuel tankers in the middle," noted McCarter, who was using his camera's zoom lens for a close-up view of the convoy.

Jahan had seen them, too. Whispered instructions were relayed to the two militia deserters who now manned a captured rocket launcher for the *mujahedeen* band.

Bolan glanced back at their guide, Darul Mirza. On the journey in from northern Pakistan he had been full of heroic stories about nighttime exploits with his guerrilla comrades. But here, cowering in the scant cover of a shallow gully, he did not seem so confident and daring.

As the spring warmth melted the mountain snows, hundreds of Afghan resisters would pour back over the Pakistan frontier to resume the fight. Darul Mirza would be busy in the coming weeks carrying messages and guiding occasional Western observers into the combat zone. He had told Bolan that he'd already brought another journalist in the week before, but where the man was now, he couldn't say.

Bolan gave their guide a reassuring nod but Mirza only hugged closer to the rocks. He wished he had left as soon as he'd introduced the cameramen to Abdur Jahan. Let Jahan take them to meet Tarik Khan.

"Any moment now," said McCarter, who had not taken his eyes off the trucks below.

Bolan used those last few seconds to film a

close-up of the man crouching immediately next to him. Shapur Rhaman was a respected marksman. Carefully he balanced the long barrel of his ancient *jezail* across the top of a covering boulder and took a bead on the caravan track below.

All the effort and determination of their cause was mirrored in his face—the assurance that he was fulfilling the will of Allah and an unremitting hatred for the infidel invaders.

Those men below were strangers from farms on the shores of the Caspian and the slushy streets of Irkutsk. But Shapur Rhaman knew these barren mountains like the back of his careworn hands.

He nestled the brass-bound stock snug against his shoulder. He would make certain that a number of the Russian soldiers would not be going home again.

The six-wheeler scout was slowing as it approached the wreckage of the tank.

One of the deserters who had joined the *mujahedeen* took aim with his missile launcher. The RPG-7V percussion-fired its projectile, then in midflight a rocket motor kicked in and sent the five-pound grenade on a streaking trajectory toward the armored car.

It smashed through the right front wheel well and erupted.

The lead vehicle spun out of control and slithered straight into the charred wreckage already littering the road.

The guerrillas, spread out in an uneven crescent behind folds of rock in the cliff face, opened fire with an assortment of weapons: Lee-Enfields, Chinese Type 56s, traditional muskets and captured AK-47s.

Bolan and McCarter watched through the drifting smoke as the Soviet troop carriers and supply trucks were abandoned or driven into the scant cover of the ditch on the right side of the track.

"What I'd give to get my hands on a Number 4 right now," said McCarter.

"I know how you feel," agreed Bolan. There was no point in taking up arms. They must do nothing that would blow their cover before they reached the camp of Tarik Khan.

Bolan kept filming as one of the local militia, trapped on the open road, was hit. He staggered blindly over the edge of the ravine.

Abdur Jahan gave a fierce yell of exultation and encouraged his men to keep up the pressure.

In an effort to escape the ambush, the driver of the second to last truck had thrown his vehicle into reverse so suddenly that he'd rammed the supply carrier behind him. Now the road was blocked at front and rear. Finding what shelter they could in the ditch, the Soviets and their Afghan comrades began returning fire up the steep slopes at a hidden enemy.

Another grenade went hissing toward the convoy. It hit the smaller of the fuel carriers. The carrier exploded in an angry twisting fireball.

The rocket man dropped the RPG and leaped to his feet, brandishing a victorious fist in the air. Then, with a small grunt of surprise, he buckled as if punched in the stomach. The deserter collapsed to his knees, blood and mucus hanging in strands from his mouth.

Shapur Rhaman fired back in reply. Through the camera lens, Bolan saw a spurt of grit puff up just above the head of a blond Russian officer. At this range it was too high and slightly to the left. Bolan shouted a correction but Rhaman only grinned. He did not understand English.

"Hey, look there!" McCarter shouted, pointing. "Next to that clump of pink flowers, a radio operator. See him?"

Abdur Jahan trained his telescope on the Soviet operator and spat out a curse.

Rhaman had reloaded. Bolan reached across and took the ancient firearm from his hands. The guerrilla watched as the American carefully took aim.

Hunched awkwardly over the camera equipment, Bolan sighted down the length of the barrel. The radioman was in the middle of a transmission.

Bolan judged the appropriate compensation and held his breath. In that eternal instant sniper, rifle and unwitting target became one as The Executioner squeezed the trigger.

The thin curved butt kicked back with an unaccustomed ferocity. Bolan never did see the precise point of impact. The force of the hit blew the man sideways. He was still clutching the microphone as he sprawled on a broken rock, staining its rough surface red.

Abdur Jahan slapped his thigh, expelling a sigh of respect tinged with awe. "You were a soldier once, perhaps?"

"This is the front line," explained Bolan, handing the rifle back to its owner. "We are all soldiers here."

"Now you will meet Tarik Khan. I will see to that." The *mujahedeen* commander was still shaking his head at the foreigner's marksmanship. "I will vouch for you myself."

Darul Mirza was already scrambling back through the rocks when Jahan signaled for his men to retreat. The convoy troops increased their fire at the weaving, bobbing backs of the fleeing fighters. They were shooting up the incline and into the sun with little success.

"Come on!" urged Mirza. "Up to that next ledge. We'll be safe in the caves."

The men scurried up the steep cleft that led to some caverns above. This network of subterranean grottoes riddling the edge of the escarpment was their getaway route. The two observers, lugging their bulky equipment, followed the others.

Bolan heard it first. He levered himself up onto the ledge and turned to look back across the valley. The throbbing of a rotor echoed between the crumpled rock faces.

"Over there!" Bolan pointed to the small blob that was growing larger with every second.

"It can't have made it all the way here from Sharuf," said McCarter.

"Must have been operating close by," said Bolan. "Or just waiting for us to strike."

The shadowy entrances to half a dozen caves peppered the stone wall at the back of the ledge. Most of the *mujahedeen* had already vanished. Bolan reached the safety of the nearest dark recess and turned his camera on the approaching chopper.

"No, come this way!" shouted Mirza. "It is not safe!"

Bolan continued filming as the helicopter seemed to slide down a track in the sky. A rocket barrage from the chopper hit the far end of the ledge. The image in the viewfinder shuddered.

The M-36 hovered over the side of the escarpment. Then the deadly machine slowly swung around and tilted its nose to face the caves.

"Let's go!" insisted McCarter.

Suddenly the menacing aircraft unleashed a jet of flame. And Bolan quickly realized why its manufacturers had designated this reptilian gunship as *Plamya drakovna*—the Dragonfire!

5

Accompanied by a terrible roar, another blazing red tongue snaked out from the Dragonfire. Bolan could hear the screams of the freedom fighters still trapped in the cave entrances at the far end of the ledge. The stone tunnels amplified their agonized death cries until they pierced the steady beat of the chopper's rotor.

He continued filming the helicopter even though he could smell the scorching chemicals that had splashed across the nearby rock face.

"Mack!" shouted McCarter, more concerned for his friend's life than with security. "Mack, come on, for God's sake!"

The nose of the chopper swung a few degrees to starboard. The M-36 was aligned with the center of the ledge now. The Dragonfire spewed another long tendril of acrid, hissing flame.

The swirling eddies of liquid fire formed golden yellow flowers that seared Bolan's memory. April Rose's eyes flickered with catlike brilliance amid those burning blossoms. And the smell of napalm was mingled with the sickly rotten scent of jungle foliage.

No! Bolan's brain screamed in silent denial. No, not Nam. The enemy seemed to taunt The Executioner, impervious in its armored battle machine. Bolan had never hated anything more than that flame-spitting deathship.

"Mack, this way!" McCarter grabbed Bolan's arm and pulled him away from the cave opening. He shoved the American up the uneven steps at the rear of the tunnel, stumbling toward the safety of the upper chamber.

A hot draft at their backs was followed by the wind rush of oxygen racing back toward the flaming puddles that lathered the entrance to their hiding place.

Every muscle was strained to the limit as they pounded up the natural staircase. The Englishman cursed the heavy film equipment tugging awkwardly at his shoulders.

Shapur Rhaman was waiting at the top. It was he who escorted the foreigners through the final shaft to safety.

A film of sweat covered Bolan's forehead. And it was not from the exertion of the long climb up through the caverns. He shook his head impatiently, as if he could shake off the images that haunted him.

McCarter was looking at him strangely, not wanting to put his own concern into words.

Bolan fingered the gold ring on his dog-tag chain as he turned away to watch the lookout clambering swiftly up the ridge at their backs. Had he frozen down there?

"I'm all right," Bolan reassured his partner.

"Never doubted it, mate," said McCarter. But his voice didn't sound quite so confident when he added quietly, "We've got to get that bloody chopper, Mack."

"With Tarik Khan's help we will," said Bolan.

From the very top of the escarpment the Afghan sentry signaled the all-clear. The Dragonfire was pulling out, heading back to its base.

"The village is hidden behind those hills," Abdur Jahan told them, pointing to a series of steep serrated hillocks about six or seven miles away. "We'll be safe there."

THEY HAD COVERED about four miles when they first saw the pall of smoke hanging over Mukna.

Three of the men, all with families there, began to run on ahead. The rest of the *mujahedeen* kept up their grueling pace. They already knew what they would find. They had been fighting this war for years and knew only too well what they could expect from the Russians.

Russia had invaded Afghanistan during Christmas, 1979, with hopes of a quick victory, but *mujahedeen* resistance had soon disabused them of that notion.

The war dragged on and the Soviets, backed by a puppet militia, seized control of the few key population centers—control by day, at least. But the mountainous terrain remained in the hands of the freedom fighters. Tanks and armored cars were useless in that region. And few men, including the Afghan regulars, would venture far into the hills that sheltered the guerrillas.

Soviet policy now dictated a war of sudden terror and indiscriminate destruction aimed at the civilian population. The M-36 was the perfect strategic solution.

Like no weapons system before it, the Dragonfire could fly right into the *mujahedeen* redoubts, literally smoking out the warriors who had caused the occupying forces so much trouble. And it could just as easily rain death on an innocent settlement, driving out the survivors to join the endless flood of refugees.

"No wonder he reached the valley so quickly," said McCarter. "He was already hard at work here!"

Ashes were slowly swirling in the air and pale strands of bitter, pungent smoke drifted above the rocky slopes that had failed to protect Mukna.

Jahan's column broke ranks as the rest of the men ran forward to find out what had happened to their relatives and friends.

By the side of the narrow track that wound into Mukna, nothing was left of some nomadic tents except powdery circles of gray ash. Farther along the path, ancient stone cottages were scorched by the Dragonfire's surprise attack.

"Their battle plan seems to be working," Bolan said, nodding toward two women who were packing the few things they could salvage onto the back of a scrawny donkey. Darul Mirza would not be crossing over the border alone.

"Over here!" Abdur Jahan signaled to the two observers. Several of the wounded had been laid out in the shelter of a low stone wall. "Things do not look good for us. You have come at a bad time."

A wizened old man, his face as brown and wrinkled as a walnut, was daubing some rancid grease on the burned leg of a child. Then he covered the raw flesh with a page torn from the Koran.

McCarter nudged Bolan's arm. "That must be Tarik Khan over there."

The guerrilla leader was dressed a little better than most of his followers. He wore a handsomely embroidered vest, stout riding boots, with two bandoliers crossing his chest and a third wrapped round his waist. He was crouching beside a young boy. The youngster was burned on at least three-fifths of his body.

Tarik Khan stood up and glanced across at

the foreigners as Abdur Jahan reported on what had happened at the ambush site. Other villagers were watching Bolan, too. Shapur Rhaman had quickly spread the story of the American's uncanny marksmanship.

The village elder, who appeared to be the local equivalent of a doctor, took advantage of Tarik Khan's distraction to bring his bowl of dubious ointment over to the boy.

"Treating him with that stuff could give the lad a secondary infection," McCarter commented.

Bolan made no reply. He had locked eyes with the *mujahedeen* leader, who tugged at the corner of his thick mustache as Jahan completed his account.

"American, I will talk with you later," Tarik Khan announced in passable English, "but for now I must attend to my son. Abdur, make sure everyone is packed and ready to leave. We move out by tomorrow night. We must pull back farther into the hills."

The two Westerners simply stood there. It was not the time or the place to intervene.

Bolan's thoughts were interrupted by the sudden brilliance of a flash. He whirled, ready for anything, but was still shocked to recognize the man standing behind them.

"Hi! I'm Robert Hutton." Unlike Bolan and McCarter, he was clean-shaven and wore a bush shirt and blue denims. "I'm on assignment for the INS wire service."

Yes, thought Bolan, that always was your cover, as he and McCarter introduced themselves by their assumed names.

"He brought me over, too," said Hutton, indicating Darul Mirza, the guide. "Been off on my own for a few days. Just getting some background color for my next piece."

Bolan forced himself to give a noncommittal nod. It had been almost fifteen years since the one and only time he had crossed paths with Robert Hutton. Mack Bolan had been wearing a different face then. A uniform. And a different rank.

Hutton had not changed much. His chestnut hair was thinner, and there was now a band of flab bulging over his belt. But even the beat-up Pentax looked the same.

He took a step closer, squinting slightly as he stared at Bolan. "Heard about that shot you made! Rhaman is telling everyone. Only knew one other man who could shoot like that."

"I was just lucky," replied Bolan, deliberately turning away to watch Jahan moving from group to group, issuing orders to prepare for the withdrawal.

"Were you in Nam?" persisted Hutton.

"Nope, I missed out on that one," Bolan lied. "I was covering the troubles at home."

"Hell of a shot from what I heard," said Hutton. "Still, it was too late for these beggars."

"Where were you?" asked McCarter.

"Just on my way back to the village. Saw the whole thing from up there." Hutton patted his camera. "Got the attack all on film."

"Yeah, well, we'd better get some coverage, too," said Bolan. "C'mon, David, we need some footage of the village."

McCarter shouldered his equipment and headed up Mukna's solitary street. Debris littered the hard-packed track.

"Watch out for that bastard," warned Bolan, as soon as they were out of earshot of the other newsman. "He's a snake. Canadian, I think. He sold out our side in Nam and then was one of the first to report from Hanoi."

McCarter pretended to concentrate on taking close-up shots of a shattered cottage at the end of the street. He dismissed Mack's misgivings over Hutton. He was more concerned about how they would get into Sharuf now that Tarik Khan's men were being forced to retreat.

They didn't get a chance to speak to the guerrilla chieftain until a meal was served later that evening. It was just a makeshift supper eaten hastily between securing packs on the donkeys and arguing whether it was better to pull back to the northeast or retreat over the border again. Parties were heading in both directions.

"Taking a risk going around dressed like that, aren't you?" McCarter asked Hutton.

"When you've been in this game as long as I have there's no need to play at being Lawrence of Arabia," answered the journalist with a patronizing sneer. "I know what I'm doing."

"I guess you must," said the young Englishman, scratching himself under his dirty cloak. "So tell me about it...."

McCarter kept Hutton talking while Bolan made his case to Tarik Khan.

"We must get close-up pictures of that new helicopter back to the West. Would you help us get into the airfield at Sharuf?"

"Why should I risk more of my men?" Tarik Khan said bitterly. "What would it profit us?"

"It would demonstrate the need you have for more support if Western audiences saw what you were fighting against." Bolan pushed the point. "It could mean more guns, more ammunition, more rockets."

"In that case show them the results of the Russian attacks! Film a close-up of Tolfi's arm. Show the burns. Show your people what it looks like to lose a hand. Wouldn't that be enough to win their sympathy? Take back pictures of my son, Kasim. Even now we do not know if he will live or die."

"We need close-range footage of the Dragon-fire," insisted Bolan. "Indisputable evidence of how the Russians are waging war."

"Evidence!" Tarik Khan leaped to his feet so suddenly he knocked over a bowl by the fire. He threw his arms out to encompass the village. "What do you call this if it is not evidence? Take your pictures here like Mr. Hutton. He has photographs of the attack."

The Canadian newsman looked up at Tarik Khan's angry outburst and nodded. "Yes, and I'll make sure they get back to the right people."

Bolan checked his temper. But he could not give away the true purpose of their mission—not with Hutton sitting there.

"Tomorrow you can come with us. We shall withdraw toward the Kajhak Mountains," said the chieftain. "Or you can return to Pakistan with Mirza. In which case I will ask you to escort my son. Tomorrow night I'm sending Kasim out with four bearers. He needs better medical attention than he can get here."

Bolan stared at the ground. It was a death sentence for the boy either way—the trip would probably kill him. Kasim needed a properly equipped burn unit if he was to be saved.

There was no point in breaching the security of their mission. What did the broader strategic implications mean to Tarik Khan? Right now he was just a father sick with worry for his injured son.

Bolan glanced across at the homemade stretcher. Kasim's eyes were open. He was staring back at the foreigner. Then he gave Bolan a small, brave smile.

"I shall see what can be done for your son, Tarik Khan."

6

"Well, Hal, you must admit that Captain Hillaby's report of the incident shows that Phoenix is at the very least, uh, potentially unstable."

Farnsworth looked around the table to see if the other men were in agreement with him. Brognola shuttled the cigar from one side of his mouth to the other. He was playing for time and sensed that everyone knew it.

Inside the small conference room the tense atmosphere was decidedly chill. The Phoenix program was on the line. And Brognola was sweating.

"Surely you have to agree that Colonel Phoenix appears to be at a snapping point?" Lee Farnsworth tapped the thick buff folder lying on the polished table. "Your assessment makes him sound like the Man of Steel. If that's the case, then he's got the human equivalent of metal fatigue. It can happen to the best of us. Not much shows on the outside but then, without warning, it just gives, breaks, snaps. Do you think that's a fair analogy?"

Brognola had to show the man some respect. It was the President who had appointed Farnsworth to chair the exclusively small committee that was to advise him on the future of the Stony Man operation.

But what could he say?

He knew he could count on Brigadier General Crawford for support. Hell, that wily old veteran and Mack Bolan went back even further than Brognola's own association with The Executioner.

Andrew Webb was young, but he seemed fair and relatively open-minded. On the other hand Glen Knopfler could twist gently with the changing breeze, anticipating each shift in the highly charged currents of feeling that swirled around the table. In the end, all Brognola could do was shrug and chew down harder on his cigar.

Realizing that he was not going to get a straightforward admission from the liaison man, Farnsworth looked for support elsewhere. "What do you say, Andy? After all, you were at the Fullerton briefings with him."

Webb immediately stopped toying with the knot of his Cardin tie. He chose his words carefully. "We were all under a lot of strain. There was a lot of ground we had to cover and very little time in which to do it. Colonel Phoenix impressed me as being very competent—"

"John Phoenix is more than competent," Brognola interrupted. "He's the best we've got, the best there is! Have you gentlemen studied his record?"

"We're not questioning his past achievements, Hal, or his technical expertise." Farnsworth did his best to sound conciliatory, but it was unconvincing.

Brognola ignored the chairman. He appealed to the others. "Do you realize how effective this man and the teams that work with him have been? He's always delivered. He's always come through for us. Here at home and abroad; the Caribbean, Africa, Italy, Japan...."

"I'm sure I speak for everyone at the table, Hal, when I say we don't doubt the necessity for the Stony Man unit. Until now, that is, when its cover has obviously been blown. But it's because we want it to continue that we must reexamine its leadership. The Stony Man teams handle the dirty and delicate missions, and that's precisely why we have to know that the man heading them up is completely stable. That's the question the President wants answered, Hal. Is John Phoenix still reliable?"

"I've given you my assessments of every member of Stony Man Farm. You've got the reports in front of you. And there's no one I trust more than Colonel John Phoenix."

"Your loyalty is commendable," replied

Farnsworth with a tight-lipped smile. "But let's face it, Hal, he's your boy."

"No, Mr. Farnsworth, you've got it wrong," Crawford gruffly corrected him. "He's nobody's 'boy.' John Phoenix is very much his own man. Always has been...."

"Are you suggesting there's even a remote chance that he might go free-lance if it suited him? Is that a hint that Phoenix might hire himself out to the highest bidder?"

"No!" Brognola cut in quickly. "I can vouch for the Phoenix program and the man who heads it."

He glanced round the table and wondered if he could do the same for the select group of advisers seated there. Could it be possible that Mack was right in his suspicions? Was there a mole, a traitor planted long ago at this level within the government? It still seemed preposterous to him.

Farnsworth's decision cut off any further speculation.

"This latest Phoenix mission to Afghanistan gives us a few days' grace before we present our conclusions to the President. I can only suggest that we still need more input."

Both Knopfler and Webb nodded in agreement.

"Hal, I want you to furnish us with a complete career profile of John Phoenix, going right back to the beginning.'' Farnsworth lifted his hand to ward off Brognola's objection. ''I don't have to remind you who convened this advisory panel, so I'm sure that all the necessary security clearance can be obtained. It'll give us a much clearer picture of who we're dealing with. Everyone agreed?''

As he chomped on his cigar, Brognola couldn't help wondering about Farnsworth's change of attitude since their meeting with the President and Bolan. Then, Farnsworth's enthusiasm to have the Phoenix program shut down could not be contained. Now, the CFB chief appeared smug; he was the soul of restraint.

Even more puzzling to Brognola was the President's decision to appoint Farnsworth chairman of this committee, which could seal the fate of Stony Man.

VICHINSKY'S NARROW FACE was reflected in the grimy windowpane. His cold gray eyes stared out through his reflection at the gloomy woods that flanked the railway line, where green shoots struggled to break through the sheaths of ice crystals that encased them. The melting snow had enlarged the footprints of a fox that had crossed the tracks the night before.

The Akinova line—like the transport system running north from Potma—is not marked on any map of the Soviet Union. Officially it does not exist. It is a private railroad run by the Ministry of Internal Affairs for the exclusive use of the KGB. But unlike the endless succession of convict cattle trucks that leave Potma for the thirty-six camps of the Mordovian prison system, this short passenger train runs only between Akinova and the main express line back to Moscow.

An American would feel quite at home in Akinova. That's the idea of the place. It is a precise replica of the kind of small town one might find anywhere throughout the American Midwest, complete with plastic pennants fluttering over a used-car lot, two drugstores and the Stars and Stripes marking the cinder-block post office at the end of the main street. It is one of the three duplicate American towns where the KGB train and prepare their agents for a new life in the United States.

Stefan Boldin was not destined to cross the Atlantic; the role of sleeper was not for him. But Vichinsky insisted on more than a mere physical likeness to Phoenix. He wanted Boldin to walk like the American, talk like him, think like him.

Perhaps, in the end, they would only need his impersonation for a few vital seconds, but Vichinsky was leaving nothing to chance. When the time came, the world would have to believe that Stefan Boldin *was* John Phoenix. Thus he was having the Pole undergo the intensive immersion program at Akinova.

On this return journey there was no one in the carriage with him, but still Vichinsky looked carefully around before unscrewing the silver top from his flask and pouring out a generous tot of vodka.

If Boldin's progress had not been so impressive—and Vichinsky was especially pleased with the prisoner's results on the rifle range—then the KGB officer might have felt guilty for having taken a whole day off from his other duties.

The Thirteenth Section had many other pressing problems to deal with: the expected expulsion of ten more agents from the embassy in London and the growing nuisance of Damien Macek and his Unity movement in the Balkans.

But after what he had seen today, he did not mind working late. The Janus Plan was very much on schedule. He turned his thoughts to his boss, Greb Strakhov.

The commanding officer of the Thirteenth Section was still compiling his report for the general secretary. It would be two more weeks before he finished, maybe longer. The KGB's activities were so widespread now that it was difficult to digest them into a single catalog. Where was Strakhov's weakness? That was the question Vichinsky turned over in his mind.

He knew his chief had recently met with Niktov, the Fabergé expert; but that was simply to pump the old man for more scraps of information about the Romanovs and not for any illicit dealings in contraband artwork.

Perhaps Strakhov's family?

Strakhov was a widower. His only son, Kyril, was a highly decorated test pilot currently serving the motherland in Afghanistan. He was untainted by the slightest whiff of scandal. Vichinsky dismissed the thought. He knew he would never find that kind of leverage to use against Strakhov.

Perhaps Janus would be enough. When the plot to cut down the Americans' top agent was successful, he would step forward and claim the credit. Then, through Vichinsky, the GRU could assert more control over the Thirteenth Section, and thus the whole security apparatus.

Vichinsky drew strength and determination from this anticipation of the power that was soon to be his. He poured out another drink and silently toasted his reflection in the glass.

7

It was a few minutes after midnight.

Bolan gave no indication he had just awakened.

He lay there for a few moments longer, looking up through the bare branches of a withered apricot tree, picking out the familiar constellations to orient himself.

"Ready?" he whispered. There was no need to shake McCarter. The British commando was prepared for what they had to do.

Crouching behind the gnarled trunk, they silently gathered their gear. Three villagers were still squatting round the fire, sipping *chai* and talking.

"What if one of Tarik Khan's lookouts sees us?"

"We'll just have to make sure they don't," Bolan said. McCarter knew that the American would let nothing get in his way now. He felt the same.

They had turned in very early, casually positioning themselves close to a ravine that angled away from Mukna to join the track on the slopes below the village. The night sky was clear and the air chill as the two men sought cover behind the nearest rocks. Bolan led the way, taking care not to send any loose stones rattling as he kept a wary eye on the turbaned guard.

McCarter half expected the subdued conversation by the fire to suddenly turn into shouts of warning. But no alarm was raised as they began to move faster down the narrow defile. Soon he settled into a mile-eating jog behind Bolan.

"I figure we should head in that direction," Bolan suggested, gesturing, when they stopped for a one-minute break.

"Yes, toward the southwest," agreed McCarter. Neither man had to consult the maps in their waist pouches; they had memorized the essential contours.

"That valley should bring us out on the Sharuf road below yesterday's ambush point." Bolan glanced at his watch. "We'll have to risk using the road. It's the only way we can make it to the airfield before dawn."

They abandoned all the camera equipment, but kept the footage they had shot of the Dragonfire. They checked their weapons and set off once more.

The turbulent stream could be heard slapping against the rocks before they reached the road itself. There were no vehicles at this time of night, and they were able to make good time along the gravel track as it meandered toward the Sharuf plain.

Finally they spotted the column of a ruined minaret perched high on a bare granite dome off to their left.

"About six miles to go," Bolan calculated. "Now it's a race against the sun."

Some goats standing on a rocky promontory above the road watched as the two men hurried past. If the herdsman was awake, he didn't hear them.

The only time they had to scramble for cover at the edge of a riverbed was when an old truck rattled down the highway, carrying a cargo of kindling for the townsfolk of Sharuf.

Bolan set a punishing pace to make up for the delay. McCarter kept up wordlessly.

Legs pumping, heart pounding, every step fanned Bolan's anger, which only fueled his determination to outwit the Russians. The physical exertion set a rhythm to what had to be done.

Reconnaissance.

Penetration.

Strike!

The game plans discussed at Fullerton had all revolved around the use of Tarik Khan and his band as a hard-hitting diversion. But now the two-man assault force was alone against the Soviet invasion machine.

Apart from those few men he fought alongside, Mack Bolan wondered if there was anyone left whom he could really trust. Perhaps it was better this way.

He thought of Able Team and Phoenix Force. But they were off fighting their own battles, so he and McCarter would have to wage this war on their own.

The Englishman would have to be a stage army all by himself. It was going to be up to McCarter to provide a noisy distraction while Bolan went in for the chopper.

Their footsteps echoed hollowly over a wooden bridge as the course of the river curved farther to the south. The road twisted through a close-packed jumble of boulders, then the ground to their right sloped away to a long expanse of bare sand and a coiled-wire fence.

Bolan found a shallow pit between some rocks that sheltered them from the road. The depression also gave them a vantage point from which to survey the newly built airstrip.

The mountains were to their rear. Ahead stretched the flinty plain of the Sharuf plateau. It was the only conveniently flat land in the whole region where the Russians could construct an air base.

Wispy columns of smoke from early-morning fires marked the town of Sharuf itself, about five miles away on the far side of the Soviet installation. The main entrance, administrative buildings, hangars and control tower were all clustered there, too. McCarter handed his colleague a pair of field glasses. He rechecked his weapons.

Both men carried compact firearms. Bolan had his Beretta 93-R; McCarter was armed with an Ingram M-10 machine pistol. They both carried six-inch-steel combat blades. And there were thin wire garrotes concealed in their belts. This was heavy-duty hardware if they prowled the back alleys of New York or Detroit. But here, facing the odds they did, it was little better than packing a peashooter.

"Looks like they've been reinforcing their defenses," Bolan said, continuing to sweep the field.

He pointed below their position to a coil of wire and a couple of spare metal poles that had been left behind by a careless work crew.

"Must have been in the past couple of days or our Afghan friends would have made off with the booty." McCarter studied the lay of the land. "Still, it makes sense. That's the most likely place for the guerrillas to break in. The Russians can't have enough men stationed here to stand permanent guard duty round the whole perimeter."

"Yeah, and my guess is that a lot of the open ground down there has been mined."

McCarter took the binoculars and scanned along both sides of the barbed wire for any telltale signs. "There's a lot of tire tracks running along the inside. They must patrol the fence fairly regularly. . . ."

Bolan's attention was still focused on the buildings at the far end of the runway. Two Hinds sat on concrete pads, and he could see an Su-25 Frogfoot being wheeled out onto the apron. But which of the three largest hangars housed the M-36? He had to be right first time.

McCarter turned to scan the jagged hillsides behind them. "I can't help feeling we're being watched, too."

Bolan began to turn when a distant speck on the road caught his eye. "Look, way back there. . . what's that?"

The Briton checked through his glasses. "A motorcyclist. Courier, maybe? He's alone."

McCarter patted the snub-nosed submachine gun.

"No." Bolan shook his head. "No shooting. Let's not bring a patrol out here. I'm going to get that wire."

Without another word, he jumped down between the boulders to the cleared sand below. There was a finger of almost-bare rock stretching out to the fence. Bolan padded along it, picked up the abandoned wire and posts, then quickly retraced his steps.

"Russian, all right," said McCarter. "Damn, I've lost sight of him."

"Quick, take this end, and the post. Make it secure." Bolan dodged across the road as McCarter used a rock to hammer in the short metal pole to serve as an anchor.

They could hear the bike coming up the far side of the slope. There was no time to conceal the trip wire, and no time to test it either. It just lay straggled over the gravel surface of the track.

Bolan wrapped his end around the post. When he jerked on it, the wire would spring taut.

McCarter gave him the thumbs-up signal and ducked behind the rocks.

The rider appeared at the top of the rise. He was wearing a Russian greatcoat, a local sheep-skin cap and had a rifle slung across his back. He kept glancing nervously up at the starkly ter-raced slopes to his left as he accelerated down the hill.

Three.

Two.

One.

Bolan pulled back hard on the pole, and the single strand of barbed wire jumped tight across the path of the speeding bike.

8

Corporal Zumarov was so intent on watching for a sniper in the hills that he did not see the wire until a fraction of a second before he ran into it. Desperately he tried to turn the handlebars, but it was too late.

The barbed wire snagged under the headlight and the bike reared upward like a frightened horse. The rear wheel slithered around under the obstruction and Zumarov landed heavily on his elbow, rolling over twice as the bike skidded sideways along the track.

Bolan raced out from his hiding place. This time he was holding a different wire in his hands—the deadly garrote from his belt. The Russian was still too dazed from the fall to unsling his rifle before Bolan was upon him.

The American's knee slammed into his back. Then the wire necklace snaked around the corporal's neck.

With his fingertips scrabbling uselessly against the choking strand of steel, Zumarov managed to twist around far enough to catch a glimpse of his attacker. As the corporal's eyes bulged horribly his last thought was that there was something odd about the man who was killing him. Zumarov was not at all sure his attacker was an Afghan. But then an explosion of red against black terminated any attempt to solve that final puzzle.

Bolan did not release the relentless pressure until the man's wild thrashing subsided.

McCarter cleared the trip wire off the road and scattered grit into the gouges left by the motorcycle. Then he walked over to pick up the machine. Bolan dragged the body of the dead man behind the rocks and began stripping him.

"Find anything?" McCarter called out. He wheeled the bike to the edge of the track.

"Yeah," replied Bolan, riffling through the officially sealed envelopes from Zumarov's leather satchel.

"Bike's not badly damaged. Headlight's smashed, one of the footrests is bent and the gas tank's got a bit of a dent. But otherwise it's all right."

Bolan shucked his Afghan disguise and picked up the Russian's tunic. The sleeves were too short. He tugged on the trousers and exchanged caps with the dead man. Then he approached McCarter.

"I'll ride through the town and see how close I can get to the main gate and the hangars. Got to find out where they're keeping that chopper.''

"What if you find a way to get in?" asked McCarter, still keeping a sharp eye on the road.

"If I don't come back here, you'd better start your diversion tactic at three o'clock. That gives you over seven hours. And it gives me plenty of time to figure out what the hell I'm going to do." The two men synchronized their watches. "If anything happens to me, you'll have to hightail it out of here the best way you can with the film we shot. Here, take this guy's rifle. But if I get to that chopper, you'll hear me coming!"

"Uh-oh, looks like company." McCarter pointed across the airfield to a streaming dust cloud left behind a speeding vehicle.

"Let's see how well this old crate runs." Bolan swung his leg over the saddle and stamped on the kick start. The engine fired first time. He toyed with the throttle for a moment.

Bolan checked the track in both directions and pulled smoothly away. McCarter watched him disappear down the road, then settled back between the rocks. He hoped nothing would arouse the suspicions of the approaching guards. McCarter did not want to start the fireworks ahead of schedule.

BOLAN GUIDED the twin-cylinder Cossack around a series of deep potholes. Lifting one hand, he tugged the scarf tighter around his face.

The Russian patrol was approaching on his right—three men in a Gaz 4x4. The driver glanced up through the fence and waved. Bolan returned the salute without slowing down. They were searching for any obvious breaches in the perimeter wire; none of them gave the passing courier a second thought. The road crested a hill and soon Bolan was out of sight.

A second track led down from the hills, and the two joined to form a single, wider road that followed the curve of the coiled-wire fence.

Bolan overtook a small caravan of donkeys and a solitary camel being led into Sharuf. The town was just ahead of him now. Freshly painted signs gave instructions on where military vehicles were to proceed. Bolan did not need indicating arrows to see that the main entrance to the air base lay to the right at the far end of town.

As long as men had traveled this land, Sharuf had always been there. The reason for its existence was its water supply, that was constantly replenished by a refreshing spring.

A network of narrow alleys and winding streets had spun their intricate web over the centuries. Nomadic tribesmen broke their journeys here. Trucks, buses and, before the Soviet invasion, camper vans full of young tourists had stopped at this market town on the edge of the Sharuf plain.

Bolan obeyed the speed-limit marker and slowed down as he approached the built-up area. At the side of the road, five men in a row prostrated themselves on their mats in prayer.

Despite the incongruous gasoline pumps, occasional plastic shop signs and the three Russian youths ordering coffee at a pavement café, some things in this ancient land never changed.

The main street was already buzzing with vendors' cries. Villagers from the surrounding hill country had come down to trade wool, scrawny lambs, baskets of mulberries and dung fuel for needed supplies of tea and sugar, kerosene and tobacco.

Bolan tucked in behind a two-ton truck loaded with sheets of corrugated tin. It seemed that a lot of construction work remained to be done at Sharuf.

When the driver flashed his turn signal, Bolan eased back on the throttle and coasted to a halt outside the deserted bus depot. He wheeled the bike to the gutter and propped it on the kickstand.

The big truck had stopped in front of the black-and-white-striped barrier. The sentry inspected the driver's pass and paperwork, gave a cursory glance at the cargo then pushed open the pole across the gateway. As the driver rolled forward into the base, Bolan squatted and pretended to check the Cossack's carburetor for some offending grit.

Peering over the gas tank, Bolan counted four men through the dusty windows of the guardhouse. And stretching on both sides of the main entrance was a strong link fence. A smooth strip of sand about twenty feet wide was marked off in front of the fence by a single strand of trip wire. Bolan had no doubt that this forbidden sector was thoroughly mined.

One of the large hangar doors was half open, and he could see a team of mechanics servicing one of the Hinds. From this angle his view of the two other sheds was blocked by a low straggle of buildings. He fished out a wrench from the tool kit and began to tinker with the fuel line. Unless he could get inside the base, it did not matter where they hid the Dragonfire.

Bluffing his way through the gate was a long shot. If the sentry took a good look at Bolan's pass it would be obvious that the man on the motorcycle was not Corporal Zumarov. And Bolan had neither the time nor the facilities to forge new ID papers. Besides, any one of the guards might well know Zumarov by sight.

There were too many ifs, and they all led to a shoot-out. And if he had to blast his way into Sharuf, the whole base would be alerted before he got anywhere near the gunship. No, there had to be a better way.

A second truck, this one loaded with sacks of cement, was coming along the road. The driver slowed to a crawl, leaned out of the cab window and shouted to the stranded rider.

Bolan pointed the wrench at the carburetor. *"Gryazni...."*

He was saved further explanation by the ear-splitting roar of the Frogfoot firing its MiG turbojets. The truck driver shrugged, shifted gears and rolled toward the gate.

Bolan felt that to linger there might be pushing his luck. From this end of town, the road followed the base perimeter and wound through a series of sculpted hummocks where the wind had pushed loose sand into an array of low dunes. It was the best location he had spotted so far for a serious probe of Sharuf's defenses. He decided to ride out that way and find somewhere to hide the bike.

The Su-25 Frogfoot had taken off, circled the field and was making a low pass overhead. Bolan was carefully studying the wing-tip pods and Phantomlike rear fuselage of the ground-attack jet when he half sensed a car approaching from behind. He certainly couldn't have heard it over the rushing howl of the twin Tumansky R-13s. Even as he turned away the car drew alongside. And Bolan found himself staring at the surprised face of Robert Hutton.

The double-dealing journalist was sitting in the back of the military limousine with a young officer. Hutton caught one glimpse of the American before Bolan pulled the edge of his scarf across his mouth. Bolan saw Hutton's lips part in a silent cry of alarm.

Bolan's foot punched the kick start. Hutton had twisted his head to watch through the rear window as the other passenger rapped out an order to their driver. The car mounted the pavement and began to swing around on screeching tires.

Bolan took off and raced through the empty yard of the bus terminal. As he came out into the market street on the far side, he found that his way out of town was blocked by a rug merchant's cart.

From the corner of his eye Bolan could see the drab limo accelerating toward him. The raucous blare of the Cossack's horn sent vendors, customers, chickens and goats scrambling in every direction.

9

Bolan zigzagged through the crowd that thronged the market center. He could hear the driver of the ZIL limousine sounding its horn behind him. Weaving a path through the busy thoroughfare, Bolan was intent on finding an escape route—some narrow alley down which he could lose his pursuers. But every possible opening appeared blocked with stalls or groups of old men squatting around brass samovars.

The *malik* of Sharuf, making his customary rounds of the market, saw the motorcyclist careering toward him. Calmly he raised his hand, palm outward. He was an official who was used to having his decrees obeyed.

Ignoring the gesture, Bolan swerved to the left. The maneuver caused the bike's handlebar to briefly nudge a heavily laden shelving unit. Goods spilled onto the street.

A farmer pushing a bicycle overladen with strings of onions ran headlong into a table of dried fruit in his effort to avoid the path of the oncoming madman on the motorcycle.

Bolan had almost reached the end of the bazaar. Now he stood a chance of outrunning the car behind him.

A lieutenant, sipping tea at an outdoor café, saw the courier pursued by an officer's car. He jumped up from the table and pulled his gun. Bolan twisted to the right as the man fired.

There was a cobbled side street not twenty yards away. Bolan aimed for the gap. A second shot hit the rear mudguard. The American hunched low over the handlebars.

A little girl, holding the hand of her younger brother, skipped out from behind a stall. Their carefree laughter turned to terrified squeals as the big machine bore down on them.

The wheels locked. Bolan plowed sideways into a table of brightly colored shawls.

Machine, clothing, the splintered display stand and Bolan all ended up in a tangled heap.

But the children were unhurt.

Hutton was right behind his officer companion as they leaped from the car. The other Russian came racing across from the café. As Bolan dragged his foot from under the bike, he found himself staring into the business end of two pistols aimed at his head.

"You! Into the car!" ordered the captain, waggling the gun just once. His English was icily correct. Evidently Robert Hutton had told him who he guessed Bolan was.

Bolan hobbled toward the car. His ankle hurt, but he was purposely exaggerating the limp. He was going to need any edge he could get.

The driver held the back door open for him. Bolan stood erect, then leaned forward to climb in, followed by the captain.

The driver was ordered back to the base.

"He's the one I told you about, Captain Strakhov," said Hutton. "He seemed very interested in the M-36."

"Ah, my little toy. She is most effective, yes?"

Bolan ignored the Russian and kept his eyes fixed on the Canadian newsman. "So after you fingered the village you stuck around to enjoy the show. I'll bet your friend here likes the pictures you took."

"I'm only doing my job," replied Hutton. "There's no law that says a neutral journalist can't report from both sides."

"Some rules don't have to be written," Bolan replied.

Hutton fidgeted and was glad they were approaching the gate. It gave him the chance to look away from Bolan.

Captain Kyril Strakhov made a small gesture with the muzzle of the Tokarev. "There are rules about dressing up in uniforms that don't belong to you. You will tell me where you got it. And why you were sneaking about here in disguise."

Seeing Strakhov's limousine returning, the sentry trotted straight to the barrier and raised it. No papers were demanded, no questions asked. At least they were taking him precisely where he wanted to go. Even if it was at gunpoint.

"I will tell you nothing," Bolan grated.

"Oh, you will talk, all right. Believe me, before we are through with you, you will tell me everything."

Strakhov turned away to watch a team of mechanics going to work. His eyes lingered on the huge doors to Hangar A. Now Bolan knew where the Dragonfire was located.

Not even the flicker of an eyelid betrayed the fact that Bolan understood the instructions Strakhov issued to the driver in Russian. They were taken to the back of a newly constructed three-story block of barracks. It did not appear to be occupied. Strakhov got out first, opened a pale green door and checked inside, then signaled for the driver to escort their prisoner into the room.

"Find Corporal Lekha," Strakhov said, "and tell him to report here." As the driver turned to leave, Strakhov gave Hutton an impatient wave. "And you can go with him. You wait in my office. The clerk will look after you."

It was obvious the Canadian was disappointed at being so abruptly dismissed. But he followed the driver without voicing any objection.

Because of the slope of the ground at the front of the building, the room was a basement. There were only three small windows set high in the back wall. Too high to see through. And Hutton had closed the door behind him.

Bolan glanced around. There was a Ping-Pong table leaning against the cinder-block wall and some baize-covered card tables stacked untidily in the corner. Strakhov, pistol in hand, picked up a metal folding chair, shook it open and placed it in the center of the bare cement floor.

The Russian motioned with the Tokarev for Bolan to sit. Despite his dismissal of the collaborator, Strakhov seemed compelled to offer some explanation. "Hutton was here just to take some photographs of me shopping in the town... that, and a short interview."

"To show the heroes of the Soviet Union being warmly welcomed by their Afghan comrades?"

"Something like that," Strakhov said, shrugging.

"Don't know why you sent Hutton away. He was present in Hanoi when they questioned some American airmen there." Bolan decided to muddy the water even further. "Of course, he brought back some useful information to our side, too. Robert Hutton has always played both ends against the middle.''

Strakhov looked interested.

Bolan continued. ''The man's a braggart and a liar. You heard how loose-lipped he was in the car. He'll be back in Pakistan next week telling them what he's seen here. He'll trade it off for some of their gossip.''

The Russian gnawed at his lip. The door opened before Bolan had a chance to smear Hutton any further, but he could tell from Strakhov's expression that the seed of doubt had been planted. Whatever happened to him now, the American avenger could take silent satisfaction that Hutton's usefulness was expended.

The morning sunlight was blocked by the huge man standing in the doorway.

''Close the door, Corporal.'' Strakhov turned to face their uninvited guest. ''I am the chief test pilot for the new M-36. So I want to know who sent you to spy on it. I am going to ask you some simple questions. You will answer them quickly and truthfully. If that proves difficult, then Corporal Lekha here can refresh your memory.''

He spoke rapidly in Russian to the noncom, who nodded eagerly and stationed himself behind the chair. ''First of all, what is your full name?''

''I'm just a cameraman for. . . .''

Bolan caught a fleeting glimpse of Strakhov's nod before the corporal's hand smacked hard into the side of his head.

The blow knocked him sideways off the seat.

Lekha's foul breath wheezed into Bolan's face as the beefy peasant hoisted him back onto the folding chair.

"I don't want him badly marked," cautioned Strakhov. "We've got to leave something for Major Krazkin."

Lekha's mouth twisted in a broken-toothed grin. He knew just what the captain meant.

Bolan glared at the corporal.

Lekha did not mistake the fury on the American's face, which only fired his enthusiasm. He raised his fist again, but Strakhov's look restrained him from delivering the blow.

"Now. We shall start again. Tell me your name...."

DAVID MCCARTER UNTIED the ragged scarf from his neck and mopped the beads of perspiration streaking his forehead. He wasn't sure if it was the midday sun or the nature of the task that was making him sweat.

From the moment that first morning patrol had gone past, McCarter had been hard at work digging up the Soviet mines from the strip outside the fence. By pressing his cheek to the ground, he could see shallow depressions where the dirt had been scraped out to conceal a mine. In one or two places the detonators had been completely exposed.

Still, the commando had worked very carefully. Using his knife point as a probe, McCarter gently brushed away the sand until he could safely lift out each mine. Then, after filling in the hole, he had relocated each explosive along a selected section of the fence.

There had been two additional jeep patrols slowly circling the perimeter, and on three other occasions local traffic along the road had forced the Englishman to take cover behind the rock.

Despite these circumstances he had transferred more than enough charges to tear out a length of the wire barrier. Now McCarter looked down at the four flat metal canisters lying at his feet. Perhaps he could use these on the road.

He scrambled up between the boulders to search for some suitable potholes. At the very edge of the track he stopped and ducked back out of sight. Half a dozen men were crossing the high ridge behind his position. He watched through the glasses and saw two more guerrillas dodging over the saddleback. McCarter knew then that he'd been right all along. Other eyes *had* been watching from up there.

The Briton continued his surveillance but lost sight of the men in the crinkled folds of tortured rock. He waited, scanning the upper slopes, but the small band of *mujahedeen* had melded into the barren scenery.

The Russians might not be the only ones to get a surprise this afternoon, thought McCarter.

The mines would blow a bloody great hole in the airfield fence. He'd found some brushwood in the ravine where he had hidden the dead courier. Together with some oily rags that had been lying by the track, the kindling should make a fair show of smoke. And he had the Soviet rifle and the Ingram to provide a noisy diversion.

McCarter went back to work enlarging the first pothole. Yes, in about three hours he should be able to put on quite a show.

He straightened up and stared at the Soviet encampment. Where was Bolan now, he wondered. McCarter had absolute faith in his American friend. He was confident that the big warrior had found some way to get inside Sharuf.

THE DARKNESS RECEDED with a roar. It sounded as if the Frogfoot was landing inside his head.

Bolan opened one eye, then the other. He was staring up at a dazzling square of sunlight. It was painful. He shut his eyes again for a moment. He tried to move. That was painful, too.

Mercifully the noise of the jet trailed off.

Bolan sat up groggily. As well as he could remember, he hadn't given any information to his captors. But the insolent mixture of silence and sarcasm that he'd stuck to had extracted its price. Bolan wondered when that giant noncom had finally gotten tired of hitting him.

Nothing seemed broken—least of all his spirit—but he carefully tested his body part by part as he slowly stood up. He had to clutch at his trousers. They had taken away his belt. And his boots. The Beretta and its holster had been stripped off, too.

Bolan looked around.

He was alone in a different room, but he presumed it was still in the new barracks. It had the same smell of cheap paint, drying mortar and freshly shaved wood. And the cinder-block walls were identical.

Blinking at the sunlight streaming through the high-set window, Bolan moved slowly across the room to check what was out there. That was when he noticed his fingers. Faint traces of black ink were still trapped in the ridges and whorls of his fingertips. He sniffed at them and detected the astringent scent of cleaning fluid.

Obviously Strakhov had taken his fingerprints while he was unconscious. Bolan guessed they would have photographed him, too. Strakhov must have been quite anxious to find out who he really was.

Bolan hauled himself up to window level. A guard stood outside, as he'd suspected. The fellow was chatting with another soldier, keeping a careful eye in both directions as he took a couple of drags on his friend's cigarette. Bolan grimaced in pain as he dropped silently back to the floor.

Judging by the length of the shadows outside, he assumed it was early afternoon. Two o'clock perhaps. Maybe two-thirty. That peasant had really put him to sleep. Bolan knew he had to make his move soon. There was little time to waste.

Of course, there would be an armed sentry stationed on the other side of the plain wooden door. Chance dictated the man was going to get hurt. Maybe badly. Bolan hoped it was Corporal Lekha in the corridor outside.

THE SU-25 TAXIED TO A HALT. Strakhov waited as patiently as he could for the turbojets to shut down before repeating his question. He was still fuming at Lekha. That dumb peasant didn't know his own strength.

"Don't worry, Captain," bellowed Sergeant Belenko over the whining engines, "your ship is all fueled up and fully loaded. I had my men check her out before we started this job."

The sergeant looked back at the Hind with an unhappy shrug. Some Afghan marksman had got lucky: a bullet had punctured the tail-rotor gear box.

"That's not what I came to see you for!" Strakhov's eyes were narrowed as he shouted to make himself heard. "I want a couple of short electrical cables, the kind with spring clips on the end."

"You'll have to ask Khomalev. He looks after that sort of thing." The sergeant jerked his head to indicate the maintenance electrician. "He'll fix you up with what you need."

It didn't matter now if Major Krazkin returned and claimed the prisoner, Strakhov thought. The American's fingerprints and pictures were already sent directly to Moscow. The package had left on the lunchtime truck. This was one intelligence coup the ambitious major would not be able to hoard and claim for himself. Strakhov anticipated the great pleasure he would derive in making the prisoner talk before the KGB detail returned from Bas-i-Dam that afternoon.

"Khomalev, I want you to find me some electrical cables."

10

Lekha was still smarting from the captain's rebuke. So maybe he had hit that damn American a little too hard. But the man had asked for it.

At least it was cooler inside. Better than standing guard out in the sun like Private Satnik. The corporal squatted on his heels, cradling the well-oiled Kalashnikov on his lap.

He spat out a curse when the prisoner started banging on the door. Lekha ambled down the corridor and unlocked the door.

He took two paces backward. He moved very quickly for a man of his bulk. He didn't want to let the prisoner get within range to grab at his rifle.

The American now stood in the doorway, gesturing that he needed to use the toilet. The corporal signaled with the barrel that he should move off to the left.

Bolan walked slowly down the passage with both hands held clearly away from his sides. Lekha snapped in Russian, "The door on your right." Bolan glanced back as if he didn't understand, then obeyed the Russian's gesture and pushed open the door to the washroom. Lekha lounged in the entrance while Bolan used the stall.

It was an inside room. The only opening in the wall was a ventilator shaft high in one corner. It was securely covered with a wire-mesh grille, the duct barely large enough to accommodate a man. The place was not completely finished yet. The towel rails still had to be installed, and soap dispensers, rare in Afghanistan stood in a cardboard box at the end of the row of washbasins. Lekha watched as Bolan moved across to rinse his hands.

"Hey, Corp!" It was the other guard shouting down the corridor. Lekha stepped back and waved that everything was all right. Bolan could hear the relief in the private's voice. "Oh, you're there. I looked in the window and couldn't see him. . . ."

From his position now, Lekha could not see Bolan. The American warrior figured this was the only chance he might get. And he seized it.

Bolan snatched up one of the plastic soap bottles and squirted its contents on the floor behind him. The oily puddle began to spread across the tiles.

Then he jumped up onto a sink and reached for the ventilator grille. Lekha heard the rattle of the wire mesh. He poked his head around the doorjamb just as Bolan had the covering half torn off.

"Stop!" shouted the corporal, stepping into the room. His foot came down squarely in the soap slick. Lekha was still looking up at Bolan and bringing his rifle to bear as his foot skidded out from under him. The startled Russian threw his arm out to regain his balance but it was too late.

Bolan leaped down as the corporal crashed onto the floor.

He grabbed the big noncom's ankle and dragged him forward, careful not to slip in his own trap.

The AK-47 clattered on the tile floor. Lekha opened his mouth to shout, but Bolan's knee, backed by his full weight, dropped across the jailer's exposed windpipe. The scream was squashed at its source.

With stiffened fingers, Bolan followed through with a rabbit punch aimed straight into the hollow of the Russian's throat. Lekha could make no more than a horrible rasping sound as he feebly tried to throw off the American.

Bolan tangled his fingers in the man's hair and dragged the guy's head up before smashing his skull onto the bare tiles. The force of the blow shattered the occipital bone.

Bolan could hear boot steps echoing down the corridor. He scooped the knife-styled bayonet from Lekha's scabbard just as the other sentry raced into the washroom. Bolan's hand swept forward in a fluid arc, hurling the razor-edged weapon with deadly accuracy.

The guard was utterly surprised to find himself grasping at the hilt protruding from his solar plexus. His jaw dropped open slackly, and he collapsed without making a sound.

Bright rivulets of blood leaked from under both bodies. Bolan took the private's boots and belt, then grabbed Lekha's assault rifle. He also recovered the bayonet from the soldier's body and wiped it on his uniform. He slipped the blade into his boot.

Bolan hurried up the steps, checked that no one was passing in front of the building, and strode out purposefully across the compound.

EVERYTHING WAS READY. A series of explosives was partially concealed by the fence. McCarter had stacked the oily rags and some broken kindling together. The potholes were enlarged to take the last four mines. The Englishman hadn't planted them yet, in case he blew up some innocent Afghan traveling to the town.

As he stood judging where he should position himself on the slope to safely make the shot that would explode the barrier wire, he heard the clink of a loose pebble. McCarter ducked back into the hollow between the rocks. The sound had come from off to the left.

There was another faint scuff of grit. It came from closer this time.

The top of McCarter's cap was just visible above the curved edge of the boulder. The head-piece was propped on the end of the Soviet rifle; McCarter himself was already crouching thirty feet away.

A cloaked figure padded into view, intently watching the decoy. McCarter advanced to intercept his unknown stalker. The man froze on the spot when he felt the hard point of the snub-nosed weapon prod into his ribs.

Abdur Jahan's eyes almost popped at being taken unawares. Then, recognizing the "foreign correspondent," his fleshy lips parted in a smile. His jowls began to shake with suppressed mirth. "Your friend shoots better than any newsman. And you're a better tracker!"

McCarter nodded. There was no point now in denying it.

"You might have taken my life, if Allah had so willed it." Jahan let out a piercing whistle. Seven more freedom fighters appeared. "But it would have cost you dearly."

Again McCarter nodded. There was no point in denying that, either. He recognized half the men from the ambush setup.

"This morning, when we found you had

vanished, Tarik Khan sent us to track you down.''

"You've been following the wrong party. Robert Hutton is the man who betrayed your village. It's not the first time he's done it.''

"And you, what are you doing here?"

"Creating a diversion for the work my friend has to do. I intend to make as much noise and smoke as I can to distract the Russians. Make them think it's a raid on the airfield.''

Abdur Jahan looked up at the steep rock-strewn slopes that towered behind them. He shook his head. "If they send the helicopter. . . .''

"If the Dragonfire comes, my partner will be at the controls.''

One of the men barked out a warning. He was pointing back to the road, where a cloud of dust signified the rapid approach of vehicles. McCarter lifted his field glasses: a jeep, trucks, a couple of tankers followed by some troop carriers. It was the biggest convoy he'd seen yet. It was time to plant the mines.

McCarter glanced at his watch, trying to figure out the convoy's ETA at the spot below. They might get there a moment or two before three o'clock, but this was too good an opportunity to miss.

"Tell your men to give me a hand! I've got

some mines over there. Let's make sure we give the Russians a proper welcome.''

BOLAN MARCHED between two rows of prefabricated huts, with Hangar A looming to his right. A door squeaked open as he passed. A soldier sauntered out, shielding his eyes from the sunlight. The man paid no attention to the ''corporal,'' and Bolan kept walking.

Bolan turned at the end of the huts and made it to the cover of a parked truck just as Strakhov appeared. The captain came out of the wicket gate set in the huge doors of Hangar A. He was humming to himself as he walked along with a pair of electrical cables dangling from his hand.

Bolan waited only a moment before hurrying along the side of the giant shed. A jumble of empty crates was heaped up at the back. The big American squeezed behind them and found a small window. It had been left open for whatever ventilation it could provide.

Bolan wriggled through into the rear of the hangar. It was a storage area for tires. New ones were laid out by size on metal racks; the used tires were stacked on the oil-stained floor. Bolan paused to let his eyes adjust to the dimness.

The noise of a drill had covered his unauthorized entrance. Three men in coveralls were standing under the tail of a Hind D. Two more were working at a nearby bench, and a uniformed guard was lounging against the far wall. He was the only one actually carrying a gun. Parked parallel to the chopper the men were working on was the Dragonfire.

Hangar A was cavernous. It had room for the maintenance and storage of at least four helicopters, but the Hind and the M-36 were the only ones inside the building. Within the confines of the hangar, the Dragonfire appeared even more sinister than against the backdrop of a blue sky.

The assault chopper was fifty-five feet in length, with a five-bladed rotor. Pairs of AT-6 Spiral missiles hung under the tips of its stub wings, which also carried launch pods bristling with S-5 rockets.

Random reflections from the working lamps trained on the Hind glinted from the bulletproof glass encasing the dual cockpits.

On the underside Bolan could see the sinuous bulges of its sensor pods, which housed the infrared, low-light television and computerized defense systems. The gunship squatted there on its retractable landing gear like a flying lizard still gorged on its last meal.

The high-pitched whine of the drill cut off abruptly. One of the mechanics shouted. Bolan stood absolutely still, ready for anything. But the technician was only calling for the guard to give them a hand moving a heavy wheeled gantry into place alongside the Hind. The soldier rested his rifle against a wall and walked over to help.

Bolan glanced at the clock over the workbench. It showed four minutes to the hour. He checked the Kalashnikov. He trusted David McCarter would hit the perimeter fence right on time. Bolan knew he was going to need the noise and confusion to cover the shooting in the hangar.

He'd only have seconds to reach the chopper and start it up because when he pulled the trigger, all hell would break loose.

He didn't have to wait.

Strakhov had discovered the sentries' bodies in the washroom.

A Klaxon blared out the alarm.

MAJOR KRAZKIN WAS PLEASED with himself. He had good reason to be. The tiring trip to Bas-i-Dam had proved most rewarding.

Krazkin was also thankful to have met up with the new detachment on its way to Sharuf; with tankers carrying the combustible mixture for young Strakhov's flamethrowing prototype, it was a stoutly defended column.

Too much firepower for those *mujahedeen* madmen to risk attacking. He felt a great sense of relief at having got through the narrow mountain passes without incident, especially with the report of an attack on a convoy near

Mukna. He smiled now as his jeep led the well-armed convoy on the last few miles to the air base. Not far to go.

Krazkin was in a good enough mood to offer his driver a cigarette. The man had just taken his hand from the steering wheel when the vehicle bumped over the last of McCarter's mines.

The right front wheel was blown off, and the jeep slewed violently before rolling over and crushing its occupants.

Krazkin was not killed outright. His shattered torso was trapped under the weight of the wreckage. He lived just long enough to see the first of the big ZIL fuel transports hit two of the mines. They exploded fore and aft, followed a millisecond later by the white-hot eruption of the bulk-chemical tank.

The driver was vaporized as the roadway turned into a river of fire engulfing men and machines alike.

The concussive force of the explosion stunned McCarter. Somewhere amid the pounding reverberations he remembered thinking that if this was meant to be just a stage-army diversion, what the hell could he do for an encore?

THE MOMENT the Klaxon began its rhythmic braying, the uniformed soldier ran back to the wall to pick up his rifle. The mechanics merely looked puzzled.

The tin sheeting of the hangar rattled as it was buffeted by the first shock waves of a massive explosion. Seconds later a mighty deep-throated rumbling reached them.

One of the mechanics raced toward the wicket door to see what was happening outside. Conflicting orders were being shouted, jeeps and trucks were starting up, and men ran about in confusion.

Even Bolan was surprised at McCarter's splendid effort to divert the Russians. He glanced at the wall clock—one minute to three! He silently commended McCarter on his timing.

He stepped out from behind the cover of the tire rack. A second violent explosion shook the building just as Bolan squeezed the trigger of the Kalashnikov, taking the guard out.

The 7.62mm bullet shattered the man's spine. Bolan let the gun drift to the right, and the same burst killed the mechanic standing by the drill bench. Jars shattered, cans bounced and cardboard boxes jumped off the shelves as Bolan sprayed the work area.

One of the technicians tried to clamber down from the work gantry. He slipped under the railing and started to fall to the floor. Bolan's next burst caught him in midair. He was dead when he hit the concrete.

The Executioner raced toward the Dragonfire. He aimed the assault rifle at the wicket door, but the panicking Khomalev had already tumbled through it and scrambled out of the line of fire.

The last two Russians were felled with single shots, neither of them understanding why he was being killed by one of his own corporals.

Bolan paused only long enough to snatch up a long rope and shackle lying coiled on top of an oil drum. Then he slid back the helicopter's portside hatch. As he fastened the shackle to the handrail, he thought he saw the small door at the back of the hangar swing open for a moment. He fired a burst into the shadows, and the magazine ran dry. But no answering fire came.

There was little room inside what in other combat choppers would have been the troop compartment; most of the space was taken up with long-range fuel tanks and containers for the flamethrowing mixture. Bolan squeezed through to the cockpit.

He checked the crawl space to the weapons operator's seat. A flight helmet lay on the floor. Bolan grabbed it and strapped himself into the pilot's seat.

The controls were eerily familiar. Geoffrey Miles had done an excellent job with the mock-up at Fullerton. Bolan scanned the crowded banks of gauges, readouts, screens, dials and switches. He shut out the noise of the camp and concentrated utterly on the start-up procedure that had been drilled into him back in the States.

"CAPTAIN!" PANTED KHOMALEV. "Captain Strakhov!" The agitated electrician tugged at the officer's sleeve.

"What the hell is going on?" Strakhov demanded.

"Hangar A...attacked...a corporal...I don't know who he...."

"I do! It's the M-36 he's after." Strakhov waved down a truckload of soldiers on their way to ward off the guerrilla attack on the far side of the field. "Follow me!"

BOLAN FLIPPED ON THE FUEL SWITCH, checked that the throttle was closed and hit the booster button. Three seconds of full-rich mixture, then he cut it back. He tried the ignition; the two Isotov turboshafts fired up.

The noise within the hangar was barely dampened by the padded flight helmet. As Bolan was making sure the exhaust fans were running he felt something nudge him on his shoulder.

Twisting around, he saw a white-faced Robert Hutton crouching in the hatchway behind him. Terrified though he appeared to be, the journalist had a steady grip on the stolen pistol aimed at Bolan's ear. So the door *had* opened then; Hutton was the rat that had sneaked into the hangar....

"You got me into this shit," shouted Hutton. His mouth worked like a struggling fish. Bolan didn't have to lip-read to catch his drift. "Now you're going to fly me out!"

There wasn't time to argue the point.

Bolan checked the revs and oil pressure, then switched on the alternator. His right hand rested on the cyclic controls, the other gripped the throttle. Hutton braced himself in the doorway as the helicopter lifted off.

The hangar door completely filled the rectangular sight within Bolan's visor. He unleashed a missile....

11

Strakhov shouted encouragement to the men bunching for a frontal assault. He turned away and signaled for the second squad to follow him to the rear just as the doors exploded outward. Jagged sheets of torn metal whirled about on the hot blast.

The Dragonfire emerged, spitting death as it clawed its way through the fiery turbulence and up into the open air. The twisted bodies of groaning men formed a carpet beneath the rising aircraft. Bolan scythed through the Russians scurrying for cover. Behind him, the front of Hangar A began to sag inward. The building swayed but held its ground.

Bolan continued to use the dual firing controls to lay down a withering hail of hot lead. Gouts of dirt spurted up in a jittery row until they reached a speeding GAZ patrol car. The driver slumped over the wheel. The vehicle swung out of control, plowed through the door of the nearest hut and exploded.

Strakhov, weighed down by the lifeless body

of Khomalev, watched as the monstrous shadow of the Dragonfire blocked out the sun. He struggled to sit up, awkwardly shifting about to scan the southwestern sector of the sky. Where was Nekrovich? He should be returning from his patrol at any moment. Strakhov pushed aside the corpse and got to his feet. And what about the helicopter the technicians had been working on—was it in flying order?

Bolan was rising steadily now. He could see the dust trails left by the troops racing toward the smoke-wreathed ambush across the field. He manipulated the rudder and took aim at the Frogfoot. Another Spiral missile belched from beneath the Dragonfire's stub wing. It plunged into the bomber's fuselage immediately below the cockpit and ripped apart the central core of the plane.

The officer in the control tower was screaming into his microphone when he glanced out of the window and saw the Dragonfire hovering outside. Two of the solid-fuel rockets leaped from their pods and turned the tower into a twisted, melting inferno.

Another touch of the rudder pedal and Bolan accelerated away from the airstrip. Strakhov watched him go, curious about the rope that trailed from the craft.

The soldier at his feet was moaning through blood-flecked lips. A fragment from the shattered hangar door was embedded deeply in his chest. He was pleading for a medic. Strakhov stepped over him without a downward glance and strode into the shambles of the hangar.

"BACK! GET BACK!" McCarter urged Abdur Jahan and his men to withdraw farther up the hillside.

The Russian soldiers in the convoy had been given a baptism by fire. The survivors from the rear of the column had taken cover amid the nearest rocks, where a senior NCO had instilled some order in them. He directed a steady stream of gunfire at the rebel hiding places above.

McCarter could see the reinforcements speeding toward the wire. The sounds of their own firefight found a popping, crackling echo in the action around the distant buildings.

There was a searing orange-red flash as the top of the control tower exploded. Then McCarter spotted the Dragonfire rising from the wreckage of the Soviet camp. His job was done. They had inflicted all the damage they could here.

The ex-SAS commando peppered the rocks below until the Ingram was empty, then, taking advantage of the brief lull he'd forced, followed the retreating *mujahedeen.*

BOLAN GLANCED OVER his shoulder. Hutton was still jammed in the doorway. He appeared composed. The gun aimed at Bolan was rock steady. The Canadian had picked the winning side again—for now, at least.

"Let's get out of here!" Hutton shouted. "We're wasting time."

"I'm going to pick up my partner," grunted Bolan. "But I'm sure you won't understand that."

He shook his head and focused the range-finder on the three truckloads of reinforcements fast coming up. There was no way Hutton would shoot him. Certainly not while they were in the sky.

Bolan looked down, the computerized nerve system transmitting the precise coordinates to the electronically controlled guns, and pushed the firing button. The desert floor churned and shook as he shredded the opposition.

He banked right. Now Bolan could more clearly see the extent of what David McCarter had accomplished. The road had been deeply cratered where the GAZ tankers had exploded. Through the bullet-proof blister he could pick out the antlike figures of the Russian resisters crawling from cover to cover, firing up the slope at the fleeing Afghans.

McCarter was trying to reach an open stretch near the top of the first ridge. It would take him a few moments yet.

Bolan zoomed down until he could see the

white ovals of the soldiers' upturned faces. They were cheering him on! They had been too occupied with troubles of their own to witness the carnage on the airfield behind them. None of them realized the Dragonfire had fallen into determinedly hostile hands. Now they were going to find out.

Hutton was shouting empty threats as the chopper twisted above the smoldering devastation of the convoy. Bolan flipped open the cover of the flamethrower switch. He was about to give the Soviets a further taste of their own medicine.

The NCO who had taken charge was flapping his arms, frantically trying to communicate that the pilot should be chasing after the departing rebels.

In the final instant, the whirring hawk hovering above him changed from a symbol of relief to one of terrifying menace. A long tongue of bright fire unfurled, spraying the unlucky survivors with the scorching agony of sudden death. Now it was the turn of Abdur Jahan's men to cheer. For once the terrifying dragon machine was on their side.

The guerrillas paused just long enough to see the chopper swooping down to incinerate their pursuers. The hunters had become the prey. The Dragonfire's attack had ensured that the rebels could safely escape over the high ridge.

One blond recruit was sprinting away down the track. The back of his tunic was ablaze. He tried to shed the jacket as he ran, but his undershirt was on fire, too. Bolan glanced down at him and pressed the trigger. A complex of integrated circuits did the rest. Victim and machine were fused into one killing event.

Bolan's face was a taut mask as he completed the grim task. He was fighting a private war now, for private reasons.

Through the flames and smoke below, Bolan could see the courageous smile of Tarik Khan's little boy. He felt the presence of April Rose with him, too.

And memories of other comrades slain or maimed on far-flung battlefields crowded in on him. No, The Executioner was not fighting because of covert instructions or in the name of some abstract ideal, but for people, very real people who had made a very real difference in this endless war.

Even Hutton was sickened by the stench coming up at them from the burning ground. They were flying so low that they would have been engulfed in the same black smoke they were creating if it were not blown away by the backwash of the multibladed rotor above.

Hutton watched as the man at the controls methodically, dispassionately eliminated his enemy. His lips pulled back in a harsh smile, because he had finally recalled the sergeant's real name.

It had come to him in a flash. It was Bolan, Sergeant Mack Bolan. From Pittsfield. The pilot of the Dragonfire was not quite as Hutton remembered him from that affair at Hoi Binh, but there was no doubt in his mind that he was indeed the same man.

Bolan made another pass parallel to the road. There was no sign of movement. The slaughter was complete. An entire convoy had been totally wiped out. Then he banked and rose, closing in on the patch of bare rock where McCarter was bidding farewell to Jahan and his band.

Bolan crooked his finger. Hutton bent forward to hear him say: "I'm going to pick up my friend now. If there's any trouble, we go down together. Understood?"

As if to emphasize the point, he decreased the collective and dropped the machine sharply. Hutton nodded. Understood.

The end of the long rope was brushing the surface of the bare rock. With a final wave to the brave *mujahedeen*, McCarter caught hold of the lifeline and hauled himself up hand over hand.

Bolan took advantage of those few moments, hovering, to switch on the radar scanners and infrared sighting systems. The glowing screen showed a blip coming in from the southwest. It was moving fast. Bolan activated the Nevski antimissile system. The Dragonfire was ready for trouble.

McCarter got his elbow hooked over the edge of the floor and swung himself aboard.

He was surprised when he saw Hutton holding a gun. The Canadian jerked the pistol, and McCarter brushed past him. The Englishman gave Bolan a thumbs-up signal for their success so far but raised an inquiring eyebrow with regard to Hutton.

Bolan waved him through to the weapons-control station and then, as McCarter's body blocked the newsman's view, made a clear sign that the Englishman should take over the controls.

McCarter clambered down into the forward section of the double cockpit. Bolan kept his hands exactly in place but released the pressure of his grip when he felt McCarter take control of the ship.

"My God, there's a chopper coming after us!" Hutton shouted in alarm. "Over there, look! Let's get out of here."

"First we're going back for Kasim." Bolan looked up as he unplugged the helmet wiring. "The boy who got burned."

"The hell with that! We're going south," blustered Hutton, sneaking another nervous glance out the door. "We've got to save our own skins. Who gives a shit about the kid?''

"I do."

"But that's going deeper into the country, you fool. They'll cut us off. . . hunt us down."

"We'll have to risk it. I gave my word, but you won't understand that, either."

Bolan got his feet well clear of the rudders.

Hutton stole another glance at the approaching Hind. Nerves fraying, he was caught off guard when Bolan leaped up and threw himself forward. Hutton felt his wrist clamped in a bone-crushing grip as he was slammed against the rear wall.

The Dragonfire was climbing steeply, trying to clear the razor teeth of the mountaintops. McCarter juggled the controls, compensating for the sudden shifting of weight as his partner went for Hutton. McCarter was powerless to help Bolan. The Englishman had his hands full eluding the Hind.

McCarter caught a bright wink of flame as the Russian pilot launched a missile.

12

Fire at the new M-36? Nekrovich felt uneasy. Despite the chaos he'd seen, he double-checked with Strakhov. The chief test pilot's angry voice had crackled through the static: bring down the Dragonfire at all costs!

Nekrovich made a last visual of the airfield. Strakhov still hadn't got the other Hind aloft. And the stolen chopper was about to vanish over the long sway-backed ridge ahead of them both.

The young pilot remembered the discussions in the mess last year concerning the South Korean airliner incident. Orders were orders—that's what had been concluded—and they were not to be questioned.

His fingers stabbed at the Fire button. . . .

McCARTER KNEW THE DRILL, but he wasn't going to place all his faith in the Nevski defenses. Not enough was known about the system. That's why they'd been sent in to steal the Dragonfire. He dropped out of sight over the looming cliffs in an effort to outmaneuver the projectile.

The sudden swooping motion threw the other two men off balance. They fell back, and Bolan found himself pinned against the bulging walls of the chemical containers. Hutton recovered first and rushed the American, ramming his knee into Bolan's groin. The pistol slithered uselessly about the floor with every sudden movement of the chopper.

McCarter made an allowance for the updrafts and let the chopper slide in a shallow cross-slope descent. The massive rock walls ended with a solitary conical spire. McCarter aimed straight for it as the missile plunged over the ridge in hot pursuit.

The Dragonfire banked sharply around the granite finger. Bolan had to release his grip on Hutton's shirt and grab at a metal retaining bracket to save himself being flung out the door.

The chopper's abrupt maneuver caused the loose band of hemp to buckle in the open entrance. Hutton snatched it and looped a coil around Bolan's neck. The Executioner's free hand snaked toward his boot, where he still had Lekha's bayonet hidden. But the next lurch threw them both rolling on the floor.

The Englishman pulled back on the cyclic stick as he decreased the collective. The M-36 responded to his touch immediately. It came to a quick midair stop on the far side of the stone column.

Hutton was winded as he slammed into the cushioned side of the doorframe, but he still had Bolan tangled in the rope. He forced the big man's head and shoulders out beyond the edge of the floor. Bolan hooked his instep around the fuel tank support to stop himself from sliding out.

The rocket was closing in for the kill. The guidance telemetry, built with components hastily designed from computer circuitry stolen from the West, made a last-minute correction. But the missile was thrown into a tight turn too late to avoid the tall spire. There was a vivid flash as the explosion tore out huge chunks of rock and hurled them into space.

McCarter was already climbing fast. Jockeying the controls, he pushed the Dragonfire into a perilous S-turn as he sought cover in the nearby crags. The enemy pilot's sensors couldn't detect them through millions of tons of mountainside.

Bolan had struggled free of the rope, but now he had to clutch at the handrail to prevent the Canadian from pushing him clear out the doorway.

Hutton made a desperate lunge to dislodge the American meddler. Bolan, still grasping the vertical handrail, swung himself bodily into the slipstream. The journalist hung in the doorway for a moment, trying to regain his balance, but he couldn't. As he tumbled past Bolan out the open hatch, his flailing hand seized the only thing left—the rope.

Hutton felt it burning through his fingers as he fell. With a desperate effort he grabbed hold of it with both hands. He was swinging in mid-air, trailing back under the chopper, his screams whipped away by the wind. The strain was intolerable.

Bolan looked down: they were positioned almost directly above the other gunship. He whipped out his blade and hacked through the braided hemp.

"Save me!"

"You had your chance." Bolan sliced through the last strands.

Hutton plummeted like a stone, still clutching the rope and screaming. It was like pushing steak into a grinder—the spinning rotor blades below made mincemeat out of him.

McCarter glanced out from the cockpit and saw the Hind momentarily surrounded by a shimmering pink halo.

NEKROVICH EASED THE HIND along the face of the reddish gray cliffs. He had heard the explosion before clearing the ridge. He saw the smoke ball and was now warily scanning the slopes below for some sign of the wreckage.

It didn't occur to him to look up and behind his shoulder. The Dragonfire was positioned slightly behind and four hundred feet above the Hind.

He felt a tremendous shudder and struggled to keep his craft under control. Then, from the corner of his eye, he caught a glimpse of the sinister death shadow of the Dragonfire. Then came the flash of a wing-mounted missile. His tail rotor disintegrated, and he lost all directional stability.

The Hind slowly began to spin in the opposite direction to its main rotor. It was still waltzing sedately as it struck the solid wall of rock and mushroomed into a thousand flying fragments of metal, perspex and fiberglass. The fuel tanks exploded, and the Hind left a smoke-blackened stain against the mountainside as the last pieces rattled down on the scree below.

"YAHOO!" WHOOPED McCARTER.

Bolan was still rubbing his neck as he returned to the cockpit.

"Never seen anyone improvise an air-to-air missile before!" said the commando, grinning. "I like your style."

"You held up your end well, too," replied Bolan. "Now let's go and pick up Tarik Khan's son."

Both men kept a sharp eye for any sign of movement on the barren terrain below. They knew that Strakhov would be coming up after them. Bolan had no idea how much work remained to be done on the Hind in the hangar to make it fully operational. But sooner or later the proud Russian captain would be dogging their trail.

Sporadic pockets of greenery marked those few places where irrigation was possible in the endless desolation below. There were regions of Afghanistan that were pleasantly fertile, but these ravaged, rumpled drylands stood in stark contrast to the well-farmed river plains of Jalalabad and the far-off Hari Rud.

"That looks like the minaret of Ghazarid! Way over there...."

"Got it," confirmed Bolan. He turned ten degrees left. "And that must be the Sufisa range ahead. I make it about six minutes flying time to Mukna."

ONE SUSPICIOUS TRIBESMAN took a potshot as the hated chopper came in to land. McCarter risked his neck by standing at the hatch, furiously waving his off-white native shirt. Every gun in the village was trained on the doorway as the two foreigners emerged. The tribesmen lowered their guns only when Tarik Khan appeared satisfied at the presence of the two men.

"So you got what you came for?" The muscles along the leader's jawline worked tautly as he indicated the Dragonfire.

"I have come back for your son, Tarik Khan," Bolan replied simply.

He gave the tribal chieftain a brief explanation: if the boy did not receive modern medical aid very quickly, he would die.

It did not take long to convince the leader, who felt instinctively he could trust the blue-eyed warrior.

"You will fly out under cover of darkness?"

Bolan shook his head. "We cannot wait. We must leave immediately."

He did not reveal the crucial timing of their refueling rendezvous to Tarik Khan. In the remote wastes of the Baluchistan desert a commercial gasoline tanker loaded with aviation fuel would be crossing the little-used Makran highway. It would wait only thirty minutes for them at the Sakshan Wells. That was when they needed the cover of darkness.

McCarter explained what had happened when he'd joined forces with Abdur Jahan and the other *mujahedeen*. Tarik Khan shouted out a brief translation of the more colorful parts of their attack and the villagers gave a rousing cheer.

"We cannot delay our departure, either," said the chief, as he watched his son being loaded onto a makeshift stretcher. "After what has happened at Sharuf, the Communists will strike out at anyone in reprisal. But Jahan will know where to find us."

McCarter made sure the pallet was securely wedged on the floor between the tanks. Tarik Khan fastened the restraining straps himself as he bade farewell to the boy.

"May Allah watch over you—" he looked up at the two Westerners and encompassed them both with a sweep of his hand "—over you all!"

BOLAN GLANCED AT THE FUEL GAUGE. He made a few rapid calculations. They would just be able to make it. He corrected their course and cut back the cyclic slightly for maximum fuel efficiency.

McCarter eased himself through the cockpit. "I'll see how young Kasim is doing."

The boy was resting uneasily. McCarter slid the hatchway back and looked out. Beneath them he saw tiny dots where a herd of karakul sheep was grazing. Farther off, he made out the plodding line of a camel caravan heading for a pass through the distant snowcapped mountains. They were the only signs of life on the barren terrain. Suddenly an angry, buzzing black speck appeared in the distance.

He tapped Bolan on the shoulder. "I think I saw...."

"I know. The radar picked him up two minutes ago. Damn, lost him again."

"He's hedgehopping." McCarter forced a tight grin. "Or maybe I should say dune jumping."

"You stay with Kasim," Bolan said. "I'll try to outrun him. We can't risk a dogfight with the boy aboard.

"Two can play at that game! Hang on. I'm dropping lower. Got to see if I can lose him."

Bolan shut the throttle, split the engine and rotor needles, and went into autorotation; at this speed it made for a dangerously rapid descent. They dropped below the skyline of the barren hills. Bolan flared out, recovered power, then accelerated away to the south.

A startled goatherd scrambled for shelter as the helicopter skimmed over his village and plunged into the broad valley beyond.

In less than a minute they had covered more than three miles. The deep trough began to swing back toward the east, toward Russian-held territory.

Bolan flew along the contours of the right slope and slipped between the jagged peaks, wheeling like a hawk as he thundered through the gap, pushing on for the safety of the Baluchistan border.

The mottled landscape ahead was split by a triangular wedge of arid hills. Bolan touched the rudder. He was going to take the deeper canyon to the left.

Just as he was about to make the turn, he saw Strakhov's attack chopper drifting toward them. The bastard had cut them off at the pass! Bolan threw the M-36 into a sharp bank to the right.

13

McCarter grabbed the doorframe to steady himself. He had seen the Hind, too, arrogantly waiting for them. Why hadn't the man fired? Strakhov must have had them in his sights long enough to launch a missile.

Bolan knew why. Strakhov's attempt to imprison and interrogate the American might have failed miserably, but the Russian wanted to show them who was the better pilot. The captain had to prove he could outfly his enemy before he blasted them out of the sky.

Bolan reoriented himself with a brief survey of the instruments. The hairs on his neck prickled. Was the Russian on his tail even now? Gloating? His internal radar told him they were still within range. Damn, Strakhov was playing with him.

"Recognize where we are?" shouted Bolan. He was pushing it flat out. The needle had just passed 330 km/h.

"Yes, I think so. This must be the top end of the Khazani Valley." It was where the German cameraman had first filmed the Dragonfire.

"Right. Any sign of him?"

"I think he's still hanging on back there. But . . . ."

"Yeah?" Bolan was concentrating on the split-second timing of what he was about to attempt.

"You're bloody low, Mack. These cliffs close right in at the pass. Remember the movie?"

"The gap's a good seventy feet across, maybe eighty feet wide." The Khazani Pass lay two miles dead ahead.

"Well, sure, at least seventy feet," agreed McCarter, "but that only gives us—"

"Seven feet of clearance on either side!"

It didn't take McCarter too long to figure the odds. "Go for it! I'll stay with the lad."

Bolan sat squarely in the seat. The slightest miscalculation now and they were all dead. He watched the narrowing gap zoom closer through the illuminated rectangle of the rangefinder. He aligned the central cross hairs with a broken-toothed pinnacle far beyond and, scarcely daring to breathe, flew straight for it.

The rotorwash dislodged stones from the surrounding cliffs, sending them bouncing down into the creek below as the Dragonfire roared through the deadly pass.

They were through and out into the open in a whirling flash. The mammoth stone walls fell back on either side like great folds in a faded curtain.

"Hold on!" Bolan kicked the rudders, skidding across the updrafts, juggling the stick and the collective as he brought the Dragonfire to a sickeningly fast stop. He allowed a half rotation as he began to ascend. The craft lurched alarmingly as the nose began to lift.

STRAKHOV SAW THE DRAGONFIRE vanish through the defile. What did that crazy American think he was doing? The Soviet pilot shook his head. It was a gesture partly in respect for the other man's daring, partly a refusal to ignore the obvious challenge. So now it was "follow the leader"; well, they wouldn't shake him off that easily.

Buffeted by the turbulent eddies left in the wake of the big gunship, Strakhov hammered through the pass. But the sky ahead was empty!

He glanced right—nothing—then swung left, suddenly fearful that he might have been outwitted.

Then he saw them. The M-36 was rearing up against the clifftops above him. Strakhov banked into a climb.

The game was over.

It was time for the kill.

Strakhov watched that horrible silhouette swinging into his sights. He had flown in her, sweated in her and exulted in her power and agility. Once when he had run out of fuel near the Arghandab River he'd slept in her. He had put that helicopter through her paces. And she'd tested him, too.

The Dragonfire was his ship.

The only thing Strakhov had never done was attack her. Now he was going to blast her out of the sky.

The M-36 was aligned dead center—just as Strakhov was in Bolan's visor.

The last thing the Russian pilot saw as he reached for the button was a blazing stream of liquid fire streaking toward him.

The cabin was instantly engulfed in a hissing, crackling smear of superheated chemicals. The cockpit imploded as the searing, choking blanket sucked out the oxygen. The wiring melted, the hydraulics wilted and the controls fused. Then the intense heat set off the ammunition supply.

SMALLER EXPLOSIONS were triggered within the already raging fireball. McCarter watched as the flaming wreckage dropped onto the valley floor, while several chunks of smoking debris fluttered down in slower trajectories.

Bolan eased the Dragonfire away from the crumbling walls of the ancient rift, soaring up to the cleaner air above. He did not look back as he touched the rudder and pointed the war machine south for the border.

THE AMERICAN FIGHTERS closed up slowly in the darkness. The lead escort approached on the port side, blinked his lights, then tipped his wings in salute.

McCarter fiddled with the radio until he made contact with the pilots.

"There's a big deck waiting out at sea for you, sir." The young pilot's voice crackled with excitement, his eagerness betraying how thrilled he was to be flying this welcoming mission. "Follow me home, Big Phoenix!"

BOLAN JUMPED DOWN onto the carrier deck as a crowd of officers and technicians swarmed around the stolen gunship. It would be lowered out of sight within minutes.

McCarter shuddered involuntarily in the crisp sea breeze.

"Careful with the boy. He's in bad shape," Bolan told the medics.

"Wake up the surgeon," said one of the junior officers. "Tell him there's work to do."

The orderly trotted away.

Bolan searched among the congratulating well-wishers for a familiar face. He finally saw Brognola standing there chewing on a bedraggled cigar butt. Bolan's friend looked older than The Executioner ever remembered. Quite simply, he looked shaken to the core.

PART TWO

THE BEAR
THAT WALKS LIKE A MAN

14

"This is the part I could do without," admitted McCarter as they were led through the steel maze of companionways to the debriefing cabin where they would be individually questioned. "Just give me a hot shower and cool sheets!"

Bolan nodded in agreement. He looked the Englishman straight in the eye. "Thanks, David. That was a tough one. I needed the job, and I needed you."

"Wouldn't have missed it for the world, sport," McCarter said. "You can call on me anytime, Colonel. You know that."

Both men had been through the procedure on countless occasions, so their initial reports were concise. Still, the debriefing sessions took a long time.

McCarter was quizzed on the *mujahedeen*. He provided details about what he had seen of guerrilla ordnance, their state of training and effectiveness, drew maps to show the latest Afghan redoubts and assessed as best he could their morale.

In the next cabin Bolan was answering a similar battery of questions about the Russians. Faceless experts came and went in the shadowy circle beyond the table lamp. He was grilled on troop movements and how he would judge the condition of their weapons. To what extent were the Afghan locals collaborating with the occupying forces? Bolan refused to speculate when he couldn't back up an answer with specific examples. He smoked almost half a pack of cigarettes during the highly detailed interrogation.

"More coffee, Colonel Phoenix?" The intelligence officer poured out yet another cup as one of his colleagues entered the cabin with a grainy enlargement of a Russian jet. "This is the best shot we've got of the Su-25—the Frogfoot. Can you sketch in exactly what you noticed about the tail assembly and the wing configuration?"

Finally it was over.

Now Bolan stood in the shower, letting the prickling needles of hot water stimulate his shoulders and neck. His muscles soon relaxed, but a burning anger remained tightly coiled within. He knew these men were only doing their job. They were doing it by the numbers. But why was he playing along?

Could any amount of questioning bring back April Rose?

Were the freedom fighters like Tarik Khan and his followers going to receive the support they deserved?

And what real edge did intel give them when everything they found out was being leaked back to the enemy?

If he was to find some answers to clear up this mess, then he had to be free to cut through the knot of intrigue. If he was to make a real difference, he had to throw away his past. Colonel Phoenix, The Executioner, even Sergeant Mercy must be peeled away as he forged himself into a new weapon capable of waging the biggest war of all.

The outline was still blurry, the details indistinct, but Bolan felt an inner force propelling him toward his destiny with the unstoppable energy of a speeding bullet. He was deep in thought when Hal Brognola arrived.

"Looks like the boy's going to make it. You know what doctors are like—they never want to commit themselves after an operation. But I think the touch-and-go part of it is over. They're going to fly him to a burn unit back in the States."

"Yeah, I'm sure he'll pull through," Bolan said as he toweled himself.

"That was a brilliant mission! And you were the only one who could have pulled it off. I've spoken to the President already. He sends his congratulations. And his thanks."

It was as if Brognola knew precisely what had been running through his mind. And right now Bolan didn't need anyone playing on his deepest feelings of loyalty and patriotism.

"How are the others? What's the condition of our people?"

"Things aren't so good," Brognola admitted. "I don't think Kurtzman is ever going to walk again. Of course, he swears he'll be up and about in no time, but Dr. Ogilvy told me the Bear will be in a wheelchair for the rest of his days. The whole operation will have to be reassessed. In fact, it is being reassessed right now. There's an investigation."

"Oh? And what conclusions have been reached?"

"Nothing yet, the report isn't complete. But I'm sure this latest success is going to weigh heavily in your favor."

"What the hell's going on, Hal? You make it sound as if I'm the one on trial!"

"No. No, it isn't that, Striker. It's just.... Look, however unorthodox the Stony Man operation is, it's still tied in to the government. So there has to be an inquiry, a committee...."

Bolan angrily flung the towel to the floor. "We've been through too much together, Hal, for all this bureaucratic crap. Tell me exactly what's happening. What the hell's eating you?" Bolan snarled.

Brognola looked almost relieved to have been cornered. "When you first suggested there might be a mole, an agent planted close to the President, I listened, said yes, maybe, and went along with your suspicions. But I didn't really believe it. I couldn't. It didn't seem possible."

"And now?"

"Now I do. Deep down in here I think you're right." Brognola patted his gut and winced, as if he had the worst case of indigestion in the world. "I'm putting the pieces together. Slowly, I admit, but I'm convinced—"

"As soon as we get back, I'm gonna nail that bastard," snapped Bolan. "Whoever he is, he's living on borrowed time. I don't give a damn who it is, Hal, but I promise you that within forty-eight hours I'll have his hide."

"That's just it, Mack. If this thing goes right to the top then it's too delicate for you to go charging in to crucify the guy. This whole situation requires careful handling." Brognola slumped on the bunk, his head in his hands. Then he looked up at Bolan as he continued, "Think about it. In Britain, France, West Germany, this sort of thing has brought down governments and often ruined the careers and reputations of innocent people as well as the guilty ones. Let's not give the Kremlin the satisfaction of destroying our administration. Give me some time, another week or two. That's all I'm asking.''

Bolan stared at the bulkhead, his fists clenched; backing off wasn't his way. He looked at Brognola who was now hunched over the phone issuing terse instructions to make a stateside connection. It wasn't easy for his old friend either, Bolan realized, to have to admit that a Soviet sympathizer seemed to have gotten so close to the President.

For years U.S. intelligence and security agencies had had their resources and energy sapped by the running battle to justify themselves with a hostile and loose-lipped segment of the media. It was this atmosphere of distrust that the top-level mole had taken full advantage of, and ruthlessly exploited.

Sitting there in his rumpled suit, the man from Washington seemed to be taking a personal responsibility for this lack of vigilance. Bolan knew Brognola wasn't after glory or the opportunity to prove his heroism; he was only asking for the chance to redeem himself in his own eyes.

Brognola replaced the phone and looked up. ''For too long I've watched you go out there in the field. I issued instructions or made suggestions, and you put yourself on the firing line. Well, it's time I picked up the ball and ran with it myself.''

Bolan nodded.

"Good," Brognola muttered, "then I want you to take a short break. Just for a few days. Actually, General Crawford has a favor to ask of you—they're patching him through now—and it comes at just the right time. You deserve a little time off."

A soft repetitive buzz signaled the call was coming through. Hal Brognola pushed the chair back and gestured to the phone. Bolan picked up the receiver and identified himself.

"I understand that congratulations are in order, Colonel." The Arkansas drawl was unmistakable. "The Stony Man operation has proved itself once again."

"Thank you, sir."

"I won't go into the developments here in Washington. Hal Brognola can give you all the pertinent details. I'm calling to ask a personal favor of you, Mack. It's about my daughter, Kelly. You've met her."

Bolan hoped the general's daughter had not gotten herself into more hot water. For the old man's sake. He didn't deserve it.

"The day after tomorrow she's flying to Zubrovna to take part in the International Students Invitational Games."

"Sir, I wasn't aware that Kelly was involved in athletics."

"Oh, yes, Mack. She's been a star athlete for

several years. That is, until the time she hooked up with that scum, Grover Jones. Fortunately that episode didn't last too long. I suppose she felt she was missing out on some of the things girls her age do. Besides, it was easy for her to be attracted by Jones's flamboyance.''

Even on the phone Bolan could sense the concern the general felt for his daughter. He was a caring man. After all, he had taken the young recruit Bolan under his wing in Vietnam. Bolan suspected he filled a gap in the general's life: the son the general never had.

Bolan thought of his own sister, who had been killed by their father when he found out she was a prostitute for the Mob. But she had only been trying to repay a debt her father had incurred with the Mafia. And there, but for the good fortune of Bolan's presence, went Kelly Crawford. Yeah, Bolan resolved to help out the old man.

"She was looking for some direction," the general was saying. "I was spared the painful teenage years because I was in the military, so I guess I'm to blame for not being there when she needed me. With her mother gone and me with my career, Kelly really had no one to guide her. So the first male who paid attention to her—that was it.

"Anyway, all these recent problems they've been having with the athletes—the steroids controversy—have opened up a position on the Olympics team. If she can win the pentathlon event at the ISIG, she gets a shot at the big one.''

Bolan could only guess what a chance to compete at Los Angeles would mean to Kelly herself but, from the tone of his voice, it was obvious what it would mean to her father.

''How can I help her, General?''

''I'd rest a lot easier if I knew you were there to keep an eye on her, Mack. Zubrovna's something of a hot spot right now. They're having problems containing the Unity movement. I'd be grateful if you were around to make sure she doesn't get into any trouble.''

Yeah, thought Bolan, he'd found out the hard way what a rebel Kelly could be. Still, what kind of mischief could she get into in Zubrovna? The athletic competition would demand her full concentration.

''It's just for eight days,'' pressed Crawford.

Bolan realized how weary he was; six days of Mediterranean sunshine and Balkan hospitality sounded appealing. He needed to conserve his strength for the brutal task that inevitably faced him at home. Besides, he wanted to think things through more thoroughly before deciding his future options. A few days R&R would give him the chance.

"We can fly you there directly," mouthed Brognola, double-teaming with the general.

"All right, General Crawford. I'll look out for her. I'll go to Zubrovna for a few days."

15

Zubrovna bore the weight of its mongrel past with bustling pride. The downtown core, known locally as the Old Citadel, was an ancient warren of cobbled laneways thronged with craft shops. In the jostling crowd, Serb rubbed shoulders with Croat, and Slav intermingled with Muslim.

Bolan felt as if he were traveling through the centuries as he turned the corner from the Street of the Silversmiths onto the broad boulevard that brushed its way past the modern administrative offices all the way out to Djakovic Airport.

The traffic cop, standing on a circular steel pedestal, jabbed his finger toward Bolan's rental car, ordering the vehicles in that lane to halt. The American waited patiently for the flick of the wrist that would signal him to proceed. He was in good time to meet Kelly Crawford's incoming flight from New York via Rome.

Sitting there with the window rolled down in that early-spring sunshine, Bolan was beginning to feel like a new man. In a way, he was—the intelligence boys on the carrier had seen to that.

His stubbly beard had been shaved, leaving only a dark mustache that gave him a decidedly buccaneer look. A passport had been prepared to match his new identity, and Bolan had filched two more blank ones. Brognola had wisely brought along a replacement for Bolan's Beretta; another garrote was threaded into his belt. The hollowed heel of one shoe concealed a short, wicked blade while the other carried a compact emergency-escape kit.

He was not expecting trouble but he was prepared for anything. Mack Bolan, or Mark Bailey as his new passport had it, was probably the deadliest equipped "tourist" ever to set foot in Zubrovna.

A brightly painted truck rattled past. A Gypsy boy, whose dark Romany looks reminded Bolan of young Kasim, sat perched on stacked cords of firewood. He gave Bolan a shy wave as the truck overtook the rental car.

For a few brief seconds the American visitor and the Gypsy boy were friendly travelers headed in the same direction. But Bolan only had to glance up at the mirror and confirm that the drab blue car was still following half a block behind to remind himself where he was—at the ragged end of the iron curtain.

Guards patrolled along embassy row, their

shiny hobnailed boots clashing on the paving. The additional hardware in the streets was supposedly there for ISIG security, but steel bayonets were standard issue and always stood watch over Zubrovna. The bleak look in the troopers' eyes and the will with which they enforced control were the results of an iron-hard ideology.

The weather was bright and clear, so Zubrovna did not have the gray, shabby look of cities in the more northerly reaches of the Soviet empire.

The sunshine found a natural reflection in the people's smiles and their ready laughter. They accepted their lot with more equanimity than the Afghans, Bolan observed, but then they had had longer to get used to it.

They had been ruled by perverted Roman dictators and Turkish despots, by the mad kings of degenerate empires and jackbooted Nazis. Now they were prisoners within the Kremlin's sphere of influence, and they would try to make the best of it any way they could.

But dissent was never far beneath the surface. Despite the current crackdown, Bolan saw posters on walls advertising the Unity rally. General Crawford was right: the situation in Zubrovna was volatile. For once, Bolan didn't mind playing the role of watchdog.

He kept his eyes on the traffic and the road signs, but in his mind the wheels were still turning over on the most important problems that faced him. Who was the most likely suspect? How best to trap the mole? And how could he continue to fight the good fight now that the Stony Man cover had been compromised?

The dark blue Zastava followed him right into the airport parking lot. But whoever had been assigned to trail the American didn't get out. Bolan saw two newspapers being unfolded as he walked off toward the terminal building. He presumed there would be other watchers inside the arrivals lounge.

Only a small group of local sports enthusiasts had come out to Djakovic to greet the visiting athletes. They waited in a very orderly fashion, not daring to push too close to the row of guards that cordoned off the entrance. There were more photographers and newsmen inside the terminal than there were fans outside.

Bolan was asked for his papers. They identified him as part of the coaching staff for the American team. A grim-faced sentry waved him through to the reception area.

Flashes were popping in all directions. It looked as if contingents from every country had just arrived.

The student games in Zubrovna had precipitated a bitter debate in U.S. athletic circles as to whether they should participate or not. Some sanctions were still in effect from the invasion of Afghanistan, and bad feeling for the Russians' cold-blooded attack on the Korean jetliner had not been resolved.

As General Crawford had explained to Bolan: "I think we should restrain our contacts with those bastards to a minimum. The Eastern bloc is our enemy; it has branded itself as such by its own actions. But isn't sports the one area where we should, at least in theory, be able to compete with one another without dragging politics into it? Maybe I'm being selfish. But I can't let Kelly pass up this chance to have a crack at a gold medal in Los Angeles."

"Any father would feel the same way," Bolan had replied.

A rippling movement surged through the crowd, spilling it closer toward the frosted glass doors of the customs-inspection area. A young man with tousled brown hair and a quick grin pushed past the American with an apology. His English was good; his lapel badge identified him as Georgi Radic. Bolan followed him to the barrier.

The dividing doors slid open, and the American team poured through into the reception lounge. Bolan scanned the incoming passengers. The group of French athletes who had joined the flight in Rome were easily recognizable by the tricolor one of them held.

Kelly Crawford was dressed in the same outfit

as her teammates: a white windcheater with red-and-blue piping, and dark blue slacks. The glossy blond hair was quite unruffled despite the long flight. And she smiled readily for the waiting cameramen. She was one hundred percent all-American.

It looked as if Kelly had already made her first international conquest somewhere en route. The young Frenchman tactfully moved to one side when Bolan approached.

"Hello, Kelly."

"Hi, Colonel! Fancy meeting you here." There was a slightly sarcastic edge to her voice that did not slip Bolan's notice. "Actually, dad had me paged at Kennedy. He said you'd be here to meet me."

"This time it's Mark Bailey," Bolan cautioned her softly. "Mark will do."

Kelly shrugged. She studied his face for a moment. "You look different with a mustache. I'm not sure I approve of it."

"How was your flight?"

She merely shrugged again, then turned to signal for her new friend to join them.

"Pierre, I'd like you to meet Mark, uh...."

"Bailey." Bolan proffered his hand. The other man had a strong, self-confident grip.

"And, Mark, this is Pierre Danjou. He's the junior fencing champion for France."

Before Bolan was forced to improvise about

his coaching responsibilities, one of the ISIG officials had plucked at Kelly's arm. "This way, Miss Crawford. Just a few moments at the microphones, please. The reporters have some questions for you."

It was too late for Bolan to stop her. Kelly gave a cheery wave as she stepped toward the crowded stand of recording equipment. "Over here, Miss Crawford!" shouted Georgi Radic. She repeated her wave for the photographer. Bolan stood patiently in the background, wondering which of the correspondents were for real and which ones worked for more sinister masters.

Kelly Crawford was certainly quick to inspire devoted admiration. Radic must have used up a whole roll of film in less than two minutes.

"Is this your first time traveling outside the United States?" one reporter asked.

"Of course not." The smile remained in place but it was undercut by a hint of impatience. "My father is regular Army. We were often stationed abroad."

"Damn," muttered Bolan. "Why does she have to remind them that she's General Crawford's daughter?"

The Frenchman had obviously heard him. "I think everyone here is quite aware of who her father is," Pierre Danjou said, a puzzled look on his face.

An English-accented voice broke in. "How do you rate your chances against the Kat?"

"The Kat?" shot back Kelly, all wide-eyed innocence.

"Katya Timoshenko. The Soviet champion."

"We'll have to wait and see. . . ."

"Miss Crawford, why did you decide to compete in Zubrovna while some American athletes are privately boycotting this meet because of what is happening in Afghanistan?"

"What are your views on the Unity movement here?" It was Radic who asked that last question.

"Naturally, I don't approve of what the Russians are doing," she fired back. "If I had my way, I'd—"

"She'd like to get to her hotel. Thank you," completed Bolan, as he gently but firmly swept Kelly away. The nearest journalists laughed at the forceful tact with which her coach had terminated the interview.

16

The room was almost in darkness.

Two oblongs of pale gray light filtered through the dust-streaked windows behind the desk. The glass of tea was growing cold as Greb Strakhov sat alone in the twilit gloom.

Alone with his grief.

And alone with his anger.

One stubby finger poked the green button set in the edge of his heavy wooden desk.

Vichinsky rapped at the door. He entered, then paused, puzzled, as if he had been summoned to an empty office by mistake.

The shadowy bulk in the tall chair moved, leaning forward across the desk top. Vichinsky heard the little brass chain rattling against the lamp stand as Strakhov searched for it. Why did he not get a more modern desk lamp, Vichinsky wondered.

When Strakhov jerked the switch, the light barely illuminated the surface of the desk and the faded carpet immediately in front of it. That was where Vichinsky stood.

Strakhov picked up the glass, sipped at its contents and quickly put it down. Belikov had left a saucer full of lemon wedges next to the tea. The security chief took one of the tart slices and sucked on it without the hint of a grimace. It always set Vichinsky's teeth on edge to watch him do that.

Greb Strakhov came from an entirely different school, a much tougher one than today's young managers and ambitious bureaucrats. Despite his years he was still broad shouldered. His narrowed eyes expressed a somber watchfulness, and although his hairline had receded, he retained a thick iron-gray mane at the back.

If circumstances demanded, he would wear his modestly decorated uniform; but usually, as this evening, he was attired in a slightly shiny dark suit.

The head of the Thirteenth Section was a serious man. Utterly serious. The years had added lines of solemnity to his broad square face.

Within these walls Vichinsky had heard him laugh on only two occasions, and neither time was the laughter shared with his GRU assistant. But through the door the laugh had sounded like a hearty peasant bellow.

Strakhov's eyes were little more than razored slits as he looked up at his subordinate. "Tell me, comrade, just how far have you got with your—what do you call it—Janus Plan?"

Vichinsky was stunned, but detected no trace of trickery. Nor was there any hint of reproach in his boss's voice. Greb Strakhov's anger was channeled toward only one goal.

"I'm sure you were going to tell me of this plan quite soon," coached the old man.

"Yes, sir. Of course I was. It, er, seemed such a long shot that I didn't want to trouble you until I was confident it was operational."

"And how far have you proceeded?"

Vichinsky reported on the latest developments in the transformation of the once-dissident Stefan Boldin into Colonel John Phoenix. Strakhov nodded at each new revelation as if he were already familiar with the details.

How had he found out so much that he could have it pieced together already? One of the guards at the safehouse where Boldin was now kept under constant supervision? Or was it the filing clerk who had originally searched out Boldin's record for him? Vichinsky seriously wondered if everyone was reporting directly to Major General Strakhov.

"Fetch me the file," the section head ordered when Vichinsky had finished his briefing.

He wasted no time returning to his office to pick up the thick buff folder he had been working on when Strakhov had summoned him.

"Who is who?" asked Strakhov when the file was placed open before him.

"This is the latest picture of Boldin." Vichinsky tapped the photo on the left.

Strakhov ignored it and picked up the grainier portrait of their American target. "Then this is the man who killed my son."

Strakhov tilted the photograph under the light and pursed his lips as he contemplated the hard-eyed visage of the deadly American agent. In the previous picture he had seen the man was obviously unconscious. "Kyril dispatched some material for my attention on the very day he died. He had this saboteur in his personal custody."

Vichinsky said nothing. Strakhov was passing judgment on his own son merely by choosing to tell his subordinate. "Positive identification has been made: Phoenix, John. Colonel. Supposedly retired. But active enough to steal our prototype of the M-36 and to kill anyone who tried to stop him. You know, comrade, this afternoon I heard that the whole assault-helicopter program might be scrapped. Well, for once a lot of people can rightfully claim they were against it from the start."

"So Phoenix was in Afghanistan.... But where is he now?"

"I've had men working on that ever since his prints checked out. Mozhenko called an hour ago, said he might have a lead. I'm waiting for him now."

Strakhov slowly began to read through the

thick folder of information Vichinsky had compiled. He felt some respect for the man's thoroughness even though he despised his GRU assistant for his deceit in attempting to conceal the Janus Plan.

The head of the Thirteenth Section carefully digested each report of the far-flung activities of John Phoenix: Japan, Africa, the Caribbean, Latin America, Germany.... The whole world was his warground! Undoubtedly, Phoenix was the main enemy—politically, as well as personally.

The KGB officer searched for a recognizable pattern, a repeated method that might indicate the man's carelessness or leave him vulnerable in the future. There was none. All he could find was a ruthless professionalism, a fighter every bit as zealous as Strakhov himself had been in the days of the Finnish campaign and the encirclement of Stalingrad.

He picked up the photograph of Boldin. The resemblance really was most remarkable.

"And you say this man is ready?"

"You can see him for yourself, sir, at any time."

Strakhov turned back to the file. He had almost completed his assessment when there was a commotion in the outer office.

"Send Mozhenko in!" barked the major general.

The administrative officer came in and flipped open his briefcase with a nervous and unnecessary flourish. "My contact at *Tass* sent these right over. It's Phoenix all right. Taken early this afternoon. He's wearing a mustache now, but it's definitely him. Don't you think so?"

"It certainly appears to be," agreed Strakhov, comparing this latest black-and-white glossy with the picture from the file. "And what do you say, Colonel?"

Vichinsky nodded quickly. He was too caught up in the tension now to worry about the abrupt disclosure that his cherished plan had really been no secret at all. They could fight for the lion's share of the credit later. He coughed to cover his excitement. "Yes, I'm sure it's Phoenix. There's something about his eyes...."

"Where was this taken, Mozhenko?"

"At a press reception in Djakovic Airport."

"Zubrovna? This afternoon?"

"Yes, Comrade General, in Zubrovna."

"And who is this girl in the foreground?"

"Her name is Kelly Crawford. She's the American pentathlete going up against Katya Timoshenko. The American girl was interviewed on her arrival at Zubrovna," continued Mozhenko. "One of our men there almost provoked her into an embarrassing answer regarding the partial boycott of the games. He took the picture, then sent it on with his report via *Tass*. As you can see, Phoenix is standing behind her. Like a bodyguard, I suppose."

"How long do these games go on for?"

"They start in three days and they'll take five days to complete," Mozhenko told them.

"Then we've got eight full days to. . ." began Vichinsky.

Strakhov lifted his hand and silenced his assistant. "Thank you, Comrade Mozhenko. The work of your unit is exceptional. I shall make sure the minister knows of your efforts."

"Thank you, sir." Mozhenko backed away. His part in this affair was ended. In fact, he was glad to be released from Strakhov's shadowy headquarters. He felt uncomfortable in the presence of these men; he was more at home with his files and computerized records.

"Crawford? I'm sure I remember that name," commented Vichinsky, as soon as Mozhenko had closed the door behind him. "It's been mentioned in connection with Phoenix before. May I see the file again, sir, please?"

Vichinsky riffled through the pages at the end, the one section Strakhov had not yet read. His nicotine-stained finger tapped at a closely typewritten report. "Yes, I thought so. General James Crawford. It's right here. Our connection in Washington says Crawford had something to do with establishing the group that backs Phoenix. In Virginia.''

''Langley? CIA?''

''No, sir. They are under far deeper cover than that.''

''You mean they might be our opposite numbers in a way?''

''I wouldn't say that exactly, General.''

Strakhov shrugged it off. The two men had simply explored the notion of a match and dismissed it; the thought never once occurred to them that the United States had no equivalent to the Thirteenth Section.

''You indicated that the double is ready?''

''I believe he is, General.''

''On the outside perhaps, but what about in here?'' Strakhov patted his chest. ''Is he committed to the success of this project?''

''I cannot vouch for that. Until now I've mainly been concerned with his appearance. Lednev is standing by in case it's a wet operation.''

''Zubrovna. A city with problems, unpredictable problems. A place of social unrest,'' Strakhov mused aloud. ''The birthplace of Unity, and the random violence it has spawned....''

Vichinsky hardly dared follow his superior's train of thought, but Strakhov let him be the one to voice it. ''Damien Macek!''

''Precisely. Macek himself is to address a rally there the day after tomorrow.''

The risk was breathtaking. Vichinsky was giddy with its implications. Macek would be a nationalist worker-martyr if they so much as touched him; but if some foreign madman were to....

"Our two most serious concerns solved in one bold stroke!" It was a temptation too strong to resist. And it was certainly more daring than any plan Vichinsky might have contemplated on his own.

"We've two birds within our grasp," said Strakhov. He held out his hand, like a bear's paw and just as strong, with the open palm cupped. Then his fingers closed as he crushed them into a fist.

17

Pierre Danjou waited for her in the lobby. He had already put in two hours training, then returned to his quarters where he had shaved, showered and changed for his late-breakfast date with Kelly Crawford. They had made whispered arrangements the night before.

Glancing around the westernized surroundings of the hotel's reception area, he thought the Americans had been assigned far superior accommodations than his own team.

Because of the uncertainty of how many student athletes would attend ISIG, and of a pressing need for a public display of economic caution, the state government had not seen fit to build showcase housing for the foreign competitors.

Instead they had pressed into service every hotel, hostel and guest house within convenient reach of the sports stadium. Interested tourists and visiting spectators had been left to fend for themselves as best they could.

Kelly stepped through the elevator doors and

gave Pierre a quick casual wave. She decided that with his fair hair neatly swept back over one side of his forehead, his blazer and slacks impeccable, and his seductively shy smile, Pierre looked, well, he looked so French.

"You look beautiful this morning, Kelly."

"Why, thank you!"

"First, I'll tell you the good news. I don't have to report back to the training gymnasium until three o'clock."

"And the bad news?"

"It's simply that I don't have the whole day off," replied Pierre, making an exaggerated show of his regret. "I wish I could spend every minute of this glorious day with you!"

Kelly nudged him playfully. "I don't have to check in until after lunch, either. My coach, Lee, says I'm not to dwell on the competition."

"I shall be glad to take your mind off the games. Come, let's go for a drive. As official competitors we have the use of a courtesy car." Pierre steered her toward the revolving glass doors. He gripped her arm. "But I thought Mark Bailey was your coach."

"Yes, well, he is, sort of. He's on the staff. A kind of special assistant." Kelly looked back across the lobby and then scanned the front entrance bay before pushing her way through the door. There was no sign of John Phoenix, but

Kelly found this cloak-and-dagger exit added an extra thrill to her meeting with Pierre.

The doorman signaled to a waiting car. It cruised forward to the main entrance.

"Better service than you get in decadent, bourgeois democracies," commented Pierre with a chuckle.

He opened the back door. Kelly got in and slid over. Then Pierre jumped in and the car pulled away.

"And where would you two like to go?" asked the driver, glancing back over his shoulder.

Kelly's mouth dropped open.

Colonel John Phoenix sat behind the wheel.

"I thought we might all go for a tour of the town," said Bolan, smiling. He enjoyed giving them a surprise.

"Yes, yes, of course. That would be great," stammered Kelly, giving Pierre's hand a squeeze as if to reassure him that she was still alone with him in her heart despite this unwelcome intrusion.

They drove down the Avenue Elena Skobla. Bolan looked in his mirror.

Wondered where you'd got to this morning, he thought as he saw the blue Zastava turn out of a side street and fall in behind them. He presumed Kelly had been briefed on what to expect before she left home: any highly visible guests at the ISIG were bound to be followed.

Still, there was no point in alarming the youngsters; they had enough on their minds with the stiff competition they faced. Bolan said nothing as he took a right turn into Zvedlo Park Road.

"I'm starving!" Kelly said. "Let's find a restaurant."

They cruised down a hill to the Petrovic Foundation. On the far side of a small square stood St. Savior's Church, with onion-domed tower and gaily colored tiling.

"Oh, it's all so quaint. I must get a photo," Kelly enthused.

"I thought you were hungry," Bolan said, indicating the open-air café on the other side of the fountain. It looked like a good place to eat. The guys in the blue car must have thought so, too; they pulled up in a parking space on the far end of the courtyard.

Bolan suddenly wished he hadn't picked this particular place to stop. A couple of press photographers were weaving and bobbing to get some close shots of the group that was getting up to leave.

The two men, one apparently a wrestler and the other his trainer, looked at the Westerners with suspicion, then with scarcely veiled hostility. The three women with them displayed a more honest curiosity.

"Some of the Russian team," murmured Pierre, without so much as disturbing his smile of greeting.

The athletes from Moscow veered to the left, giving their rivals a wider berth than was needed. The last woman stopped briefly, looked first at the older American before turning her attention to Kelly.

The Russian was tall, perhaps five foot eight, but her lithe-limbed grace and perfect posture made her seem taller. Her face was a study in contrasts, with the line of her delicately angular cheeks running down into a strongly defined jaw. And her eyes were a self-confident blue, almost as fathomless as Bolan's.

"Hello, Miss Crawford." Her English was faultless.

Kelly stared back. "Hello, Katya."

As the Soviet woman traded glances with the American blonde, the faster of the two photographers got his shot of two superpower athletes facing off.

Bolan detected just the slightest deepening of the smile lines that framed her mouth, then the young woman whom the world had taken to its heart as "The Kat" turned away and followed quickly after her companions.

One of the paparazzi decided to stick with the

Russian party for his story. The other hadn't made up his mind, but Bolan's hand closing on his shoulder took care of that decision. "You're not going anywhere for a moment."

Bolan propelled the fellow to the table chosen by Pierre and Kelly. He recognized the photographer from the reception at the airport.

"Mr. Radic, I want that film in your camera—the picture you just took of the two girls. No need to stir things up."

"What!" exclaimed Radic. "But that's my best picture! Miss Crawford, I appeal to you...."

He glanced over at Kelly, his brown eyes pleading.

Kelly fell for the man's act. "Oh, let him keep the pictures, Mark."

"Then may I take some more?" Radic pressed his luck. "Some shots of Miss Crawford relaxing here in my beautiful city before the games get under way."

Bolan shrugged impatiently. Customers turned to watch Kelly being photographed. Kelly ordered a coffee and croissant for Radic, too, when the waiter came.

"Thank you!" Radic snapped half a dozen shots or more. Kelly did her best to appear quite blasé about the young cameraman's attention.

The Frenchman picked up a sheet of paper that he thought the Russians might have left behind. It was a flier advertising the Unity rally to be held the next morning at Revolution Square. "If I can get a couple of hours off tomorrow, I might go along to watch some of it. Kelly, would you like to go?"

Kelly was about to voice her acceptance when Bolan, who had temporarily been watching the blue car, shook his head. "You're not to go anywhere near that meeting."

"I think we should all hear what Damien Macek has to say," Pierre suggested. "It will be a rare opportunity to see history in the making."

"What do you say, Georgi..." Kelly began to ask.

"George. Please, call me George."

"Do you think there's going to be any trouble at the Unity rally?" Kelly continued.

"I think perhaps that you should not go, Miss Crawford," he replied gravely. "The authorities are very angry. They have let it be known they want this meeting canceled, but they dare not impose martial law while all the visitors are here for the games."

"Unity is taking a tactical risk that might very well backfire," added Bolan.

"But Pierre has a point, doesn't he? It's like meeting the Pope, or seeing the space shuttle land or something. It really will be history as it happens!"

"Miss Crawford, I tell you sincerely that even those among us who are committed to the cause of Unity—" Radic's voice had dropped to a conspiratorial whisper "—are asking if this is the wisest course of action."

Kelly's cheeks flushed slightly; she was excited by the tensions the argument had generated. She knew that several of the other customers were watching them closely. "Well, we'll see...."

"No, you won't," Bolan shot back.

BOLAN TURNED RESTLESSLY. The sheets and thin blanket had become as confusingly tangled as his thoughts. Baby-sitting Kelly Crawford was not turning out to be the rest and recreation that Brognola had promised him it would.

He had left Kelly Crawford in the care of her regular coach, Lee Brebner. Then Bolan had spent the late afternoon playing cat and mouse with the two guys in the blue sedan. One was a fat operative in a greasy raincoat, the other man wore leather gloves despite the warm weather.

Just before returning to the hotel Bolan shook off the two men in a crowded department store, doubled back and left them stranded with two flat tires.

It was a provocative risk, but it released a little of Bolan's frustration. He still hadn't heard anything from Brognola. How much time did he need? That was where he should be, thought Bolan—in Washington. And a long way from Kelly Crawford.

The sight of Kelly with the dashing French fencer forced Bolan to think of April Rose. He missed her deep in his heart, in his guts. Yet in a way it still had not struck home. Bolan toyed with the ring he wore on a chain around his neck. It was almost as if she were still waiting for him back at Stony Man Farm.

But the enemy had turned his headquarters into just another blood-soaked killzone.

Yeah, April was gone, and inside Bolan knew that part of himself had died with her.

For years he had been putting out the brushfires of international terror. But it hadn't worked; even with the loyal support of Able Team and Phoenix Force. The body count mounted—now on both sides—but the inferno raged on, as uncontrollable as ever.

It was no good to merely hack away at the limbs and heads of this monstrous Hydra. He had to attack its central nervous system, again and again, as many times as were needed to paralyze the beast.

Bolan lay back, one arm cradled behind his head, and tried to organize this chaotic stream of semiconsciousness. First, they had to identify the mole who had burrowed so close to the President, isolate him and destroy him. If Hal

Brognola hadn't got the job done by the time Bolan returned from these games, then he would attend to the matter with brutal dispatch.

Secondly, he would have to discuss the whole notion of a new unit. If Brognola didn't go for the suggestion, then he would resign.

But, would they let him quit? Would they allow John Phoenix to simply walk away—and live? Not likely, not after all he'd been through and what he knew of current American security measures.

Nobody resigned from that.

Unless it was a terminal retirement.

THE AIRPORT MANAGER and his deputy, together with his most experienced controller, were all in the control tower to watch the landing of the unscheduled Aeroflot night flight. It touched down at Djakovic at 0240 local time.

The airport was closed to the public. Normally there were no flights coming into Zubrovna at this time of night.

Branislav Pepovski mopped his brow with the limp handkerchief he'd been clutching for the past twenty minutes. Looking down across the tarmac, he could see the local commandant of the state-security forces with Mr. Novikov, a Soviet official.

Pepovski was quite certain the Russian was not a press attaché. Both men turned to look up at the tower windows as the Yakolev whined to a halt close to the cargo terminal.

Pepovski's assistant, who had been monitoring the walkie-talkie, repeated the garbled instructions more clearly. "They want us to kill the lights."

"Do what they say!" the manager urged. The man extinguished the tarmac floodlights just as the ramp was wheeled in place under the door of the jet. "And the ones in here. Turn everything out!"

There was another delay while the ground crew left the area. A long black limousine, sleekly reflecting the moonlight, cruised to the foot of the ramp.

Four men came out. They hurried down the darkened steps. Pepovski couldn't resist taking a look. After all, they had called him out with scarcely an hour's notice, and surely he was entitled to know something of what was going on in his own airport. But there wasn't much to see. He could have sworn the man in the middle had a coat or cloth pulled over his head.

The passengers quietly piled into the waiting Mercedes.

STEFAN BOLDIN TOOK THE JACKET off his head and glanced out of the tinted windows.

"Zubrovna," said Vichinsky. There was no point in concealing it anymore. In less than six hours they had an appointment to keep in Revolution Square.

Boldin's upper lip was filmed with perspiration. He pressed the false mustache back in place.

Lednev, the very best marksman in the Thirteenth Section, stared out into the darkness and cracked his knuckles in anticipation.

18

Kelly woke up when the door rattled open. She hadn't ordered a room-service breakfast and certainly wouldn't have done at this ungodly hour.

She was about to complain when she caught sight of the single long-stemmed rose lying on a breakfast tray and an envelope with her name written on it. As soon as she was alone again she ripped open the letter.

Dearest Kelly,
    Meet me in one hour outside the Church of St. Savior. Let's spend a little while together by ourselves—without the company of Mr. Bailey!

In anticipation,
Pierre

Kelly plucked a strip of bacon off the plate and nibbled at it as she ran the bath.

Forty minutes later she left the hotel. This time by the staff exit at the rear.

Less than five minutes after Kelly's departure a maid entered the young woman's room. She scooped up the message supposedly written by Pierre Danjou, ripped it up and flushed the pieces down the toilet. Then she replaced it with a brief note that she had brought with her. The maid took a last look around the room, picked up the rose for herself and left.

MACK BOLAN was nearly always awake before his wristwatch alarm went off. This morning was one of the rare exceptions. A buzz summoned him back to consciousness. It was six-twenty.

He let the shower wash the sleep away, and with it the dreams and memories and unanswered questions that had disturbed his night. He had left a message for Kelly that he would meet her at seven. They were to go jogging in Zvedlo Park together.

He was five minutes early when he knocked on the door.

No reply.

"Kelly, are you awake?"

Still no sound from inside the room.

Bolan tried the handle. The door swung open.

He raced across the empty room and checked the bathroom. She was nowhere in sight.

The remains of a pecked-at breakfast lay on the tray at the foot of her bed. He saw the note right away and picked it up.

Mark,

Pierre Danjou was right. I've gone to watch the rally in Revolution Square. It is history in the making.

K

Bolan scanned the note a second time, shaking his head at her foolishness, but quickly looked up. Georgi Radic was standing in the open doorway.

"What the hell are you doing here?"

The young photographer started to reply but Bolan cut him off. "Just how did you get up here? How come the desk clerk let you in?"

"He didn't see me," Radic said, shrugging. "I parked at the back and used the service entrance."

"You've got your own car? Out there now?"

"Yes, but excuse me.... Where is Miss Kelly?"

"That's what we're going to find out. Come on, show me that entrance you used."

Radic's car, an ancient Citroën 2CV, was parked in the alley.

"Revolution Square, as fast as you can," ordered Bolan. The minute they pulled away, he asked, "And what were you doing at Kelly's door?"

"I wanted to catch her before she went to practice," replied the cameraman. "I was going to ask if she would allow me to accompany her, to take more pictures for my photo essay, 'A day in the life of an American athlete.' I thought she liked me. I like her."

They now headed directly toward a location both of them had wanted to avoid.

The Citroën was rattling along in the general flow of the morning traffic. Bolan checked through the rear window. There was no sign at all of the Zastava, but then Fatman and Gloves weren't looking for him in a beat-up wreck belonging to a local journalist. As the car swept down the road toward the square, the press of vehicles became a fuming, honking flood of commuters.

Radic stuck his head out of the window. "Looks like a detour ahead. They must have cordoned off the whole area around the square."

An overworked policeman was waving all the cars to the right; the street behind him was already clogged with a slow-moving column of pedestrians. Obviously the authorities had not dissuaded too many people from attending the rally.

"Hold on!" shouted Radic as he bumped over the curb and drove into a narrow side street.

There was a butcher's shop at the corner ahead, with four floors of accommodation above it. "I live there," Radic said as he drove past. "Top floor."

He turned to the left and pulled into a small courtyard. There was just enough room to park his car next to a rack of bicycles.

Radic, camera case swinging from his shoulder, led the way down an alley, which brought them out on a boulevard leading back toward the square.

"Why is Damien Macek taking this risk?" Bolan asked as they strode along the sidewalk.

"He wants to show who is in control." There was an undercurrent of skepticism in Radic's voice that belied the image of Macek as every worker's hero, the image that had been portrayed in the Western media. "Not just the authorities; he wants to show that all of Unity is behind him, that it really is a united movement."

"Isn't it?"

"Well, some factions just want to work out a new deal with Moscow. Others want to develop stronger ties to the West."

"And you? How did you get involved?"

"I was working at the paper. One day the editor was ill, so I wrote the editorial. I'm still not sure which sentence offended them, but that's when I was relegated to sports reporter permanently. It's also the day I joined Unity."

Two truckloads of soldiers were parked to

one side of the street. They did not attempt to stop any of the passersby heading for the rally; they just watched everyone with hostile eyes.

Bolan began looking for any sign of Kelly and Pierre, but he continued to question Radic. "Being a sports photographer can't be all that bad, can it?"

"It does have some advantages. I enjoy a relative freedom of movement and that has been useful."

"As a courier?"

Radic quickly turned to look at Bolan. This tough foreigner was no more an assistant coach than Radic was merely a sports cameraman. But there was something about the man that instilled an implicit and immediate trust.

The street ended, opening out into a broad square. Its proper name was Karadjordje Place, after a Serbian guerrilla who had rallied the resistance to Turkish rule, but everyone called it Revolution Square. There could not have been a more appropriate nor dangerous place in all of Zubrovna for Macek to stage his Unity rally.

The crowd pushed forward, jostling Georgi Radic and his tall American companion. It was often difficult for the two men to make headway through the throng, but at least Bolan could see over the heads of most of the onlookers.

The people were hushed as they listened carefully to the translation of a message from Lech Walesa that had been smuggled into the country. Bolan's eyes roved along the perimeter of the square, hoping that Danjou had enough sense to keep Kelly away from the middle of this crush.

Radic did not look out of place among these office workers, tradesmen and students. In fact, Bolan spotted several of the photographers who had been at the airport. They all knew where the real story was this morning. He couldn't blame Kelly for coming along. This was history, in the raw.

Bolan was about to suggest that he and Radic split up when he spotted Fatman and Gloves. They were on the steps of the war-memorial cenotaph, with a camera mounted on a tripod. But the 35mm Zenit was not focused on the slogan-covered speaker's stand; the long lens was pointed upward at a large building on the opposite side of the square.

It was built in the seventeenth century, its classic architecure cluttered with baroque afterthoughts. In the prewar years it had been occupied by a French banking concern. The financial institution had not been welcome in the new socialist state. Now it housed an obscure branch of the cultural affairs ministry.

Bolan automatically swiveled to see what was attracting the attention of his two former shadows. What could be so important for them to photograph over there that they had abandoned the trail of a potentially suspicious American?

"George, let me have your camera for a minute." The photographer looked puzzled but complied.

Bolan used the zoom lens on Radic's camera to inspect the facade of the building. A clock over the left-hand entrance read seven-forty.

Bolan swung his attention to the right, to a fifth-floor window. A movement caught his eye. He studied the shifting shadows behind the glass. He discerned two figures up there and thought there might be a third man standing behind them.

They were looking down on the rostrum where Damien Macek was stepping forward to address his followers.

The window slid open, the protective glare on the glass disappeared.

The pale oval of the assassin's face was pressed against the hard dark lines of the sniper-scoped rifle. The ugly slits of the SVD's long flash suppressor poked over the sill. To the left, farther back and perhaps two feet higher, another gun was being brought to bear.

Bolan could not believe it. The assassin was the spitting image of Bolan, right down to the new mustache!

Fatman made a final adjustment to the focus of the Zenit's zoom lens.

The sniper's finger curled around the trigger.

"Find Kelly for me!" Bolan shouted as he pushed the camera back to Radic. But his instructions were drowned by the roar of the spectators as they returned the greetings of the Unity leader. The gut instinct of the news photographer made Radic snap off a shot just as Bolan turned to plunge into the crowd.

The American elbowed his way forward. Several bystanders dodged aside as Bolan raced toward the entrance of the ministry building. He felt the comforting weight of the Beretta beneath his jacket as he charged the front door.

Someone had only a few seconds left to live!

19

With his personalized Steyr-Mannlicher, Lednev could group three rounds within a one-inch spread at four hundred yards. But he was a dedicated marksman who specialized in the one-shot kill. The cross hairs of the Kahles scope tracked down from Damien Macek's face to settle on his chest. Lednev took a shallow breath and held it.

The Unity leader was still trying to quiet the large crowd so that he could begin his speech. He raised both hands, palm outward, in a subduing motion. . . .

The 7.62mm bullet clipped the knuckle of his little finger, deflected downward and hit the cheekbone.

Blood sprayed in a crimson arc over his wife's arm and the top of her cheap flowery dress. Instinctively she reached out and caught Macek as he staggered back. Their nine-year-old daughter screamed hysterically.

A dream was dying as a nightmare came true.

BOLDIN SWALLOWED THE BILE in his throat. Lednev alone was responsible.

The Polish prisoner knew now that he could never have done it, no matter what he'd promised them. Boldin had spent long enough on the rifle range to tell what the difference in his weapon's recoil meant. Vichinsky kept him kneeling in the window for a fraction of a second longer.

Fatman took his picture as pandemonium broke loose.

The Russian colonel still held his pistol loosely. It wasn't pointed at the double, but Boldin knew Vichinsky would not hesitate to use it. He waggled the muzzle toward the door. "Quickly! Into the other room!"

Lednev snapped shut the catches on his rifle case and ran for cover.

BOLAN, taking the broad marble steps two at a time, heard the double report of the rifles in the room above. He pulled out the Beretta. A door opened...pounding feet...another door slammed shut. Breath rasping in his throat, Bolan raced up the last flight of the twisting staircase.

A STUDENT STANDING at the back of the crowd pointed at the ministry building and shouted the alarm. Then a factory hand who had been jostled as Bolan ran past added his cry. Gloves looked at Fatman, shrugged, and joined in the chorus.

Two of the crowd-control police ran in the direction that several people now pointed out. A nearby army officer signaled for his patrol to follow him. Only Georgi Radic began walking quickly in the opposite direction.

THE SOUND FROM OUTSIDE was a muffled roar, punctuated by angry shouts of disbelief and wails of protest at the obscene horror of Macek's assassination.

The top landing was deserted. The door to the room at the front was standing ajar. Every sense on alert, Bolan moved with speed and precision. He shoved the door open wider with his left hand and he came through fast and low, the 93-R sweeping the room. But it was empty.

The place reeked of cordite.

Bolan ran to the open window. The square was in total confusion. As a former sniper, the American dispassionately assessed the shot: tough angle, long range. Whoever did it knew his business. Someone down below saw him standing in the window and screamed, ''Assassin!''

The crowd really began to panic.

Bolan instantly drew back, but in his hand he held one small key to the puzzle—a shell case that had landed on the inside window ledge. It wasn't a NATO round; it was a Russian-styled 7.62mm. There was no time to figure it out, but from the splintered crimping it looked like a blank!

He was almost certain there had been at least three men up here. But which way had they gone? There were four other doors on the top-floor landing.

Bolan heard boots stamping up the first flight of steps. Rifle bolts clicked as the soldiers levered live rounds into their weapons. The officer barked out a guttural order for his sergeant to lead the way.

Bolan saw a decorative recess in which a large empty vase was standing on a plaster column. He grabbed it and tossed the container over the railing. It plummeted down the stairwell. The shattering vase would keep the men down there frozen for a few precious seconds.

Bolan was already running toward the doors at the rear before the vase hit the tiled floor at the bottom and exploded into tiny porcelain fragments.

He couldn't hang around to work out how the real hit team had vanished so completely. He was the one the police and soldiers were after now.

Bolan tried the left-hand door. It was locked. The other one opened into a carpeted office. A plain wooden chair was standing against the wall. He spun it around and jammed the top edge under the door handle, then he crossed to the window.

Behind the impressive houses that faced onto Karadjordje Place was a grubby maze of ancient dwellings. Bolan leaned out just as three small figures ran through the narrow alleyway below. They were not soldiers, just onlookers smart enough to escape from the melee in the square.

The guttering didn't look as if it would take his weight. Besides, he didn't know who or what was up there or where the rooftop led; it might be a dead-end trap.

He would have to risk the ledge that ran around the outside of the building. It didn't look safe, either, but it was better than staying where he was; a shoot-out here could only have one eventual outcome. Bolan holstered his gun, shoved the shell case in his pocket and swung a leg over the sill.

The corner of the building was twenty feet to his right. In the other direction, but farther away, was a fire escape. He decided to go for the rusted ladder. His pursuers had reached the fifth floor. Bolan could hear them shouldering the door. With his cheek pressed against the crumbling brick, he began to inch his way along the ledge.

The soot-stained structure on the other side of the alley might have been a warehouse; most of its broken windows were blocked with cardboard or old canvas. At least there was no one staring out at the big man who was testing each new step as he edged toward the escape ladder. Two more feet to go and he would have to pass in front of the window to the locked office.

Bolan heard a door being smashed open. He hugged tighter to the masonry. Three men charged in, saw the place was empty, then two ran out. The last guy came over to check the window.

Bolan's palm was pressed flat, his fingertips digging into the dusty mortar, as with his other hand he began to reach down for his ankle sheath. But caution cost time.

The soldier stuck his head out the window, saw the fugitive balanced there and sucked in a breath to shout the alarm. Bolan struck with the speed of a cobra. His free hand snaked forward, fingers grabbing the man's windpipe.

The scream was trapped in his throat. He felt only a hot giddying rush as Bolan twisted savagely. The big warrior pushed the unconscious body away, and the unwary soldier collapsed limply back inside the room.

Bolan eased his way past the office window. A loose flake of tiling rattled down over the broken gutter. They were searching the roof above. And two more frightened demonstrators sprinted along the alley below. Bolan froze—he was still about fifteen feet short of the ladder.

He reached up to steady himself. His hand closed on the heavy metal bracket supporting the ceramic insulators of two thick telephone cables that stretched across the alley. He used these few seconds to draw the razor-sharp combat knife from its sheath.

Bolan glanced up and saw a policeman's head bobbing out over the eavestrough. The guy was standing directly over the fire escape.

There was no time to weigh the options as the uniformed officer reached for his holster. Bolan hacked through the phone wires with three rapid strokes.

The policeman yelled out that he'd found the man they were after; he was grinning as he drew his pistol.

Bolan grabbed a firm hold of the two wires and launched himself from the ledge. He swung down in a sickeningly swift arc across the alleyway. The cop had only a second to snap off one hasty shot as he saw the fugitive smash feet first through a fourth-floor window of the warehouse opposite.

Bolan landed bruisingly in a jumble of flapping cardboard and old sacks. Knees flexed, he had rolled forward to break his fall, becoming even more tangled in the sacking. His tumbling momentum came to an abrupt halt as he bumped into a musty jute-wrapped bale.

The frustrated cop aimed a second futile shot into the dark space of the window frame.

Bolan shook off the sacking and padded

across the wooden floorboards to a narrow, open staircase. His eyes had already adjusted to the gloom.

No one was working on the third floor. Bolan quickly descended. He could hear movement on the next level down. He looked over the railing at the top of the steps and saw some men moving about.

Half of the workers had abandoned all pretence of appearing to work. They were huddled in small whispering groups.

Attention was suddenly focused on a panting newcomer who had arrived with the latest rumor.

But a dozen of the older men were still carrying cartons over to a loading chute, down which the packages were slid to a waiting truck. They were not going to let the foreman catch them slackening off, no matter what the commotion outside was all about.

Bolan picked up the smallest wooden crate he could find, hoisted it on his shoulder and marched over to the elevator cage. He pushed the red button and the cables shuddered into life. No one turned to see who was standing in the shadows at the back of the cage as it descended past the second floor.

Reaching ground level, Bolan shifted the box to his other shoulder to hide his face from a group of workers engaged in a heated argument over the events in the square. Bolan strode down the short ramp in front of him and vanished around the back of the half-laden truck.

He simply dumped the small crate next to a rear wheel and ducked into a tiny pedestrian passageway that threaded past the backyards of some deserted tenements.

"Police!" One of the workers shouted a warning to his mates. They all scrambled to appear busy. Bolan could hear the clatter of running feet and then a car screeching to a halt outside the warehouse.

He vaulted a fence, hurried through a damp smelly hallway and emerged into the street. It was swarming with people still escaping from the square.

He walked swiftly along in the swirling flow of humanity. Right now Bolan didn't care where he was headed as long as he put some distance between himself and the building-by-building search of the Revolution Square district.

He could only hope that Radic had managed to find Kelly.

Bolan had more pressing matters to attend to: he knew he'd just been framed for the cold-blooded assassination of the charismatic leader of Unity.

The whole world had been watching Damien Macek.

Now they were going to want his killer.

20

Bolan had no choice but to go to ground. Fast. The state-security forces had thrown their drag-net over the city. Now they pulled it tight.

The soldiers were working in conjunction with the regular police. People were being asked to produce their papers, say where they were from and why they were not at work. A truck cruised past with a loudspeaker system barking orders. Several of the pedestrians scurried faster to get out of the area.

Bolan turned in to a narrow side street that ran parallel to the boulevard he and Radic had used when they approached the rally. The crowd was thinning out; there seemed to be more cops on the streets than civilians. The tall American hunched over a little more, trying to cover his face with a handkerchief as he passed an army patrol. He fell in step with a worried-looking couple as they crossed at the intersection.

He cursed under his breath. Of course! The real killers hadn't gone anywhere. They didn't have to. All they had to do was conceal themselves long enough to mix in with the milling throng.

A job this big could not have been a local operation. It had to have been initiated, perhaps even supervised, by the KGB. The hit team could pull the right strings all the way to the Kremlin. And no one would dare challenge them.

Bolan took his bearings. He was sure he was heading in the right direction. He didn't want to involve civilians, but Georgi Radic was the only person who could help him. The young photographer had been reluctant to get mixed up in this from the start. He hadn't even wanted to go to the rally, but now he was in it up to his neck.

The KGB left no room for innocent bystanders.

The butcher was pulling down the shutters in front of his shop windows as Bolan approached; like other storekeepers he was closing up in anticipation of the military crackdown that was certain to be announced at any moment.

But the shop was the landmark Bolan was looking for. He resisted the temptation to glance up at the fourth-floor windows. He did not know who else might have their eyes on him.

Bolan turned the corner and slipped through the back entrance. A door on the first landing clicked shut as he came up the stairs.

The light bulb over the last steep flight had

burned out. Bolan waited in the darkness outside the apartment at the top. A floorboard squeakily protested as someone inside crossed the room.

Bolan loosened the Beretta in its holster, then he tapped once. "George!"

The door opened instantly.

"Phew! I guessed it was you," Radic said with a nervous grin. He quickly corrected himself. "I hoped it was you!"

He tugged Bolan into the room and locked the door behind them.

"Did you find Kelly?" She was Bolan's first concern.

"I saw Miss Crawford as I was leaving your hotel. She was in a car. Monsieur Danjou was driving. And there was another man with them: about forty-five, graying hair, thin on top. He had a military air. . . ."

Bolan nodded. He sounded like a fair description of her coach, Lee Brebner. So Kelly was in safe hands. He did not blame her for leading him into this mess. In fact, he was beginning to doubt if she had even written the note that sent him to Revolution Square in the first place.

There were no loose ends. Nothing this morning had happened by chance. The KGB and their local minions would not have left anything to chance.

The men from Moscow had pulled the perfect

suck play. But Bolan wasn't going to be suckered into fighting for his life on their turf. That was their game plan, not his.

Bolan was going to fight them, yeah. He would settle his score with that blood-red murder machine. But it would be on his own terms only.

There were two things he must try to do now—escape from Zubrovna and clear his name.

His suitcase was standing beside a worn leather armchair. "You said you were at the hotel again?"

"The crowd panicked. The police started clearing the square. I still had not caught sight of Miss Crawford so I ran back here, got the car and drove to the hotel."

"Using the back entrance again?"

"Naturally. I bribed a maid to let me into your room. I threw your things into the case and then drove on down past the American consulate thinking you might make your way there."

"Was it surrounded by guards?"

Radic nodded. "I showed my press card to the officer in charge. He told me that the state-security troopers were guarding the foreign embassies in case there might be demonstrations."

"Well, I wasn't going to run that gauntlet. That's why I made my way here."

Radic, hesitant to speak what was on his mind, looked at his guest. Finally he got it out. "Mr. Bailey, are you a spy? Are you with the CIA?"

"No," replied Bolan truthfully, "but something like that." He bent over the nylon flight case and began to remove the handle. "Tell me how you saw Kelly."

"I saw a truckload of state troopers drawing up at the front of the hotel. Then I saw the car with Kelly and the others going into the parking lot. She seemed to be in no danger."

Radic watched Bolan as the American stripped off the webbing that formed the carrying straps.

Bolan removed his jacket, turning it inside out to reverse it to black. He draped it over the back of the armchair, then pulled on a dark polo-neck sweater. He rearranged the webbing straps and clipped them around his chest as a combat harness.

Picking up an oblong pack of ballistic nylon, he tore open the Velcro fastener and tipped out the hairbrush-and-comb set. He refilled the pack with loaded magazines for the Beretta, then snapped the ammo pouch into place on his new belt.

Bolan selected another small pack that looked like an ordinary traveler's first-aid kit and hooked it onto his shoulder strap. Next, he pulled an extra large tube of toothpaste from the toiletries bag, opened the end and shook out a compact silencer. He secured it by adjustable loops to his other shoulder. Quickly, he added the sheathed combat knife and the Beretta holster. Finally he pulled on his jacket.

Radic felt a cold prickling at the base of his spine as he followed the big man's economy of movement.

He knew he was watching Death get dressed.

When Bolan looked across at him, Radic lightly slapped his own forehead. "I forgot to tell you.... When I parked the car around the corner, I saw a policeman stop a couple of passersby. He showed them a picture. What do you call it? The kind a police artist draws of a suspect...."

"An identikit picture."

"Yes. I couldn't look too closely as I went by, but I'm sure it was a very reasonable likeness of you."

"But that couldn't have been more than, what, fifteen minutes after the shooting." Bolan shook his head at the efficiency of the secret police. Absolutely nothing had been left to chance.

"But I may have some interesting pictures of my own," Radic said, holding up a small canister of 35mm film. "I took a last shot of you just as you went through the door of that ministry building; then, a moment later, the gunshots were fired from the upper window.''

"Did you have time to wind it on?"

Radic smiled and reached across to pat his camera. "A sports photographer's best friend—motor drive! It fires off six frames in three seconds. It all happened so fast. I panned up to the window on reflex."

"So you have the whole sequence on film?"

"We won't know until it's processed," Radic warned. "Let's develop it and find out. Through there—I use the bathroom as my dark-room."

In the tiny washroom Radic had everything neatly organized. Three chemical trays lay on the bottom of the bath; the enlarger stood on a plywood sheet fitted over the basin. The air was permeated with the smell of the developing mixtures. It was a tight squeeze with both of them in there.

"Hand me that." Radic indicated a dark rectangle leaning against the wall. He had simply tacked a piece of thick black cloth over a wooden frame to form a light-tight cover for the small window.

Radic stood on the toilet lid to reach the window. Bolan handed him the blackout screen. He was leaning forward to put it in place when he stiffened.

"We've left it too late. There's a police car

coming up the street.'' He stretched to press his face closer to the glass as he checked the opposite direction. ''A black van. Probably with a squad in the back.''

He jumped down to the floor.

''I'm sorry I got you into this,'' said Bolan, pocketing the roll of film.

''I was in it long before you came to Zubrovna. We've no time to waste. Follow me!''

A narrow door at the back of the kitchen alcove led out onto a small balcony cluttered with flowerpots. A wooden partition divided it from the adjoining balcony.

''Come on.'' Radic moved some geraniums out of the way and clambered around onto his neighbor's balcony. ''There's nobody home at this time of day. We can get up to the roof from the other end there.''

Bolan hoisted himself up the outside of a building for the second time that morning.

The roof was not too steep, and the rough surface of the tiles provided a secure grip. Hunched low, the two men moved swiftly along the rooftop. Radic led the way as they hurried to cover the second side of the square that surrounded the open courtyard.

''Take cover!'' rasped Bolan. They squeezed behind a brick chimney stack as a state-security patrol rushed through the cobbled yard below. Five men in dark blue uniforms, two with their guns already drawn, charged into the back of Radic's place.

"Now, over the top!"

This part of the town was not as ancient as the warren of the Old Citadel, but the shops and apartments ran close together in a packed jumble of architectural styles.

Bolan followed hard on the heels of the photographer as they clambered over red tiles and chipped gray slates. They jumped from roof to roof, climbing up ladders, skirting water tanks and running along wooden walkways. They were one long block away from Radic's tiny apartment, and both panting for breath, when they reached a gap too wide to negotiate.

"We have to go down to the street here," Radic said, pointing to a rusted drainpipe. It looked as if the slightest weight would tear it away from the wall. "It's meant to look unsafe! It was installed by Unity workers last year. Don't worry, I use it all the time."

To prove his point he double-checked the back alley below them and swung himself out over the gutter. Bolan shinned down the pipe after him.

The daytime curfew was already in effect. The streets were eerily deserted. Once, they were forced to duck inside a shop doorway, and twice they had to hide behind garbage cans to avoid being seen by the police who were patrolling the area in pairs.

"Where are we going?" Bolan asked.

"Saraci Street. It's the nearest . . . ."

The nearest what, he didn't say—they were off and running again.

Bolan thought he caught a glimpse of a net curtain falling back into place as they loped past; he was certain that hidden eyes were watching their progress.

Radic had reached the next corner. He waved Bolan back. "Patrol coming!"

They turned on their heels and fled back the way they had come. It was a long street of terraced cottages. The nearest intersection was two hundred yards away.

As they were running down the sidewalk a car raced across the junction. They heard the brakes squeal as the vehicle skidded to a halt.

"We've been spotted!"

Now the cops were both behind and in front of them.

There was nowhere left to run.

21

They both knew that within seconds armed policemen would appear at both ends of the street. Bolan began to unzip his windbreaker.

Suddenly the front door of a house on the other side of the road flew open. A white-haired lady, wearing a crocheted shawl, beckoned them briskly with a sticklike arm.

The two fugitives raced across the pavement toward her. There was no time to ponder her offer of refuge, no time to consider what further risks they might be taking. It was a decision that had to be acted upon instantly; the kind Bolan was used to making. They ran straight past her into the narrow hallway.

She shut the door the moment they were safely inside. When the two patrols turned into the street, it would be empty.

"Bless you, little mother!" Radic gasped.

The old woman looked at their faces. In that very instant, time had raced backward for her—to another war, another enemy. She had sheltered the Resistance fighters through the long

GET THIS MACK BOLAN BUMPER STICKER FREE!

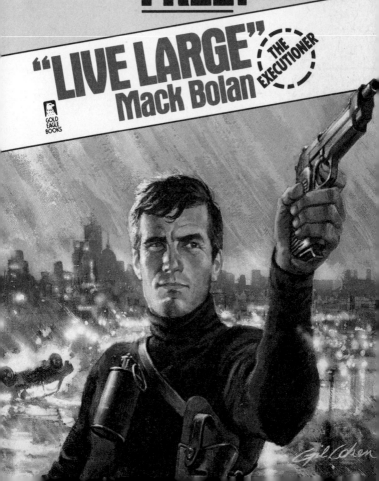

"LIVE LARGE" Mack Bolan THE EXECUTIONER

GOLD EAGLE BOOKS

HE'S UNSTOPPABLE. AND HE'LL FIGHT TO DEFEND FREEDOM!

FREE! MACK BOLAN BUMPER STICKER
when you join our home subscription plan.

Gold Eagle Reader Service, a Division of Worldwide Library
2504 W. Southern Avenue, Tempe AZ 85282

YES, please send me my first four Executioner novels, and include my FREE Mack Bolan bumper sticker as a gift. These first four books are mine to examine free for 10 days. If I am not entirely satisfied with these books, I will return them within 10 days and owe nothing. If I decide to keep these novels, I will pay just $1.95 per book (total $7.80). I will then receive the four new Executioner novels every other month as soon as they come off the presses, and will be billed the same low price of $7.80 per shipment. I understand that each shipment will contain two Mack Bolan novels, one Able Team and one Phoenix Force. There are no shipping and handling or any other hidden charges. I may cancel this arrangement at any time, and the bumper sticker is mine to keep as a FREE gift, even if I do not buy any additional books.

166 CIM PAC2

Name	(please print)	
Address		Apt No.
City	State	Zip
Signature	(If under 18, parent or guardian must sign.)	

This offer limited to one order per household. We reserve the right to exercise discretion in granting membership. If price changes are necessary, you will be notified. Offer expires August 31, 1984

PRINTED IN U.S.A.

GET THIS MACK BOLAN BUMPER STICKER FREE!

See exciting details inside.

dread night of the Nazi occupation. Now it was the state police and the Moscow-trained security agents who hunted down patriots. Only the uniforms had changed.

She said something to Radic. He translated for Bolan. "She thought we looked like honest men who badly needed help."

Bolan smiled and nodded to the woman.

"But we've got to keep moving," he whispered to Radic, "before they start a house-to-house search."

"This way." She led them down the passage, where the stale smell of cooked cabbage and potatoes seemed to cling to the faded wallpaper.

He was thankful he hadn't opened his jacket all the way. The hardware he was carrying might have surprised their benefactress. But then again it might not have shocked the old lady at all.

Without another word she steered them through her kitchen and opened the back door. The tiny yard was immaculately maintained, complete with a postage-stamp-sized vegetable plot.

She pointed to the wooden gate at the end of the short brick path and again said something to her compatriot. Picking up a battered but still serviceable flashlight, she gave it to Radic.

He nodded in gratitude. "She knows exactly what we're looking for."

"I think she's done this before...."

"Yes. I sensed it."

They ran to the gate and crouched behind it. The old woman took one last look at them, her frail fingers tracing the sign of the cross as if to give them a blessing, then she closed the door.

Radic reached up and unclasped the latch. He eased the gate ajar, peered through the gap, then opened it a little wider.

"There!" He pointed with the flashlight.

Bolan looked over his shoulder. The stretch of the alley they could see from the gateway was clear. Radic was pointing to a sloping metal cover set in an old concrete dome. It was four backyards away. It looked as if it might have been the doorway to an air-raid shelter left over from the dark days of the German invasion.

"Saves us going to Saraci Street," Radic said. "It's an entrance to the storm sewers. Once we're down there, they'll never find us. I promise you that."

Bolan's grimace revealed his distaste.

"Don't worry! It's not the city sewage system," Radic explained. "We get storms off the Mediterranean here. The sewers handle the flood of rainwater. Right now, I doubt if they're half full. The walkways will all be clear."

"Are you ready?"

"Yes. I'll go first," Radic said, tensing to race toward the metal door. "You cover me."

"Okay, let's do it!"

Radic prodded the gate right back, and they sprinted down the lane one after the other.

The photographer tugged at the handle of the door leading to the sewer system. The hinges were very stiff. Radic pulled on the handle again. This time the door shuddered open with a nerve-jangling scrape. Radic switched on the flashlight and ducked into the shadowy chamber beyond. Bolan was right behind him.

"Quick, George, the cops are coming!"

Bolan grasped the edge of the door and heaved it shut behind him. The slam of the entrance plate echoed down the steep chamber stairway. It was immediately followed by a second metallic clang as a bullet flattened itself on the heavy-gauge steel where a moment before Bolan had been crouching. Now the big blitzer stumbled down the dank steps, chasing the glow given off by Radic's flashlight.

Twenty feet down they found themselves on a catwalk spanning a huge brick-lined tunnel. A dark watercourse gurgled lazily below them. A weak light at the far end showed a series of metal rungs leading down to a ledge built out from the tunnel wall.

Bolan reached into one of the pouches on his combat harness and fished out a compact but powerful light of his own. The small inspection lamps, and the occasional ventilation shaft that led to the surface, provided only dim patches of twilight in an otherwise pitch-black world.

Bolan directed the pencil-thin beam at the water. It was murky with grit, but otherwise quite clean. Some twigs and a sodden newspaper floated past.

"About three feet deep. Maybe less. As a courier, I have to know these things," Radic said.

"Which way are we heading?"

"Downstream. Toward the river. It's about a mile."

The squeaking hinges of the entrance plate gave an amplified warning that their pursuers were determined to follow them.

"Get going!"

Radic started off at a trot; it was as fast as he dared. From experience Radic knew that if they could just reach the junction where this tunnel met up with those that drained the lower slopes of the Old Citadel, they could lose the police in the complicated network of filtration pools and overspill chutes. But still they had to exercise caution. To slip and break a leg now would kill any chance of escape. "Watch out, there's a step coming up."

The flagstone shelf had single steps at about fifty-yard intervals to compensate for the down-hill gradient. Bolan glanced back over his shoulder. He thought he saw a moving silhouette partially block the catwalk light above and behind them.

A guttural order bounced off the walls in a spiraling echo. The American did not have to speak the language to know he was being ordered to halt.

Gunshots! Two muzzle-flashes. Bolan heard the angry whine of bullets ricocheting within the confines of the storm drain. The police were firing blindly into the darkness.

Their flashlights now switched off, the two men hugged the wall. Bolan had the Beretta in his hand, but firing from this range would only waste ammunition. And tip off their hunters that the quarry was armed.

"It's about four hundred yards to the next major junction," Radic whispered. "Do you think we can make it?"

They could hear the policemen climbing down the metal rungs.

Bolan reached into a pouch and extracted the thin plastic tube to be used in emergencies as a water-purifying straw. Today it would have to serve double duty as a breathing device.

"You go on," instructed Bolan, whispering in Radic's ear. "When you reach the next step, flick your light on for just a second. Then duck out the way."

He patted the photographer on the shoulder to send him on his way. The policemen were arguing. As soon as Radic took off, one of the cops shouted, and Bolan could hear their footsteps slapping against the stone shelf.

He lowered himself under the water. It was not as cold as he'd imagined. With hardly a ripple, Bolan submerged himself completely. He gripped the plastic stem between his teeth. He kept himself in position with one hand stretched out to grasp the weed-choked retaining wall.

As the dark waters swirled over his face, they carried with them memories of another battlefield in this unending war, of night patrols to harass the VC supply lines. Bolan could recall lying in a fetid jungle stream—just like this, but breathing through a length of bamboo—to get the drop on Charlie.

He felt the vibration of pounding feet through the stones; had the walkways been better lit, the police might have spotted him.

As Bolan surfaced, the leading policeman was firing a burst at the momentary flicker of Radic's light.

The night warrior rose from the water like a demon from the netherworld.

The muzzle-flash of the second burst lit up both cops against the curving wall. The Beretta barked in reply.

Two slugs tore through the side of one of the policemen, smashing him against the bricks.

He bounced off, took one faltering step on the flagstone and fell headlong into the murky stream.

The other official thug was hit, too. He went down with a scream. The howl of pain and rage was prolonged by echoes. The weapon, a Skorpion, had clattered on the stone floor.

Crouching beneath the edge of the walkway, Bolan could hear the man's labored breathing and the desperate scuffing of his fingers searching for the fallen gun. Then, with a small grunt of relief, he gave away the fact that he'd found it.

Bolan vaulted back onto the path, rolled to tuck himself against the wall. The policeman fired at the sound of the splash.

There was no time to be surprised at how close they were. In a single reflexive impulse Bolan had homed in and pulled the trigger. Three times he fired. And the hollow acoustics turned his attack into a ragged fusillade.

No more breathing.

No more furtive fumbling in the darkness.

No answering fire.

Bolan risked his flashlight, holding it forward and well away from his body. The man lay supine, staring at him with three eyes: the third one glistened blankly in his forehead.

"Mr. Bailey, is that you? Are you all right?"

"Yeah, I'm okay, George. How about you?"

The photographer switched on his light and retraced his steps along the tunnel. His jacket had been sprayed with brick dust gouged out of the wall by the police bullets. Radic brushed off the dirt while Bolan removed the dead man's wallet with its official ID.

"Never know if this may come in handy," Bolan said. He rolled the body over with his foot and shoved it into the drainage canal.

Radic played the beam of his flashlight on the bobbing corpse, but within moments it looked like just a sodden log drifting through the sewers.

IT SOUNDED LIKE A BATTLE of mechanical monsters out there. Bolan stared through the heavy grille at the boxcars slamming into each other as the locomotives steamed and groaned to assemble another long freight train.

The military crackdown cleared the civilian population from the city streets but did not hamper the vital work of the railroad yard.

Bolan gave an involuntary shudder. His clothes were beginning to feel cold and clammy.

It had taken Radic half an hour to lead them through the main tunnel complex, over a bridge across an underground waterfall, and then up a smaller side channel to this barred opening.

Near the banks of the river stood the main marshaling yard of Zubrovna's extensive railway system.

Radic used his fingernails to scrape away the mud plastered around the end of one of the iron bars, revealing the neat incision of a hacksaw. He grinned at the American and began to clean off the next cut. The seemingly secure metal grille was held in place by dried mud!

Bolan wiped down the Beretta as best he could while the Unity courier loosened the bars.

"Ready? We'll sneak down to the back of that track-walker's shack." Radic pointed to the tar-papered hut at the edge of the tracks. "I've been watching it. Nobody's in there."

A concrete ditch provided cover to the halfway point. Then they waited a few minutes for a long line of grain carriers to shunt slowly by on the nearside track. It screened them from the rest of the yard as they crossed the open ground to the hut.

When the train had passed, Radic began to scan the other wagons for likely transportation. "South. That's no good. We've got to head north for the border." Many of the freight cars had their destinations chalked on the side. "Kremac...Alexsova...both in the wrong direction. There, got it! To our right. Three tracks over. See it?"

"Northbound?"

Radic nodded. "Several of the wagons are taking sugar beets and sunflower seeds to the processing plant at Mokravina."

"There's a flatcar in the middle that we should be able to.... Keep down!"

A workman in a blue cotton jacket walked slowly along the length of the train, checking off each wagon on the clipboard he carried. He paused at an empty boxcar, peered inside and rolled the door shut.

"It must be almost ready to leave," Radic whispered. He looked around the other end of the hut to make sure the inspector had moved on.

"The signal's just gone up," said Bolan.

The big diesel strained forward. A tremor of movement rattled through the freight cars as the wheels slowly began to turn.

Bolan took a long last look at the distant control tower. They would have to risk it. Hopefully the signalmen were already concentrating on the next task at hand.

They ran across the tracks, turning to race parallel with the departing train. Bolan caught up with the flatcar, leaped up onto the step and scrambled aboard.

Radic charged alongside, reaching out for Bolan's hands. With the American's aid, he hauled himself onto the wooden platform.

They sat there catching their breath as the train followed the bend of the river, heading out of Zubrovna toward the forested hills to the north.

22

Belikov carried a circular tray into the major general's office. He placed the envelope that had been delivered from Mozhenko's department on the blotter. Then he set down the steaming glass of tea and the saucer of lemon slices.

"Thank you, comrade."

"Colonel Vichinsky has just arrived."

"Good." Strakhov checked his watch. "Tell him I want to see him immediately."

Belikov withdrew from the room.

Strakhov picked up a lemon wedge and crossed to the window. The gloom of dusk had settled over the square. The sky was clear, but the glare of the city lights dimmed the first display of stars. He chewed on the tart fruit, wishing he could get away to his dacha on the Black Sea coast. Instead, within the hour, he had to attend a very secret meeting inside the Kremlin.

The funeral for his son had been a grueling round of formal condolences and military courtesies. Strakhov had read the preliminary report that detailed the events at the Sharuf air base. He knew others had studied it, too. And yet no one had made any mention of the American invader or his theft of the M-36.

The official version of Kyril's death, full of self-serving heroics, was acknowledged as the truth even by the men who had the facts at their disposal. Greb Strakhov accepted that. It had happened so many times over the years. He would settle the score with this Colonel Phoenix. But it was a private war.

How he would have liked to be strolling through the low hills behind his dacha at Dnestropol. Spring would already be in full bloom. There, he would have the peace needed to further ponder the mystery of the Romanovs.

Strakhov sucked the last pulpy flesh from the lemon rind.

Vichinsky coughed to announce his arrival. Strakhov turned away from the window. "How was your visit to Zubrovna? It appears you stirred up quite a hornet's nest."

Vichinsky looked tired from the exhausting return journey, but a sense of accomplishment glittered in his gray eyes. "I am pleased to report that the first phase of the operation has been a complete success."

Strakhov seated himself behind the desk. He cupped his hands around the tea glass.

"Damien Macek killed in a 'senseless act of provocation.'" Strakhov quoted from the official statement he himself had helped prepare. "The games will continue, of course. We will not be intimidated by the reckless ambition of an international terrorist."

Vichinsky's lip curled in a tight smile at Strakhov's straight-faced recitation of the party line.

"Did Janus perform as expected?"

"He fulfilled his role, Comrade General. But Lednev made the kill."

"And where is he now?"

"They have both returned to Akinova. I have them under close watch. Boldin can be disposed of as soon as the real Phoenix is apprehended."

"They haven't caught him yet?"

"The whole country is alerted. All exits are being guarded. I am confident we will have him within twenty-four hours."

"Let us hope the security forces will get Phoenix for us quickly." Strakhov paused for a moment, then made a sweeping dismissive gesture. "If not, the package we shall have delivered will make certain that he has nowhere left to flee, no place to hide. He will be a dead man on the run. It only remains for us to convince the Americans that their own man has turned."

"I bring you indisputable evidence of that." Vichinsky opened his briefcase and pulled out a folder of photographs.

"Good work, comrade. Let us review the material." Strakhov checked his watch again. "I have to be at a briefing in forty minutes."

He picked up the earlier photographs first. He wanted to examine the evidence they had contrived in its chronological order.

The picture he held beneath the lamp showed Phoenix talking with a Soviet agent.

"Taken in Munich," commented Vichinsky. "One of our men there stopped him in the street supposedly to ask for directions."

"Do the Americans know this man works for us?" mused Strakhov. Then he answered his own question. "They'll find out quickly enough."

A second shot clearly depicted Phoenix sitting at a café table. A swarthy man on the left was placing a folded newspaper on the empty chair between them. "There was nothing in it, of course, but it looks like an exchange is taking place. That one was taken in Central America."

Strakhov slit open the packet from Mozhenko. It contained copies of two bank slips. Both were receipts for monies paid into a private Swiss bank account. It had been opened in Zurich under the name of John Phoenix.

"One hundred thousand dollars was paid into the account yesterday morning." Strakhov examined the other slip. "This shows he has received a total of nearly a quarter of a million dollars. But now it will be obvious what services he has rendered to justify this generous payoff."

"And here are the prints from Zubrovna," said Vichinsky. "Grainy and amateurish, but clear enough. Just as if a tourist had caught the assassin on film by chance."

Strakhov looked at the photos taken by Fatman in Revolution Square. John Phoenix was sighting down a sniper rifle from a window overlooking the Unity rally.

"Conclusive proof," said Strakhov, gathering together the "evidence" and putting it all in a fresh envelope. "Everything is ready for the delivery?"

"The air force has a plane standing by for immediate takeoff. It will be handed over in Berlin tonight."

"Excellent work, Comrade Vichinsky," Strakhov approved. He closed up the package and laughed. Vichinsky was startled. It was not the earthy bellow he had overheard before, but a dry death-rattling chuckle that chilled him to the bone. "This should seal the fate of Colonel John Phoenix."

IT WAS VERY LATE. But the soft drizzle did little to dampen the sounds of celebration coming from the city streets behind him. Paul Kaplan could hear the raucous farewells of partygoers taking their leave of each other.

The other sector of the city, lying beyond that

somber wall, was quieter, but neither side was sleeping.

Kaplan turned up his collar and lit another cigarette as he watched the East German checkpoint. Guards with submachine guns slung on their shoulders prowled restlessly behind the barricade.

A small group was being let through. A young man pushing a bike was quickly in the lead. Next, a couple sauntered across. In between walked a tall man, wearing a fur hat that was really too warm for that time of year but afforded him protection from the rain.

The man caught sight of Kaplan standing by the phone kiosk and strode confidently toward the waiting contact.

"Erich," Kaplan greeted the visitor. He gestured to his Porsche. "Shall we use my car?"

"It's not necessary. I have the package." Erich reached inside his coat and produced a large square envelope. It was secured with red blobs of old-fashioned sealing wax.

Kaplan walked back to his car and climbed in. He didn't start up immediately. He sat there for a moment watching the East German courier walk off into the misty rain.

"How ELSE WOULD YOU INTERPRET IT?"

Farnsworth's question was a direct challenge to Hal Brognola. The pictures and papers laid out along the conference table told their own story.

The five members of the special presidential commission were summoned as soon as the package had been delivered. Webb and Knopfler had been working all night digesting intelligence reports, trying to piece together what might have happened in Zubrovna, when they got the call.

Andrew Webb, uncomfortable at feeling so rumpled, cut in before Brognola could respond. "It looks very much as if John Phoenix has sold out to the KGB. And they're making damn sure we know it. Somebody over there must be gloating!"

"What if we went public with some of this material? It could be carefully leaked to the media. Then Moscow would be implicated in the assassination of Damien Macek," suggested Brognola.

"That would reveal a whole lot more about the Stony Man operation," said Farnsworth, tapping the thick top-secret folder that lay open in front of him, "and blow Colonel Phoenix's cover wide open."

"They'll stonewall it," added Knopfler. "Those bastards will brazen it out just as they have been doing with the Bulgarian connection behind the attempt on the Pope's life."

"It's a setup, I tell you," Brognola grunted. "They've framed him."

"I'd like to agree," Knopfler ventured cautiously. "But I'm not sure anyone in Moscow Center has that much imagination."

"Maybe you've been underestimating them," snapped Brognola.

Crawford remained silent. In the past twenty-four hours he had in turn been frightened, angry, and now for the first time in his life the general felt truly indecisive. Bolan had deserted his daughter, broken his word...but a phone call from Kelly had at least set his mind to rest about her safety, even while it magnified the mystery around the man he had chosen as her bodyguard.

But the sequence of photographs stretched out on the table offered a comprehensible scenario of what had happened. Even Hal Brognola could not deny that it was *one* explanation of what might have transpired in Zubrovna.

Bolan had always been a loner, Crawford recalled. Even in Nam he was a man who had done things his way; that had been his strength. But now.... Could he have gone over the edge? Crawford had seen too much—in love and war—to entirely rule out that possibility.

The red light on the console in front of Brognola flickered briefly. He picked up the phone, turning away from the others to murmur his reply.

"Excuse me, gentlemen."

Farnsworth watched him walk heavily from the room. The summons of only one man could take precedence over this extraordinary meeting. The President must have read Farnsworth's hasty note and now wished to discuss the matter directly with Hal Brognola, the man who had served him diligently as liaison officer with Phoenix since the inception of the Stony Man program.

"I do not deny that there might be some other explanation," Farnsworth conceded to the others, as soon as Brognola had left. His tone was calm, reasonable. "But we must proceed on the assumption that we've got a very dangerous renegade on our hands."

"That's my opinion, too," said Webb, fiddling with his tie. "It's time to cut our losses."

"And cover our asses," added Knopfler. The presidential adviser turned to General Crawford. "Mr. Brognola would like us to give Colonel Phoenix the benefit of the doubt. But we cannot risk being wrong. It's too big a chance to take."

"Then I take it we're in agreement," announced Farnsworth, shutting the Stony Man file with a snap. "Put out the word to all agencies, all operatives: Operation Bad Apple is to take effect immediately. It's a global sanction. Eliminate John Phoenix. Find him and kill him!"

23

The couplings slackened and the buffers clanked into one another in a noisy rippling succession as the train began to slow down. Bolan peeked out from beneath the canvas cover. There were ghostly patches of mist still drifting in the deceptive half-light just before dawn.

They had stopped twice during the night. Once they had pulled off the main track for an interminable delay, waiting for an overdue passenger express to come whistling past them. Then they had stopped again outside Novigrad for a change of crew.

Radic squirmed over the lumpy cargo of sugar beets to join the American. "Look, there are the mountains," he said.

A low jagged line, frosted in patches with a scattering of snow, spanned the northwestern horizon. Radic shivered and peered through the gap in the canvas. Those glittering peaks, reflecting the first rays of sunlight, still looked a long way off to him. "What are we stopping for this time?"

Bolan risked lifting back the corner of the tarpaulin a little more. The flatcar was immediately in front of them, so they had a good view of the front of the train.

"Someone's waving a light. Three men, no, four, standing beside the track. Here, we'd better trade places. See if you can catch what's going on."

The freight train came to a complete halt. The driver leaned out of the diesel cab window and spoke to the fellow holding the lamp. He shouted in reply.

"He says the train's got to be searched... wanted men...two murderers from Zubrovna," Radic translated. "Now the engineer's telling him they've already received orders to pull into the yard at Trajevo. There's an army squad waiting to search the train from end to end."

The two railroad workers stared at each other in a frustrated standoff.

"It's a bureaucratic foul-up," commented Radic. "Typical!"

"Shh. Listen!"

"The local official says he's got his orders to follow."

The driver ducked back into the cab for a hasty conference with his assistant, then he spoke to the men waiting by the track.

"He's invited them to climb aboard and start

the search, but he's going on to Trajevo. He's got to follow his orders, too."

Two men climbed up into the engineer's compartment. The other pair started walking toward the rear of the train.

"They're coming this way. Two of them, carrying pick handles."

Bolan pulled Radic down inside the wagon and tugged the canvas back in place over their heads. His fingers curled around the Beretta as the railroad men approached. Their feet scrunched in the gravel as they trudged past.

"What were they saying?"

"Complaining about their boss, wishing he'd left everything up to the army," Radic whispered.

"It's time for us to get out onto that flatcar."

The train rolled forward again.

Bolan went first. He slipped over the wooden wall of the freight wagon, balanced on the buffer bar and jumped onto the flat planking of the car ahead. Radic followed him.

Scanning the ground on both sides of the track, Bolan pointed to a gap in the trees ahead. "Looks like a small river coming up on the left. Stay loose, and roll when you land."

There was no time for further instructions or encouragement. The ground sloped away to form the marshy banks of a shallow stream that meandered through the woods. They were fast approaching a low iron bridge.

Bolan jumped. His feet hit the incline and skidded in the damp grass. Then he sprawled forward into a dead bramble bush.

Radic stood on the edge of the flatcar watching Bolan's precipitous landing. The reporter froze—the train was going too fast. The trees rushed past in a blur. Suddenly he was looking down at the river.

"Halt!" A man was standing on the roof of the boxcar in front. He was pointing his pick handle at Radic.

The young Zubrovnan leaped for his life, barely missing the end of the bridge. He tumbled headlong down the steepest part of the bank, arms and legs flailing wildly.

The diesel continued rumbling down the track.

Radic landed in a clump of rushes with one foot twisted awkwardly under him and the other in the water.

Bolan trotted over to the far side of the bridge. The photographer sat up groggily, rubbing his shin.

"You okay?"

"Nothing seems to be broken," said Radic, assessing his condition. He climbed to his feet, took one step, winced and swore. "Must have sprained my ankle."

"Can you walk on it?"

"I think so. Give me that stick, will you? We've got to get away from here."

Bolan led the way, glancing back over his shoulder to make sure that Radic could keep up with him.

The young man hobbled along, occasionally leaning on the walking stick to catch his breath, then pushing himself a little faster up the path that led away from the stream. Overgrown in places with a tangle of weeds, the narrow dirt trail wound through the trees until it merged with cart tracks that skirted the edge of a meadow.

Bolan did his best to bolster his companion's spirits, but it was becoming obvious that they would soon have to secure some sort of transport. The honed warrior could make it alone. Bolan knew he could reach the safety of those mountains in little more than a half-day's hard march, or in one night if the enemy sent up spotter planes. But Bolan would not desert the Unity worker who had helped him escape the trap in Zubrovna.

He saw Radic force a grin when he turned and caught him limping badly.

"Take it easy, my friend. Rest for a while. I'll scout around and see if I can find us a car or something."

Radic looked relieved. "I'll wait for you in those trees over there. Good luck, Mr. Bailey."

Bolan moved fast. He was not motivated solely by a concern for George Radic; he wanted to get out as quickly as he could. He had no doubt that the KGB had mounted a far-reaching campaign to completely discredit him before he had the chance to unearth their mole in Washington. They had provided both sides with an excuse to blow him away—if they could. Bolan did not intend to give anyone the opportunity.

He returned within forty minutes. Radic had torn his vest into strips and used them to bind his ankle. He still looked pale. The jump from the train had shaken him up badly.

"There's a quarry on the far side of that hill. It's less than two miles."

Radic nodded. He could make it that far.

"I saw a truck drive in. It's our best bet. We have to steal it."

"They know we're in this area. The theft will not give us away," agreed Radic. "So, as you say: let's do it!"

They kept watch from the cover of some bushes until they saw the truck driver summoned by the quarry foreman. Radic was close enough to overhear the conversation. They talked, then the driver shrugged and the two men walked toward a wooden shack sheltered behind a steep mound of broken rock.

"They are going to detonate some charges in the cliff face," Radic translated.

"Let's go," Bolan said. With machine pistol

ready—the 93-R was set to fire 3-shot bursts—
the Executioner skipped nimbly from cover to
cover. His companion zigzagged more slowly
behind him.

They ducked behind some dust-caked hoppers
waiting on a narrow-gauge track and approached the truck from its blind side.

"Climb in," ordered Bolan, "and slide a-
cross."

Radic grunted as a shaft of pain lanced
through his ankle. He struggled past the steering
wheel, cleared some of the driver's gear from
the end of the bench seat and huddled in the corner of the cab.

The unsuspecting driver had left his keys in
the ignition.

"Stay down till she blows. . . then we go."

They both crouched below the level of the
windows.

A massive explosion split the air.

The concussive effect made the truck sway on
its springs. The rocks shook. Streamers of dust
escaped from a thousand new fissures; the
whole cliff face seemed to slide down to the
quarry floor in slow motion.

Bolan hit the starter. It fired first time. Loose
stones were rattling off the roof as he rammed
the gear lever into reverse for a fast turnabout.
The truck accelerated down the quarry road,
plumes of grit spewing from the tires.

Radic sat up, his ears ringing, and glanced in the side mirror at the choking cloud that blotted out the sky behind them.

"If we're lucky they'll hang around in that shack having a smoke until the dust settles. Then they'll come out and find the truck's missing...."

Bolan slammed on the brakes, reaching across with his right hand to prevent Radic from sliding forward. They skidded to a halt and Bolan jumped down from the cab. There was a series of short poles running alongside the gravel track carrying two telephone cables. To buy them time, he slashed through both the wires before proceeding.

Radic began to examine the things he'd swept off the seat. He opened up the driver's grease-stained lunch bag.

"Hmm. Bread, some slices of sausage and a piece of cheese!" He put on a flat cloth cap and divided the food.

"Those hills look a whole lot closer now, don't they?" said Bolan, between mouthfuls of a king-sized sandwich.

Radic stared out at the thickly forested slopes ahead of them. "The only pass I know is the one beyond Mokravina. It's the main highway through the mountains."

"No good. It'll be guarded night and day. I don't think we'd stand a chance of bluffing our way through."

"There are other paths that were used during the war. But I don't know who could show us the way now."

"There are some houses coming up. Stay down. Here, give me that cap."

It was a small village—twenty or so dwellings drawn up around a muddy market square. Bolan slowed down. He figured reckless speeding would only attract unwelcome attention.

Glancing through the rear window, Bolan noticed a small wooden crate in the cargo box.

"What's that we're carrying?"

Radic turned to look. "Just a wooden box."

"Can you read what's stenciled on it?"

"My God! It says Handle with Care: Dynamite!"

"Well, it hasn't blown us up yet. It'll just have to stay there."

Radic did not look too happy about the arrangement. He sat fidgeting for a while, staring out the window.

The truck rattled around a tree-lined bend. Ahead of them Bolan saw a car approaching.

"Short-wave antenna. Must be cops! No, don't move, George, it's too late to duck. We'll just drive right by them."

Bolan steered as close to the ditch as he dared, leaving plenty of room for the unmarked cruiser to pass.

Radic exhaled in a noisy rush. He had to look

through the rear window. Nothing could have stopped him. "They're going straight on! I guess they can't have heard about the truck."

Bolan was still watching the mirror. The police car was vanishing around the curve. In the last fraction of a second he caught sight of a taillight blinking red. "No, they're braking. They know who we are all right."

The morning sun flickered faster through the trees as Bolan pushed the truck to its limit.

"You're right," shouted Radic. "Here they come."

"How's your leg? Can you drive?"

"Yes, but... but you're not going to stop now?"

"No. Slide over. I'm going to open my door. Got the wheel? Now wedge your toes on top of the accelerator."

Bolan eased himself out of the door. Radic was doing his best to avoid the potholes. Bolan hooked one leg over the edge of the cargo box, judged the right moment and levered himself into the back.

A cop leaned out of the chase car and fired a round. It whizzed over Bolan's head as he dropped to the floor. He was now shielded by the tailgate. The policeman did not fire again. They were gaining steadily.

Bolan forced the lid off the crate with the flat of his knife. Several fuses of different lengths were coiled on top of the box. He brushed off the sawdust and started pulling out the dynamite.

He bound five sticks together with the longest fuse. The shortest one he used for its proper purpose.

"Faster, George! They're getting too close."

He tried one shot from the Beretta, but bouncing along at this speed it was pointless.

Bolan risked bobbing up again to check the road ahead. The woods were even thicker now. There was no place to turn off.

It was a straight race. And they were losing. He lit the fuse. Holding the explosives until the very last moment, Bolan tossed them ahead of the truck at the base of a large pine.

The bomb went off on impact. The shattered conifer keeled over the road as the explosion shattered the windows of the truck. Radic peered over the wheel and brought the truck through the diminishing gap between toppling tree and road. The trunk bounced off the back of the truck. The police driver tried to stop but the car smashed head-on into the tree.

Bolan leaned over to speak to Radic through the cab window. "Are you okay to keep going?"

"Yes, I'm fine, Mr. Bailey—" Radic frantically tapped the fuel gauge "—but I don't think this truck will take us much farther. We're almost out of gasoline!"

24

"Did you hear that? Listen!"

Radic rested heavily on his improvised walking stick, turning to cup his ear in the direction indicated by Bolan. The sound came again, clearer this time—the baying of eager dogs.

"They're a long way off," Radic said with a sigh of relief. "Those hounds are farther away from us than we are from the mountains. Let's stay on this footpath for a while. We're heading the right way."

It had been two hours since they had abandoned the truck. They were moving toward the mountains. The leafy track wound along the slopes of a river valley.

Bolan surveyed the terrain to their left and ahead of them, searching for the best route through the high country beyond. Bare outcrops of weathered rock towered over the greenery of scattered timber. Only the tallest peaks still shouldered a mantle of snow; the lower elevations were clear.

The sun was hot overhead. Off to their right

the river sparkled through the willows that fringed its banks. The two men paused behind cover to watch a military jeep speeding along the road on the far side of the water. It was not cause for immediate alarm; there was no bridge in sight.

They walked on in silence for another twenty minutes. Bolan abruptly signaled a halt. The trees thinned out ahead, giving way to a boulder-strewn meadow. He could see the outline of a vehicle parked behind a clump of bushes.

A danger signal had alerted the Executioner—they were being watched.

From behind. In the rocks they had just passed.... He whirled, drawing the Beretta from beneath his jacket. A startled Radic was standing right in the line of fire.

The stranger already had them covered with a double-barreled .410 shotgun. It was aimed true and looked big enough to blow a hole in them if they did not obey the man's gesture to walk on ahead of him.

A second man appeared, his shirt-sleeves rolled back to reveal walnut-brown forearms. He tilted back his battered felt hat and said something to his partner who had the gun. Bolan could not recognize the language.

As they turned into the sheltered dell, Bolan got his first good look at the vehicle, then he understood the strangeness of their tongue. "They're speaking Romany."

"Gypsies." Radic said, nodding. He tried addressing them in the local dialect. After a moment's hesitation the older man replied.

Bolan let them talk. He was brooding over what had happened back there. His reactions had been slow, dangerously dulled. He and Radic were being worn down, exhausted by the chase, and those mountains still stood between them and the freedom of the frontier.

The Gypsies' caravan would have lifted anyone's spirits. Built onto the chassis of an antique Italian truck was a traditional Romany *vardo*, the kind of gaily decorated wagon that might have been drawn by plodding horses.

A young woman leaned on the sill of the Dutch door at the rear, nursing a baby swaddled in an embroidered shawl. She made no attempt to adjust her blouse but, at a signal from the man with the shotgun, her husband, she retreated modestly into the interior of the caravan.

Two other women appeared from the woods. They were carrying a wicker basket full of mushrooms. The younger one, presumably the daughter, was extremely pretty, with luminous eyes and dark hair pulled back beneath a cotton print headscarf.

"They are all one family," Radic explained. "The old man and his wife, their two daughters and the son-in-law. They've come for a fair to be held near Mokravina.''

The man placed his firearm against the wheel rim and crouched by the small open fire. He picked up a blackened pot and poured tea into two tin mugs.

"These folks don't like the central government any more than we do," said Radic, sipping on the strong brew. "They refuse to settle down. It's not their way. They've always been wanderers.''

"And that kind of freedom can't be tolerated.''

"No. Yet the Gypsies still crisscross the borders of all the eastern European countries. An underground society quite apart from the state.''

"Do they know we're on the run?''

"Yes, they guessed as much. They heard the dogs, too.'' Radic looked puzzled when the unmarried daughter came over and knelt at his feet. She tugged off his shoe and began to unwind the strips of torn vest. He seemed rather embarrassed to receive this kind of attention and turned his head to talk to her father again.

Radic asked a question—Bolan heard him repeat it twice—but the Romany leader chose not to reply. Instead, he ordered the younger man to resume standing watch by the rocks.

"I asked him how they got over here. They

must have crossed the river someplace," said Radic, as the girl wrapped a fresh compress into place.

Her father glanced toward the nearest mountain, fingering a necklace heavy with silver charms and carved amulets. After careful consideration, he replied with a nod toward the river. Radic translated his directions with a grin. "There is a ford down there. A traditional crossing place used by horse traders. If we know of it, others will, too. There are many paths through these hills. See that spur up there, it covers one of the old trails.... Go through those pine woods and behind the ridge you'll find a way leading up to the high pass."

"Thank him for us," Bolan said.

Before he could convey their gratitude, Radic was interrupted by a shout from the lookout. The Gypsy ran into the encampment, brandishing his gun toward the south. "Soldiers! Six or seven of them coming through the trees."

"Dogs?" asked Radic.

"I didn't see any."

"We've got to leave, Mr. Bailey. There's a patrol heading this way."

The older man scuffed the dirty bandages into the fire. "You'll find an old monastery—in ruins now, I think—that marks the very top of the pass. A mile beyond that is the border. Hurry!"

Bolan set off for the belt of pine trees above them. Radic waved goodbye to the women and followed his friend.

They scrambled up the hill, ducking behind the boulders and sprinkling of young evergreens. Both realized that the Gypsy folk they left behind would be given a hard time by the government forces.

Bolan stopped.

The photographer had just caught up with him when he realized the American wasn't going on.

Bolan turned around to look in the direction of the Gypsy camp. He shook his head.

It was time to make a stand. Bolan was tired of being herded, tired of having a hungry pack snapping at his heels.

"One lousy shotgun against a whole squad. That's no odds to leave them with," he said.

Bolan palmed the 93-R. He double-checked the magazine, pushed up the safety button, set the weapon for short bursts and deployed the fore grip.

"You wait here," he said briskly.

"I'm going back, too," Radic replied evenly.

"Then keep behind me and stay down."

They retraced their steps toward the dell, careful to use every scrap of cover. Bolan could see the roof of the caravan behind the bushes.

Suddenly they heard a shotgun blast. It was

quickly answered by the sharper crack of rifle fire.

Fifty more paces and they reached a quartz-studded block that gave them a sheltered view of the grassy depression below.

The old Romany's son-in-law's body lay crumpled beside the path. The soldiers were laughing among themselves as they surrounded the wagon in a loose semicircle. Still clutching her baby, the woman ran between the troopers to where her man had fallen. No one tried to stop her.

The sergeant had the older Romany and his wife standing against the side of the painted truck. The sobbing woman was bent over her husband's corpse. The shotgun lay next to him on the ground.

"Bastards!" muttered Radic, impatient for the big man to make his move.

One of the soldiers dragged the young girl out of the *vardo* door. He made a lewd suggestion that amused the others. Her father rushed forward to help his daughter, but a hard clip on the side of the skull with a rifle butt sent him to his knees.

The sergeant started shouting.

"He's threatening they'll have her daughter one after the other, unless the old woman tells them which way they saw us go."

"Move down to the left. Toss some stones

into the back of those bushes," ordered Bolan. Radic wriggled away to create a diversion.

One of the soldiers sat down on the grass to enjoy the show. Another handed his rifle to a comrade, shed his tunic and started to unbuckle his belt. The sergeant tugged at the old woman's gold earrings, forcing her to turn and watch what was about to happen to her daughter.

There was a loud rustling through the nearby undergrowth.

"There must be more of them back there!" Two of the men unslung their rifles and warily approached the thick screen of bushes.

"Find me another dark-eyed beauty like this one," called out the squad leader.

Five men were left in the open.

The Executioner reared up from behind the rock. Three times the 93-R delivered its message of death. The three men nearest the fire lay suddenly lifeless.

The soldier who was undressing saw the cold-eyed stranger taking aim. He tripped over his own pants in his haste to squirm away.

The sergeant reached forward, trying to use his captive as a shield. She struck back unexpectedly, clawing his face so fiercely that the skin was stripped off in shreds. The daughter, her blouse torn open, seized the officer's leg and pulled backward. He sat down with a thump. The next 9mm parabellum slug blew off the back of his head.

The two privates near the bushes both fired at once. Bolan rolled away to one side as the top of the rock exploded in zinging chips of grit.

Radic chucked another handful of loose stones right at them. Both men were distracted. Bolan sighted, snapped off two more bursts and the soldiers staggered back into the weeds. Ugly red stains soaked through their tunics.

The last man, still clasping at his trousers, tried to escape down the path. He glanced over his shoulder at the black-clad doombringer on the slope above the dell; in his terrified flight he paid no heed to the newly widowed woman crouching beside her dead husband. She had placed the baby on the grass and now held the shotgun in her hands. The soldier was less than ten feet away when she pulled back on both the triggers. The blast all but cut the man in two.

"That makes seven," said Bolan.

Radic stood up, too. His legs were trembling. He glanced across at the American. The man looked drained, empty. There was no arrogance or pride in what he had done, only a bleak pity for the persecuted wanderers.

They threw the bodies in a ravine behind the trees and covered the spot as best they could with brushwood. The Romany family would bury their own.

The leader approached Bolan. "You helped

us," the old man said. "We do not forget such things. You are brother to the Rom."

Radic translated the remarks while the Gypsy chief removed an amulet from his necklace.

It was a small ivory dagger with a curved blade, less than two inches long, delicately carved and yellowed with age. The pommel was shaped in what looked like a pig, and scratched into the surface of the blade were the stick-figure of a hunter with a bow, and seven stars.

"It was fashioned from the tooth of a boar," said the old Gypsy. "Wear it always! It will protect you and bring you good fortune when you need it most."

25

The overgrown trail was there all right, just as the old man had said, but it was difficult to follow; obviously it had not been used as a regular footpath for many years.

As Bolan and his companion toiled up the steep slope they were soon able to view the sweeping vista below. Curving away to the northeast, the river valley widened into a checkerboard of rich farmland. In the distance, grayish smudges from the processing plants on the outskirts of Mokravina rose into the sky. Three tall steeples marked the town itself.

"I thought I caught a glimpse of the old ruins," Radic said, panting. He shaded his eyes to scan the notch between the craggy peaks above them.

The way ahead was partially blocked by a landslide of tumbled rock. Bolan guessed that it must have happened some seasons before. Thick weeds and young saplings were already sprouting in the crevices. He tried to estimate how long it would take them to reach the pass.

Scrambling through that pile of stones was going to cost them precious time. Still, if they could make it to the top in three or four hours, they might be able to slip across the frontier under cover of darkness.

He clambered over the last of the fallen rocks, and waited for Radic to catch up. The reporter's limp seemed even worse than before, and his pale forehead was slick with perspiration. Bolan would have said nothing, but Radic glanced back down toward the river bottom and saw the soldiers too. "There's a whole platoon coming across. Difficult to tell from this distance, but it looks as if they've got the dogs with them."

Bolan fingered the boar's-tooth dagger he'd been given. It hung round his neck on the same chain that carried April's ring. "Even if the Gypsy family is safely away, the hounds could pick up our trail. They might even find those bodies."

Off to the right, Bolan spotted the insectlike figures of another patrol crossing a path in the woods. He urged his companion on.

Half an hour later the gradient eased a little. A faint trail of beaten earth forked off to the high pastures that were already brightly speckled with alpine flowers. They could hear the tinkle of a sheep's bell somewhere above them. Radic's labored breathing was beginning to worry Bolan. He pushed on for another five

minutes and then sat down on a springy tus-
sock.

"They'll gain on us if we stop now," Radic
said.

"You're right," Bolan admitted. "But they'll
catch up with us for sure if we get so tired we
can't go on at all. Take a ten-minute break,
George. I could use a breather myself."

The photographer slumped on the grass. It
took him only a few moments to drift off.

Bolan used the time to inspect his weapons
carefully. Then he double-checked their bearings with the miniature compass from his survival kit. There was a good chance they would
leave those men behind them stranded on the
mountainside at nightfall; they wouldn't risk
moving after dark.

Radic sat up suddenly. "Sorry!" he blurted
out. "I didn't mean to. . . ."

"It's okay," Bolan told him. "We both need
the rest. I'm going to catnap for five minutes.
You keep watch. Then we'll try to make the pass
while it's still light."

Trained to sleep anywhere, even under the
most adverse conditions, Bolan shut his eyes
and willed himself to relax.

But the darkness of his mind was not complete. The horizon of his subconscious flickered
red with gunfire and flames. Battles fought long

ago and far away still raged within. Ghastly images that might have driven another man mad floated past in grisly succession.

The distant throb of a helicopter rotor scudded along the threshold of his awareness: gunships in Nam. . . the Dragonfire. . . .

He was snatching for his gun, rolling off to the side, as the shadow swept over him. A troop carrier heading straight for the pass rose like a raptor on the updrafts and vanished between the peaks.

They could have been spotted. Bolan was angry. ''Why the hell didn't you. . . .''

But Radic wasn't there.

Bolan looked around. Not ten feet away, anchored by a pebble on a large rock, was a rolled-up note. Radic had torn the paper from his reporter's pad. Bolan flattened out the message and read:

I am only slowing you down. I have gone back to see if I can mislead our pursuers. Take the film and make sure the world knows who the real culprits are. Good luck, Mr. Bailey.

G.R.

Bolan did not race after the photographer. Radic knew what he was doing and Bolan respected his decision—Bolan would not want to be chased out of his own country, either.

Bolan's eyes skipped to the bottom of the note again. "Mr. Bailey" it read. The brave young man had gone off to almost certain death without knowing Bolan's real name. In his warrior's profession, Bolan had met several truly courageous men; he would always number Georgi Radic among that rare elite.

He put the other survival items in his pocket. The note reminded him to check the small film container in the hollowed heel of his boot. Then he touched a match to the corner of the note and let the curling ashes drift away on the breeze.

The chopper had not reappeared. Bolan reasoned that the pilot had found a clearing along the border fence broad enough to set down the troops. Now they would dig in and wait.

Even if Radic did succeed in drawing off some of the trackers, and perhaps confusing them for a while, their dogs would still sniff out the other trail. And, with reinforcements now in place in front of their quarry, they could finish off the squeeze play when it suited them.

Bolan traveled faster, unburdened by a companion, but with a heavier heart. As he walked he kept a fix on the weathered stone walls of the monastery, which grew closer with every step.

Bolan pondered his grim situation as he willed himself up the final incline.

He was framed for a murder he did not commit. Stranded and alone in an alien land, he was unsure of which man's hand was against him or where he could turn next. And now he faced a hostile frontier.

But these impossible conditions, coupled with the kind of heroism displayed by Georgi Radic, only strengthened Bolan's resolve to survive and take the battle to the enemy.

There were people everywhere who were willing to risk their lives to rid themselves of the burden of tyrannical leaders, secret police, criminal bureaucrats and the cruel hand of stale ideologies whose demand for innocent blood could never be sated.

Bolan was going to fight—for people like Georgi Radic who made the final sacrifice. Their battle for freedom was Bolan's battle.

As long as he lived and breathed, he was going to strike back.

He was equipped with the skills and experience to wage a war every bit as ruthless as that waged by the foes of freedom and dignity.

Colonel Phoenix had been tied up in red tape, trapped by double-talk. And now, having failed to kill him, a highly placed mole was trying to tame Bolan to serve a traitor's whims.

But no more!
Mack Bolan was going to be himself again.
He would attack before dawn.

26

Only a part of the small monastery was in ruins. The front wall had crumbled away to reveal the cracked flagstones of the courtyard within; the roof of the main hall sagged badly, and its gradual collapse had sent the slates slithering down onto the walkway that surrounded it. But the squat tower was still intact, and a wisp of smoke curled from the kitchen chimney.

Bolan approached the open gateway. The wooden door leaned drunkenly, its hinges rusted beyond use. He unholstered the Beretta but concealed it behind his leg.

A small plot of land in the corner of the courtyard had been planted as a vegetable patch, with a trellis for beans against the wall.

Bolan was wondering who the gardener was when a voice came from a window in the keep.

Bolan turned at the sound, though he could not make out the words. The voice spoke again in German, then in a gruff and throaty English.

"You won't need that here. I shall not harm you."

The American fighter made certain that whoever was up there could clearly see he was putting the pistol back under his jacket.

The door at the bottom of the tower opened with a squeak and out stepped a monk. Bolan guessed him to be about sixty-five. He was bald, apart from an unkempt fringe of white hair. He wore rough homespun clothes and had a firm handshake.

He ushered Bolan into the kitchen, sat him on a bench at the table and served him an earthenware bowl of hot potato soup without asking a question.

"What is this place?" Bolan waited for the food to cool.

"Originally it was a monastic retreat built in the early fourteenth century. It was later seized from the monks," explained his host. "By 1800 it had changed hands again, and so it went, slowly falling into disrepair. Now I tend it alone. My name is Brother Josef. I have found peace here...."

His voice trailed away in a sigh, as if he knew the arrival of this man marked a shattering of the quiet contentment he treasured, but he accepted that as preordained.

Bolan sipped on the soup. It was good. He looked around. "This place is never going to get back on the map."

"A shepherd takes shelter here when the

storms come. In return he brings me the few things I need: razors, salt—" and the old monk looked a little guilty as he added "—and tobacco sometimes."

Bolan fished in his pocket and produced a battered cigarette pack. "Here. Keep them."

Brother Josef carefully extracted one bent cigarette. His gnarled fingers gently stroked it straight, then he broke it in two, selected the slightly longer part and lit up. Bolan watched him. It did not seem to be the gesture of a man of the cloth.

"You followed the old pilgrims' path up from the river?"

"Yes," replied Bolan, intrigued as to who this man really was. "How did you get here? I mean, originally."

The monk ignored his question. There were more pressing matters to be discussed. "You know they are waiting for you, don't you?"

Bolan nodded. "Do you know how many men have landed on the mountain?"

"Yes. I saw them." Brother Josef moved to the kitchen window and pointed to the lip of the pass. "From that outcrop you can look down on the border wire. They maintain a bare strip about a hundred yards wide. The helicopter has landed on a level ledge near the watchtower. I counted fourteen men. They are entrenched, with machine guns covering the path...others are constantly patrolling through the trees.''

Bolan stared into the flames of the kitchen fire. The 93-R, his knife and a wire garrote—not much artillery to take on a squad armed with machine guns. And these men were expecting him. But his plan remained the same: strike before dawn.

''You can rest here.'' The monk indicated a pallet hidden in the shadowy corner of the kitchen. ''I shall keep watch for you. I can wake you at four.''

Bolan's only advantage was to remain more alert than those soldiers stuck out on that bare mountainside. There would be no sleep for them this night. Bolan trusted this mysterious old man enough to take the risk.

The cleric brought him a blanket, then went to fetch some more wood for the fire. By the time he returned Bolan was asleep.

This time there were no dreams.

BROTHER JOSEF shuffled over to the corner. Bolan was already awake, lying with his head in the crook of his arm. He was watching the monk.

''It's almost four o'clock. There's a rainstorm brewing; it's beginning to cloud over.''

Bolan stood up. Brother Josef handed him a steaming mug of herbal tea. Its warmth helped him wake up. They both squatted in front of the fire.

"I came here a long time ago." It seemed that the monk had decided to answer the question after all, as if he wanted to confess his secret before the big stranger went out to face the men who were waiting for him. "I, too, was a soldier. I fought in Poland in 1939, then Belgium, France...and finally in Italy."

"You were with the Wehrmacht?" At least that explained his accent.

Brother Josef nodded sadly. "The Allies landed and pushed north. The Italians threw down their arms. Hitler ordered us not to yield another inch of ground, but I had made up my mind to leave such madness behind. I turned my back on it all, retreating farther northward by train at first, then I stole a motorbike and headed east, then I walked. I walked for days, always moving east, heading deeper into the mountains."

"Until you found yourself here?" Bolan took another swallow of tea.

"Yes. I was taken in by Brother Stefan. He gave me sanctuary. New clothes. And another chance at life."

"What happened to Stefan?"

"He was an old man when I arrived. I looked after him. But he died; in 1956, I think it was. And I have stayed here ever since. But perhaps there is no escape...."

"You mean from men like those?" Bolan tipped his head toward the dark square of the kitchen window.

"I was never a Nazi. Just a German soldier called up to serve my country. I was glad when I heard that the Allies had finally defeated Hitler, although the news did not reach us here until months after the war had ended."

Bolan picked up a log and placed it on the fire.

"I do not know what you have done that they want you so badly," the old man continued, "but I feel I must support you. You have chosen to fight, and that is the braver decision. Come, I have something to show you."

He picked up a candle stub and led his guest to a small storage chamber adjoining the kitchen. There was a large wooden trunk, a finely constructed container, standing against the far wall. Brother Josef knelt in front of it and opened the lid. He had to exert considerable effort since the box was almost airtight.

In the box Bolan glimpsed the distinctive flared shape of a Nazi helmet. Brother Josef lifted it out and placed it on the floor. Next he pulled out the field-gray tunic of a German trooper. Concealed beneath it was a long bundle of waxed paper.

The monk unwrapped the hidden object. *"Maschinenpistole,"* he said.

It was a Schmeisser MP-40, one of the most effective submachine guns of World War II. Brother Josef reached down and produced two 32-round magazines, plus a pouch full of loose ammunition.

The paper in which he had carefully packed away the ordnance crackled as the older man lifted it out of the bottom of the trunk. Lying on the cedar lining were four "potato mashers," the unmistakable hand grenades used by the Wehrmacht.

"Why didn't you discard these things?" Bolan asked.

"I had no intention of being taken alive," said Brother Josef, "by the partisans, the Russians or by my own comrades."

Bolan nodded. He understood only too well what it meant to have every man's hand against you.

A tremor ran through the monk's shoulders as if he were recalling memories of only yesterday. "I disobeyed the regulations of the army I served in. Desertion was instantly punishable by death. I broke the laws of my own country; at least, the laws that were then in effect. My illegal entry must certainly have contravened the laws of this country."

"Looks as if everything you did was wrong," Bolan summarized without judgment.

"It is sometimes necessary for a man to do

what others claim is wrong if he is to live at peace with himself. Laws can be changed to serve the most perverted ends, but justice remains immutable. Sometimes a man must become an outlaw to do what is right. I trust you understand me now.''

"Better than you think, old man."

"Then take these weapons...and may they be of some aid for what you have to do."

Bolan felt the odds tipping in his favor.

Sometimes a man must become an outlaw....

27

Tongues of lightning were flickering within the serried banks of clouds sweeping in from the south. Bolan held the Beretta in one hand. The Schmeisser was slung over his shoulder by its strap. In the other hand he carried the soup pot. It was full of glowing embers from the kitchen grate. A cast-iron lid prevented any random sparks from giving away his position. He moved along the dark line of stunted pines toward the deep notch dimly outlined against the storm-racked sky.

Brother Josef had sketched the layout of the pass, and Bolan could match the silhouetted landmarks against the clearer picture he held in his mind's eye.

He left the sandy track and padded out along the bare overhanging rocks that looked down on the far slope of the mountain. He came to the edge of a cliff that fell sheer for nearly two hundred feet.

The moon was obscured by fast-moving rain clouds, but Bolan could make out the trail wind-

ing through the woods below. Now the path
ended abruptly in a strip of open ground that
cut along the flanks of the high country.

Running down the center of this barren clearing was a single fence, six strands high, with
heaps of coiled wire pushed up against it at occasional intervals. It was not a formidable ob-
stacle in itself—Bolan could see the pale outline
of the path still continuing through the thick
forest on the far side.

But almost directly below his position was a
watchtower rising above the treetops, with an
unobstructed view of the old crossing point and
the no-man's-land.

The windows of the cabin at the top were
faintly lit, and Bolan counted four men inside.
He could barely make out the silhouette of the
helicopter parked on a flattened area where all
the stumps had been pulled.

Big, soft drops of rain started to spatter
down. The hot soup pot sizzled briefly as Bolan
spotted one of the machine guns dug in close to
the path. The other one would be in the opposite
trees to provide an effective cross-fire pattern.

He squatted on his haunches to observe the
woods. A cigarette glowed intermittently, as a
bored sentry waited impatiently for the end of
his nightwatch. The lay of the land was exactly
as Brother Josef had described, and the soldiers
were deployed much as Bolan had envisaged.

A white-hot fork split the sky. The storm was getting closer. It was almost time to make his move.

For aeons, pelting rains, freezing cold, blistering sun and bolts of lightning had worked on these stones. The exposed cliffs were dangerously eroded, with rocks balancing on weathered columns that threatened to collapse at any moment.

Bolan moved cautiously along the ridge, constantly wary of dislodging any loose pebbles, as he searched for the fissure. It was about a hundred yards from where the trail descended dizzily toward the border wire.

Some bushes grew about sixty yards farther on. Here he put down the iron pot and removed its lid. The embers were still quite hot but covered with a soft layer of ash. Bolan's pocket was bulging with the old German ammunition. He scattered the bullets on top of the embers, then ran back to the spot he'd located on the cliff edge.

He kept the handle of one potato masher tucked through his belt. He held the sticks of the other three grenades in one hand, waiting for the signal from the overheated rounds.

One of the guards circled the platform at the top of the tower, decided everything was quiet, and began to climb down the long wooden ladder.

It all seemed to happen at once.... .

About a mile away a lightning stroke cleaved the sky, splitting a fir tree apart with a frightening crack. And as the pealing thunder died the first of the bullets exploded.

Bolan pulled the fuses on the grenades and immediately dropped them down the crack in front of him. Unslinging the submachine gun as he ran, the lone warrior raced back to plunge down the path.

The grenades went off in rapid succession. Their muffled reports were followed by the grinding creak of the stones moving outward. The unsafe rocks at the top tumbled first, knocking larger chunks out of the cliff face as they fell.

Another lightning bolt struck the woods, even closer this time. Then the rain started pouring down.

"There! Over there!" A machine gunner opened fire toward the sound of the exploding ammunition. His steady stream of bullets only chipped more stones from the cliff top.

"No. He's coming down the path!" yelled a guard. He had seen the fast-moving figure illuminated by the lightning. Then, from the corner of his eye, he saw the whole rock face giving way. Huge slabs mixed with jagged stones collapsed, gathering force as they rattled and rumbled down the scree. The soldier knew he had no chance of outrunning the landslide. His shout of warning turned into a high-pitched scream.

Bolan dodged along the track. Below him and to the right, the falling rocks tore out trees and buried large bushes in their mad rush.

One of the sentries reached the trail, seeking shelter from the rockfall. He turned, thinking another comrade had reached comparative safety with him. What he saw was a black-clad death-dealer, hair plastered wildly by the rain, a gun in either hand.

Bolan fired a single burst from the Beretta, scoring three hits less than two fingers apart, as he simultaneously swung the Schmeisser across to target on the muzzle-flash of the second machine gun. The shuddering incandescence of the machine pistol was answered by the brilliance of the raging sky.

He was a living blitzkrieg of stone and fire and flying lead.

The enemy had been struck by a one-man storm of such ferocity they were taken completely by surprise.

Only seconds had elapsed since the first round had exploded. The man on the ladder heard the terrible groaning roar of the rock slide and clung there for a moment, undecided whether he should go back up or continue down. He began to ascend.

The force of the rolling rocks was almost spent by the time it reached the watchtower. But the momentum of the moving wall of debris swept away one of the support struts. Another began to bend. The whole platform tilted alarmingly as the structure leaned backward. Then it collapsed on top of the helicopter. The watchtower's guardroom itself landed square on the rotor assembly and squashed the chopper cabin flat.

The dust cloud was being beaten back into the dirt by the pouring rain. Bolan, his face a battle mask streaked with grime, had reached the last long run to the fence. A three-man patrol was charging in from the left...but a raking broadside of Schmeisser-fire shredded into them before they could get off a shot at the speeding shadow.

The flaring storm lit the avenue he had to cross. The frontier fence was fifty yards ahead. He slammed home fresh magazines and ran into the open as bullets danced in a crazy pattern across the earth. Bolan skidded to a halt, spun about and dropped to one knee. Both his weapons spurted flame as a staccato stream of destruction cut down the machine-gun crew.

The MP-40 was empty. Bolan dropped the gun, tugged the last grenade from his belt, yanked the fuse with his teeth and hurled it at the nearest fence post. He hit the ground. The explosion splintered the upright, severing the wires. They peeled open with an angry twang.

Bolan fired a last burst at the trees, then he

was up and running through the hole. His soles were caked with mud as he raced for the deep cover of the forest.

Behind him, a few smaller stones were still slithering onto the scree; and one of the survivors fired a single rifle shot after the weaving figure.

But Mack Bolan, like the storm itself, had moved on.

28

The promise of springtime had been dashed by
sheets of silver-gray drizzle as Bolan, damp and
chilled, struggled westward. He had managed
only a few short snatches of sleep in the past
forty-eight hours.

He was contemplating stealing a motorcycle
from the blind side of a country café when a
trucker pulled over and offered him a lift.
Thankfully, the fellow at the wheel was not the
talkative type, so Bolan curled up in his corner
of the cab and dozed off.

The driver stopped at a gas station on the outskirts of the city; when he returned from the rest
room his passenger had disappeared.

Now Bolan waited near a phone booth beside
a bus terminal. He scanned the cars heading
north on his side of the highway, watching for a
green Fiat. He saw two of them before the third
squelched to a stop at the curb.

"Hop in," said Wetherby. Bolan could sense
the uneasiness lurking behind the smile. "We'll
soon have you safe...."

Lawrence Wetherby was the agent who had fielded Bolan's call. He hoped he could distract the renegade Bolan with small talk until they reached the secret CIA office. Thank God, Dave Hamilton was riding shotgun in his sports car.

Wetherby signaled he was about to turn back toward Zubrovna. "Keep going! Straight on... north. And move it!" Bolan ordered the agent.

He pulled out the Beretta and held it across the front of his body.

"So they were right. They said you'd gone bad." Wetherby's voice cracked with fear. The fact that the gun was pointed at his stomach only confirmed the stories that he'd heard.

"If you don't lose the white Alfa Romeo that's trailing us," warned Bolan, prodding the driver in the hip, "I'm gonna turn you into a real soprano."

Wetherby pulled a fast maneuver, first signaling right, then accelerating left across three lanes of traffic to drop onto the autoroute. They had shed their escort.

"You're dead on your feet, Bad Apple," Wetherby told Bolan, trying to bolster his own courage and wondering why he'd been crazy enough to think he could score a coup by bringing in the renegade alive. "You're all through— you just don't know it."

"Tell me about it."

Wetherby was happy to—as long as he talked he was still alive—and he spilled everything he knew.

Bolan realized that if he went back to Washington right now, any one of his closest colleagues—even Hal Brognola—was duty bound to turn him in. And if he surrendered Radic's precious photographs they just might get "lost." Whatever happened, he'd never get a crack at the mole.

Bolan let Wetherby drive for another half hour before he ordered him to stop. They were miles from anywhere when Bolan gestured with the pistol for the young man to get out of the car.

"Take off your shoes. Hurry. Now drop them on the back seat." Bolan kept the agent covered as he moved behind the wheel. Just before pulling away he glanced up at Wetherby's startled face. "No, I'm not going to kill you. Now you figure that out."

The oncoming lights were a hypnotic blur flashing over the rain-streaked windshield as Bolan sped northward.

When the fuel gauge indicated empty he abandoned Wetherby's Fiat in a dilapidated barn and started walking again. The weather was shifting.

Bolan pulled up his collar. A cold wind was blowing from the east.

Bolan knew he had only one chance.

Find the man he'd seen in Zubrovna.

The man with his face.

PART THREE

SPLIT IMAGE

29

Vichinsky took a sip from his vodka flask before going into the major general's office.

"So it would seem he has slipped through their fingers," Strakhov remarked. The head of the Thirteenth Section did not look up from the map of Europe spread out on his desk. He had suspected this might be the outcome. He had never liked relying on local operatives. "Amateurs!" he raged.

"The body of the journalist, Radic, was brought back to Zubrovna," Vichinsky offered in an effort to mollify his boss. He had to try to salvage what he could of a botched assignment. It would have been different if he had stayed on to supervise the manhunt, but his continued presence risked directly implicating the KGB.

Nothing was ever allowed to attract attention to the Thirteenth Section. But he gave no voice to the confidence he felt that he could have trapped the American. His fear of being scoffed at by Strakhov bordered on paranoia. He stuck to the facts. "Nothing more has been released to the press except for the pseudonym Phoenix was using.''

The department head continued perusing the map. His finger hovered over Switzerland, wandered toward eastern France, then swung back up to Germany as he tried to gain some insight into the resourceful mind of his enemy. Strakhov's tracings paused at England. He tapped the pale blue ditch of the English Channel and shook his head.

''It was a good plan to send the package to the Americans. They have had time to inspect the evidence, I am sure. It should guarantee that we will achieve our primary goal.''

''Our American contact has just reported that there is now a worldwide sanction on the life of Colonel Phoenix,'' Vichinsky said enthusiastically.

Strakhov sat back in the tall leather chair. He linked his stubby fingers across the front of his stomach. The major general's eyes bored through his assistant. But they were unseeing as he pondered the immediate problem. He could not be as proud of eliminating the main enemy in this manner. But the final result—the death of John Phoenix—would net him every bit as much satisfaction.

DAVID MCCARTER HOOKED BACK the edge of the curtain. He could see the hood of the beige

Rover barely poking out from beyond the alleyway. He sighed as he let the drapery fall back
into place. They were still down there. The
move to Lynn's apartment had not shaken them
off; a switch now to Karen's place in London's
West End would only encourage their vigilance.

The phone rang.

"David, shall I—"

McCarter signaled Lynn away from the
phone. He crossed the room and picked up the
receiver.

"Hello."

"David, it's Yakov." McCarter recognized
Katzenelenbogen's accent immediately. The
Phoenix Force commander sounded tense and
irritable. "Are you alone?"

"No, I've got company—even on the street
outside."

"Someone else knows about the number?"

"We must assume so." McCarter had heard
no telltale clicks or buzzes, but it seemed prob-
able the line was being tapped by now.

"Brognola has called a special meeting of all
Stony Man associates. New York. Tomorrow
night. Same place where we discussed the Grenadian affair."

"Got it. I'll be there." They hung up without
any farewells. McCarter paced over to the window again.

He saw a red post-office van stop in front of

the entrance. He watched as the driver jumped out, heading toward the building's main doors. Seconds later, McCarter heard the buzzing of Lynn's intercom.

"Telegram for Mr. McCarter!" came the tinny announcement through the speaker. Lynn pressed the button and let him in. When the man's knock came, she opened the door.

"Sign here, please."

"Thanks."

McCarter ripped open the cheap brown envelope as soon as the man disappeared. It was from Paris. Although it was addressed to David McCarter at Lynn's fall-back address, it read: Dear Hilary, Waiting off Juno. H plus 12 for 3. Love, Mike.

The ex-SAS commando read it through twice, the tumblers turning in his mind as his memory unlocked the secret of the message.

No doubt the telegram had been screened by other eyes before it was delivered. Had they managed to read between the lines, too? Juno... love... Mike: that particular combination of words meant only one thing. McCarter thought it unlikely that anyone who might have seen the cable would share both his own passion for military matters and his retention of small details. But he was certain someone would make the right connections.

He grabbed his coat from the hallway rack.

"I have to go out for a while, darling. Look, as soon as I leave here those blokes in the Rover are going to follow me. When they do, drive my car to the back of the public library, okay? Stay on the side streets and leave it there for me."

"Take care," she said

His lips brushed Lynn's forehead as he handed over the keys. "I'm not sure when I'll be back...."

DAVID WAS RIGHT. Lynn watched as the Rover waited for a double-decker bus to go by, then the beige car slipped into the lunchtime traffic before the tall raincoated figure could gain too much of a head start on them.

Six blocks later, McCarter heard a car door slam as he went up the broad stone steps of the library. He glimpsed the Rover in his peripheral vision as he entered the building.

The librarian gave him a hearty smile. "You'll find our military history collection over in that far corner, sir."

It took him only a few moments to locate the volume he was looking for: *The Greatest Invasion, 6 June 1944.* His friend Stuart Farson, the controversial historian, had scoffed at the book in his review, dismissing it as a shoddy rehash but conceding that the illustrations and diagrams were first-rate. McCarter stood by the window and riffled through the pages to locate the double-spread map of the D-day landings.

His fingertip traced along the Normandy coast, past Omaha and Gold, to the beaches around Courseulles code-named Juno. The western flank, stretching toward La Rivière, was divided into two sectors—Mike and Love. A small black circle on the chart marked the offshore position of the headquarters ship for the Juno assault; it was the *Hilary*.

McCarter scanned the text to check on the timing of the landings. Because of the heavy German obstacles, H-hour on Juno had been delayed to 0745. Add 12, as the telegram had instructed, and that made the rendezvous time 1945 hours.... So Mack would be waiting for him off the French coastline between Courseulles and La Rivière until a quarter to eight for the next three evenings.

He glanced through the shelves at the man apparently poring over a newspaper spread out on the library table. It was time to leave these watchdogs behind. He sauntered to the washroom, made a rapid exit through the frosted-glass window at the rear and was long gone before the other man realized McCarter wasn't coming out again.

As McCarter drove, he thought of Peter Stevens, an ex-SAS comrade. He had restored a fast patrol boat for the questionable adventures he now pursued on both sides of the Channel. No man knew the treacherous shoals of the

French shoreline better than Stevens. It would take about two hours to reach his place on the south coast.

McCarter eased onto the motorway and accelerated. New York would have to wait.

THE OTHER LARGER FISHING VESSELS had already returned, threading their way back to port through the rocky shallows. Bolan waved as one of the commercial fishermen passed him by. He started the motor and cruised in a circle as if he intended to give it one more try before heading back to shore as well. Actually, he was holding his position as best he could with an approximate triangulation off two church spires that poked up above the low dunes.

The old fishing skiff had cost him the last of the funds hidden in his belt. The light was fading fast as Bolan picked up the tin can he was using as a bailer. The wind was freshening.

Bolan's upper lip felt raw and naked since he had scraped off the mustache. He had neither the contacts in France nor any money left to create a new identity from one of the blank passports he carried with him. Anyway, in this fix, who else could he count on besides David McCarter?

The last glimmering rays of sunset shot through the clouds with a lurid glow of reds and purples. The dark shadow of the patrol boat, riding on a curling bow wave, came arrowing in toward Bolan's craft. He signaled with his flashlight.

With its powerful engines throbbing, Stevens's sleek vessel slowed long enough for Bolan to reach up McCarter's extended hand and get a tug aboard. Then, with the helm hard over, the boat turned back for the refuge of the Channel night, leaving only a phosphorescent wake streaking the sea behind it.

Bolan wrapped his fingers tightly around a steaming mug of coffee served him as soon as the brief introduction to Peter Stevens was completed. It had been a long, cold wait.

"They've declared open season on you, Colonel," said McCarter, lacing their mugs with a shot of rum. The Briton was careful not to use Bolan's name.

"So I heard. A guy named Wetherby told me all about it."

"Well, whoever he is, what he probably didn't tell you is that you've still got friends."

Bolan lifted up the fingers of both hands. "Yeah, I counted already."

"You may find there are more people than that who are willing to help you."

The American conceded as much with a nod. He took a final drag on the cigarette then flicked the butt over the side. "I was sitting in that damned boat waiting for you to pick me up... thinking things over." He faced McCarter squarely. "I've been framed, David, and the evidence against me is too damning. I have to clear my name. If I don't, the Phoenix program will cease to exist and everything that we, Yakov, Hal and the others have ever fought for will have been in vain. Besides, the group lobbying against me in the States won't be satisfied with just closing down Stony Man Farm. They want my head."

He chose not to tell McCarter of his suspicions about a highly placed mole in Washington. Bolan put his hand on McCarter's shoulder. "I have a lot to ask of you, my friend."

"I'm ready, Colonel. Just say the word."

Bolan shook his head. "This is one battle I have to fight alone. But you can help. I need funds, supplies, a new passport, intelligence on the inner workings of the KGB. . . ."

"That's a relief," said McCarter, grinning. "For a minute there I thought you were going to ask for the impossible!"

30

McCarter's destination was about an hour's drive from Peter Stevens's private mooring.

Professor Stuart Farson had turned a lifetime's study of espionage and subversive warfare into a series of often shocking bestsellers. His popularization of this shadow world, especially with his embarrassing revelations, had not won him many friends among his peers, but the royalties had financed his freedom from any further academic backbiting. He now lived in a small manor house tucked into a fold of the southern downs.

"I put in a call to the States yesterday," said McCarter, slowing down for a roundabout in the road. "To the Easthill Burn Treatment Center. Kasim is making good progress. Oh, yes, and there's news of another friend of yours, too. Check that paper on the back seat. Look at the sports section."

Bolan flipped to the back of the newspaper. "She did it! Kelly won first place."

"Yes, she beat the Kat. By a whisker...."

"That's all you ever have to win by." There was a photograph of a radiantly smiling Kelly Crawford on the arm of Pierre Danjou, himself a champion in the fencing competition.

"How much does this friend we're going to see know about Stony Man?"

"I'm not sure, but whatever information he's put together didn't come from me," replied McCarter. "Stuart has built up an amazing network of contacts. He might surprise you...."

The light over the front porch went on as their tires crunched up the gravel drive of the old house. It was sheltered behind tall hedges and a row of elm trees. Farson came out to greet them; he glanced up at the stars and sniffed the breeze. "More rain's on the way. Do come in, both of you."

He wore a light cardigan and tweed trousers, which did nothing to disguise the comfortable bulge of his paunch. However, a mischievously cherubic smile made him seem much younger than his years. They were ushered into a parlor where the dying embers of a log fire still glowed hot in the grate.

"I could easily get used to living in America," Farson told his late-night visitors, as he poured out three stiff tots of brandy. "Unlike my fellow countrymen, I see no particular virtue in being constantly damp and chilled to the marrow." They raised their glasses in a silent toast of acknowledgment. "This is an unexpected pleasure. I'm glad to have the chance to meet you at last, Colonel Phoenix."

"Bolan. My name is Mack Bolan."

"Very well, Mr. Bolan, how can I help you?"

McCarter listened to Bolan's story as he recounted the events for the attentive writer.

"Here's the shell I found on the window ledge." Bolan handed it to his British colleague. "What do you make of it, David?"

"It's Russian all right. Seven point sixty-two millimeter. One of their old-style rimmed cartridges." McCarter examined the rosette crimping, which had burst open into tiny jagged flanges. "But it didn't kill anyone. It was definitely a blank."

"Probably used in a Dragunov SVD," Farson offered. "Most of their other weapons fire the shorter M-43."

Bolan looked at McCarter. "I want you to take that shell case with you to New York. Take it to the meeting."

McCarter checked his watch. "I can make it if there's a seat on the Concorde."

"And I want you to take this as well." Bolan handed over the canister of Georgi Radic's 35mm film. "Deliver it to Hal Brognola personally. Those pictures will substantiate my claim that the Russians have a double working for them."

"The use of doubles has a long history," Farson offered, lighting his pipe. "And, ironically, it has become increasingly common in our own media-dominated age. Roosevelt, Churchill, Montgomery—they all used impersonators at one time or another. In peacetime, doubles have been used to fill in when a leader has been too ill to appear, or to mislead his rivals, and no doubt sometimes out of sheer cowardice."

"What about the Russians?"

"Ah, they're masters of the art. They lead the field when it comes to such deception. They even found two look-alikes to impersonate a couple of cosmonauts who were killed on re-entry—a fact that the Politburo did not want to come to light. And so it never has." Farson tamped down the top of his tobacco, struck another match and relit the pipe. "A few years ago I learned that a certain casting director at Mosfilm had located an excellent likeness of Brezhnev. The old man even attended a couple of state functions when the real Brezhnev was too sick to go himself.

"This brought my attention to a small enclave within the KGB. I do not know its name or its exact function, but since the Department for Executive Action mishandled the attack on the Pope, then botched the Grenadian coup, they have been accumulating great power. This small but lethal unit is under the command of Major General Greb Strakhov and his...."

"Strakhov!" exclaimed McCarter. "But wasn't he the man who...?"

"I recently crossed paths with another man named Strakhov," Bolan said.

"Kyril Strakhov? Afghanistan? So you were behind the hijacking of the M-36...." The network the British professor plugged into was fast *and* accurate.

Bolan gestured toward his commando comrade. "Actually, it took both of us to steal that chopper."

The historian smiled with renewed respect for the ex-SAS officer who was his friend.

Then his expression became serious. "The late Captain Strakhov was one of the most decorated test pilots in the Soviet Union. He was Greb's only son. If the major general did not know of you before, Mr. Bolan, you have now made a formidable enemy."

Bolan could feel the pieces falling into place. "Tell me what you know about him."

"As a very young officer Greb Strakhov distinguished himself in the Finnish campaign in the winter of 1940. He transferred to security, then attracted the attention of Khrushchev during the battle for Stalingrad. No doubt he used his political connections to further his postwar career, but always kept a sufficient distance so as not to be dragged down when his partners fell from grace...a not inconsiderable feat."

"What about the private man? Any known weaknesses?"

"It would seem he has an obsessive interest in the fate of the Romanovs, especially young Anastasia." Farson held up a hand to caution Bolan. "But he can hardly be accused of harboring reactionary sympathies—although I suspect that might be the case—since he is now in charge of the long-standing KGB dossier on the last czar and his family."

"If this Greb Strakhov did not mastermind the Macek plot himself then, from what you've said, he probably knows who did," mused McCarter.

"There must be a way of reaching him," Bolan said darkly.

Farson stared into the ashes piled up in the fireplace. "Strakhov has managed to keep an extremely low profile over the years. I doubt if any of the agencies have much of a file on him. But there is one other person who might be able to help. In Paris. I'll put a call through. It's awfully late, but she has a younger companion and he very rarely sleeps...."

"She?"

"Yes. Marijana is an elderly lady now. Never leaves her Paris apartment. She's one of the very last surviving members of the czar's inner circle." Farson rose. "Excuse me. Do help yourselves to some more brandy."

They heard the study door click shut as Farson withdrew to place the call to Paris.

"Can you get me back to France?"

"Peter can," McCarter assured him. "He's standing by until he hears from me again. I wasn't sure where you'd be heading for."

"All the way this time—to Moscow."

McCarter gave a low whistle. "What other help do you need?"

"A new identity."

"Right. I know a chap in Portsmouth who can fix that. It's about forty minutes from here. What else?"

Bolan lifted the Beretta from its holster. "I hoped there would be time for a thorough overhaul of all my weapons. This has been dragged through sewers and mud, avalanches and seawater...."

But there was no more Konzaki; his master armorer and friend had fallen, victim to the everlasting war.

The Briton opened up his jacket to reveal a Beretta 92-S. "Here, let's trade."

"Thanks, David."

"There's ammunition in my car."

Farson came back into the room. He carried a piece of paper with a series of numbered instructions. "This is all rather complicated. I hope you can read my handwriting. Once you've met them, you'll know why you've got to go for a runaround of Paris first...a sensible precaution, I can assure you."

Bolan accepted the directions. He would memorize them and then destroy the paper before landing in France.

Professor Farson had something else for his American visitor. He reached into his pocket and produced a miniature camera.

"Let's call it a parting gift. Handmade in Switzerland. As you can see it's even smaller than a Minox," Farson said, then added dryly, "You might take some snapshots of your trip for me."

31

With a purposeful stride Bolan made his way through the crowds at Gare St-Lazare. He spotted the familiar caps of two gendarmes and veered to the right. The first leg of his Paris journey was to ride the Métro to Concorde.

It felt good to be taking the offensive. Bolan wore an olive trench coat to cover his combat suit. In a small Cordura duffel bag he carried his personal gear, some spare clothes and additional ammo. The Beretta was fitted snugly into its custom-made holster.

He hurried down the subway tunnel and slipped through the platform door at the last possible moment. He played the same trick when changing to the westbound train to Etoile. He was walking down the Champs-Elysées when he first spotted the man in the dark blue raincoat. He was pretending to study a film poster plastered on a billboard.

Halfway down the broad avenue Bolan skipped into the traffic and weaved his way across to the other side. One more train ride and he was walking over the bridge to the Ile de la Cité. He had memorized Farson's instructions. Now he turned left, walking past Notre Dame cathedral, then doubling back over the Seine to Ile St-Louis. Each time he changed direction, Bolan quickly checked to make sure he was not being followed. All the time he kept his head low, as much as possible buried in his collar, so as not to be recognized.

A solitary visitor, taking a photograph of a barge plowing through the powerful currents of the river, gave him a friendly nod. Sensing danger, Bolan hunched deeper into his trench-coat collar and strolled along the water's edge uneasily.

He glanced over his shoulder. No one there. He moved forward again and suddenly the man in the raincoat was standing at the end of the cobbled quay. He was much younger than Bolan, perhaps an inch taller, with shoulders just as broad but a thinner trunk. His face was quite expressionless.

As Bolan studied his pursuer, only one word came to mind. Knife. The Executioner was carrying steel too, and he knew how to use it. Whoever this guy was, whichever side he was working for, he could not be allowed to make a report. He was standing directly between Bolan and the stone steps to the street above. Bolan came straight at him, forcing the other man to make his play.

He stretched out an open hand. "Mack Bolan? My name is Alexei Kirov."

Bolan shook his hand. "I haven't been followed—except by you."

"I had to make certain that no one was pursuing you."

"What's the next move?"

"I am to take you to the duchess. The car is waiting for us at the top of the stairs."

Bolan was driven across town, past the Eiffel Tower and over to the Right Bank.

The duchess lived in a quietly fashionable cul-de-sac just east of the Bois de Boulogne. The house was set back behind a high stone wall. Bolan caught a glimpse of a small front courtyard through the narrow wrought-iron gateway. Two dogs—an Alsatian and an even larger Russian wolfhound—were stretched out on either side of a sundial, watchful to warn off any unwelcome intruders.

Kirov touched a button in the vehicle's control console and waited while the garage door slid silently upward. He drove in, shut the sturdy metal door with the same switch, then turned off the engine.

"This way, Mr. Bolan."

A side door led directly into the house. The passage, which needed a fresh coat of paint, led past the kitchen.

The main rooms were not as gloomy as Bolan

had anticipated. Kirov took the American up to an airy room on the second floor and left him there.

Bolan was looking down on the small, carefully trimmed lawn at the back of the house when Kirov returned.

"Her Imperial Highness, the Grand Duchess Marijana Sophia Mikhaylovna Rytova," he announced gravely.

Bolan found himself standing at attention as the elderly aristocrat entered the room. She was blessed with a fine bone structure and regal bearing; her white hair was pinned back, and yet she retained a hint of youthful vigor in her bright green eyes. The duchess must have been a strikingly beautiful woman in her prime.

"You come to us with the highest recommendation, Mr. Bolan." She sat on the couch and gestured that her guest should also be seated. "Professor Farson rarely displays such trust and certainly never misplaces it."

"I am honored, ma'am."

"I think it is we who should be honored. Few men will still fight for a cause that is considered so futile, if not utterly lost."

"I'm just trying to set something right. I'm fighting my own war, not yours—not one that started nearly seventy years ago."

"Perhaps they are the same," she murmured in reply. She was intrigued by the serious dark-haired stranger. Her war with the usurpers would never die as long as she could enlist the aid of a man such as Mack Bolan. She would extend to him whatever support was in her power. "I understand you wish to get into Russia unnoticed."

Bolan nodded. "As quietly and quickly as possible."

"That much can be arranged." She leaned forward. "And once you're there?"

He hesitated; he was used to playing long shots, but this time the odds seemed overwhelming. "I must find some way to establish contact with a high-ranking KGB official, Major General Greb Strakhov. And the meeting must be dictated on my terms."

The duchess glanced across to Kirov, who was still standing silently near the door. Bolan caught a flash of recognition at his mention of the name. "Do you know this man Strakhov?"

"We know of him, Mr. Bolan." She turned and issued her young bodyguard an instruction in Russian.

"What has a diary to do with all this?" asked Bolan.

Marijana faced him quickly. She was amused at being caught by surprise; so he understood the language.

"I was born with the turn of the century, Mr. Bolan. I am in my mid-eighties and I rather hope to live to the turn of the next. If only I could see Russia free again, I would die a happy woman.''

Bolan realized she meant just that: her first priority was freedom, not merely the reestablishment of the Romanov dynasty.

''As a young girl I often played with my cousins, sometimes Maria, but more often Anastasia. . . .''

For a brief instant Bolan saw a distant look in the duchess's eyes as she remembered her childhood.

Kirov returned with a slim leather-bound volume, securely fastened with a brass lock. He handed the diary to his elderly charge.

''There is no one left but myself who knows the full truth about Anastasia. I have met or interviewed all those women who have claimed her identity. My conclusions are written down in this diary.''

''Stuart Farson mentioned that Strakhov is absorbed by the mystery of the missing girl.''

''Greb Strakhov would kill me to lay hands on this book. He would kill anyone who possessed it.'' She placed it on the side table between them. ''Vasili Tretyakov is an art dealer here in Paris. He does business on both sides of the iron curtain. I know he has already supplied Strakhov with other memorabilia regarding the Romanovs. It was Tretyakov who warned us of

Greb Strakhov's passion and the lengths to which he would go.''

Bolan reached for the journal. The duchess did not stop him. He weighed it in his hand; it would fit easily in his inside pocket.

"If you were a thief who had broken into this house, Mr. Bolan—" Marijana sounded doubtful, though she realized that if any man could breach the security Alexei had installed it would be this American "—it is not likely that you would take only the memoirs of an old woman. Alexei, open up the safe again and bring me the Fabergé egg.''

Kirov hesitated for a moment, but one imperious stare from the duchess sent him on his way.

"How did you two...?"

"Alexei's grandmother was my private nurse when I was forced to leave Russia. The Kirovs have always been retained in the service of my family. Now we are both the last of our lines. It is an appropriate partnership.''

This time Kirov came back with a cylindrical leather case, dull with age. He placed it on the wooden table.

"This is what you would have stolen," said the duchess, accepting the key from Kirov and unlocking the container.

The side walls of the case opened out like two small doors. Nestled on a cushion of velvet was a single unblemished nugget of turquoise, the color of a robin's egg, smoothed into a decorative Easter egg about three inches high. It was enclosed in a delicate latticework of silver branches, and each junction of this shining tracery was pinpointed with miniature flower petals that held within them a sapphire as a bud.

Marijana lifted out the egg and with a gentle twist opened it up. Cleverly hidden inside was a tiny bird perfectly carved from lapis lazuli. And the base of this whole incredible confection was a tangle of silver filigree representing a robin's nest.

"That's worth a fortune," said the soldier.

"Oh, more than that, Mr. Bolan. It is priceless. There are more than thirteen thousand works by Picasso. But Fabergé created less than sixty of these famous jeweled eggs. In the realm of art and craftsmanship, you are looking at the very definition of rarity."

"I must agree with you—if I were a safe-cracker, this is what I would be after."

"Then in the morning, once Alexei has laid a trail of 'breaking in,' I shall report the robbery. Within twenty-four hours several key people in Paris will know all the details."

"Would one of them be Vasili Tretyakov?"

Marijana nodded. "Undoubtedly. And the news of the theft will be in Moscow before you arrive."

"The egg will prove that I broke into your home and am therefore in possession of the authentic diary. It will be too much of a temptation for Greb Strakhov."

"It is a calculated risk." Marijana directed this remark to Kirov. "I have faith that you will return to us, Mr. Bolan. And I trust you will bring back both these invaluable objects to my safekeeping once more."

"First I have to get there."

"I am the principal patron of the Gospel Light Mission. They specialize in taking the Word to the enslaved peoples of Russia. Bibles and other tracts are smuggled across in specially constructed vans and cars. They will also be able to arrange for the necessary documents."

Bolan watched as the duchess carefully placed the Fabergé creation back in its velvet-lined box.

He was going to engage the KGB in their own game.

Treachery.

The lure was dangling in front of Strakhov's nose.

And Bolan had the bait.

32

Bolan flew from Paris to Munich, where he was introduced to Rudi Dietz, a German evangelist. Together they traveled to Graz, Austria. The Volkswagen van was loaded and waiting for them. Dietz did the driving right across Hungary. The Hungarian border guards gave them little trouble. Now the frontier checkpoint was just ahead. Bolan watched the Russian soldier amble toward the small Peugeot that waited at the side of the road less than twenty yards ahead of them. The roof of his mouth was dry. This would be the real test.

"Where is he?" Dietz asked aloud, impatiently drumming his fingers on the steering wheel.

Two more men appeared from the corrugated-metal shed that served as the guard post. But there was still no sign of Fat Ernst. Dietz glanced at the American and watched as he calmly took a drag of his cigarette. The preacher had never smoked in his life but at that moment he almost asked for one.

Bolan judged Dietz to be in his early thirties.

He was sandy haired, with a short beard trimmed to follow his jawline. Bolan thought him rather dour for someone engaged in spreading the Good Word. Dietz did not offer any explanation of why he had chosen this dangerous ministry, and Bolan didn't ask him. Their silence was mutually acceptable.

They were traveling on the second set of papers from the documents provided in Munich. Bolan's new name was Karl Kelsen. The two of them were supposed to be engineering consultants on their way to supervise repairs on the natural-gas pipeline outside of Dashava.

Gospel tracts were hidden in a false compartment within the enlarged gas tank. More pamphlets were bundled in the metal tool case. And one wooden crate marked Electrical Equipment contained a consignment of Bibles. Bolan's duffel bag, holding the diary, the priceless egg and his gun, was in the same box. His personal effects were now in a cheap suitcase that lay on the floor of the van.

"How do we work it at the border?" Bolan had asked Dietz as they drove over the bridge spanning the Latoritsa River.

"Mostly we use the quietest checkpoints. We have contacts who find out the rosters. Sometimes a guard is so stupid we risk brazening it out; sometimes we find an odd one who is sympathetic, but the most common method is to bribe them."

"And today?"

"Fat Ernst has been bought."

But there was no sign of him. The three soldiers in front had the family out of the Peugeot and were opening their luggage for inspection. Bolan stubbed out his cigarette. Dietz's lips were moving in a silent prayer. It must have worked—the German gestured toward the shack.

"Here he comes." There was no mistaking the fat Georgian corporal. Right behind him was a poker-faced officer. "*Meine Güte!* What's he bringing him over for?"

Bolan's hand moved instinctively.... Then he remembered. The gun was buried in the spare crate.

Ernst was panting as he marched past the others, who were beginning to hassle the Hungarian visitors. He looked far too agitated to be coolly setting up a trap.

The serious young lieutenant walked right up to the open window of the van. Dietz surrendered their papers. The officer glanced at the travel permits and handed them to the corporal.

"Why are you driving? Why not take the train to Lvov?"

"We want to get there quickly, Lieutenant. And the minute we've done our job we want to get back home." Dietz swallowed as soon as he had spoken. He hoped his remarks would not be taken as an insult.

The Russian officer stared into the cab to where Bolan leaned back into the darkness. He was just about to ask another question. . . .

"Come over here, comrade. Look at this!"

A soldier leaning against the Peugeot held up a brown paper bag. It had split open to reveal half a dozen oranges and apples.

"Check them out!" the lieutenant ordered Ernst before he turned to walk away.

Dietz gulped down his first breath in what seemed an eternity as he watched the man stalk toward the unfortunate Hungarians. The discovery of fresh fruit gave the customs detail the license to search the car to see what other contraband they might be trying to smuggle over the border.

The corporal thrust the papers back into the evangelist's hands. They were both sweating. His jowls shook as he jerked his head. "Go on! Drive on through!"

It took the missionary three attempts before the engine roared to life. They lurched forward and steered around the group probing the Peugeot.

"How far is it to Dashava?" Bolan inquired.

"We can follow the pipeline all the way to Kiev. You can make your own way to Moscow from there. I have to travel south."

Dietz slipped onto a secondary road—little more than a dirt track—that wound through the wooded hills of the Transcarpathians. He broke the silence only to have the American memorize his alternate routes out of Russia. The preacher himself would be coming back through Kiev in exactly a week.

Two days after that, another Gospel Light driver would be leaving Minsk for the run through Czechoslovakia. Failing either of those rendezvous, Dietz could only give Bolan his own backup escape route: a fisherman named Zakop who lived in a small village on the coast outside Odessa. For a price he would risk a run across the Black Sea.

The preacher cared not at all about the identity of his passenger. He wished only to carry out the bidding of his good duchess.

They slept in the van that night. Late the following afternoon, still sticking to the side roads, they drove into Kiev. The German left Bolan in the hands of the Malinovsky family, devout believers in the evangelist's underground crusade.

As they said their farewells, Bolan could tell from his companion's expression that he hoped the American would decide to return via Minsk.

Dietz made the sign of the cross, then shook his head as he departed.

THE NEXT MORNING Mr. Malinovsky drove his guest as far as he dared. He followed a circuitous route to avoid the militia posts strung along the main roads in and out of every major city like Kiev. He left the "engineer" at a junction on the way to Gorzhin, warning him not to hitch a ride on any truck heading into the restricted zone. There, a traveler's papers were sure to be examined closely.

A farmer returning to a collective near Novabelitsa gave him a ride. He was a talkative fellow, and Bolan had to do little more than mutter *da* or *kharoshi* to keep the conversation going. The chatter continued until the driver dropped off his grateful passenger.

The day was getting hot and the highway very dusty. Bolan draped his coat over his arm and unbuttoned the top of his shirt. He carried his suitcase into a truckers' café and ordered lunch. A bovine waitress with thick ankles brought him a bowl of tepid *charcho*—mutton soup reddened with tomato sauce. She almost tripped over his cardboard valise. Bolan muttered an apology and pushed it farther under the table. He knew the absence of newspaper and television served to preserve his identity, but he wished to raise no fuss.

Through the flyspecked window he could see a couple of workers waiting at the crossroads ahead, ready to thumb the next ride. He didn't want their company; they might be overly curious. Bolan casually glanced at the other customers, wondering which of them were pushing their rigs on through to Moscow.

The woman was standing by the counter sipping cola from a bottle. It was only now, when she was half turned toward him, that Bolan realized she was in her mid-twenties. Their eyes met, and she didn't take hers away.

She wore a pair of sturdy boots and much-laundered coveralls; the seam on the shoulder of her T-shirt was torn, and her dark brown hair was tucked into a cloth cap set back at a jaunty angle. Bolan could see the feminine curls at her nape, and the way her full breasts strained at the denim bib. She had a very rich, even tan for this early in the year, which almost hid the scattered dusting of freckles on her fine cheekbones.

Her eyes swept over him, too, and finally settled below his throat where the shirt was parted. She must have glimpsed April's ring, for she looked away sullenly.

The café door flew open. The newcomer was in uniform. He was a cop!

He surveyed the diners and took his time moving to the far end of the room. "Hello, Leo. What are you carrying this time?"

The trucker mumbled in reply.

"I can't hear you, Leo. Speak up."

Bolan put down his spoon as the policeman continued his informal interrogation.

The woman was watching him again. She raised her eyebrows and fractionally tipped her head to indicate that Bolan should proceed outside.

Bolan placed a couple of coins next to the soup bowl and slowly stood up. The woman swigged the last of her drink, then walked over to the policeman. "What shall I bring you back from Moscow, Shapkin, a *beryozka* from the corner of Kutuzov Prospekt?"

While his newfound ally was distracting the cop with her banter, Bolan walked out into the yard. Six trucks were parked out front. Bolan slipped behind the first diesel rig to get out of sight of the café window.

"This way," came the woman's voice. "It's the old Roman at the end of the row."

Bolan and the woman climbed into the cab of the Rumanian-built truck. She gave him a knowing grin, rolled the vehicle smoothly onto the concrete and began to accelerate.

"That pig policeman's always on the take!" She spat out the window. "He just bothers us enough to make sure we don't forget him."

"Thanks," said Bolan. "I owe you one."

She glanced at him long enough to study his face. She liked what she saw. "Are you truly Romany?"

So it was the boar's-tooth carving she'd noticed back there, not the ring! Bolan touched the tiny talisman. The old man had said it would bring him good fortune.

"No. But I am their friend. It was given to me." Bolan watched her expression and for the first time he fully understood what an honor had been bestowed upon him. Treasured amulets were a Gypsy's most prized possessions. He looked again at her dark skin. "You're Romany yourself?"

She nodded. She was pleased to be recognized for what she was without jeers, insults or abuse. She was glad she had trusted her instincts about this man.

"Zara." She stretched her hand across in friendship. "My name is Zara."

"And I'm...Karl. Karl Kelsen."

"You're heading for Moscow?"

"Yes. Are you going that far?"

"All the way."

"Where are you from, Zara?"

"Near Krichovka. They barred the Romanies from traveling as we always have done. Forced us onto collective farms. But I've got this old truck. I'm as free as my ancestors. There's always a way around the system."

They crossed over a sluggish, muddy river. There was a neatly kept battle shrine on their right. Bolan watched two children at play, using their fingers as pistols as they chased each other around the steps of a statue of the local partisan leader.

The road signs were no longer posted in both

Ukrainian and Russian, as the kilometer markers clicked off the distance to Moscow.

"Know what I've got back there?"

Bolan shrugged. He'd noticed the outline of several small crates under the torn canvas sheet.

"Paperwork. Five years of records must be taken to the central office. Meaningless! No one will ever look at them. But I'm also taking the best of our vegetables to the Sunday market. And some homemade liquor, too."

Without the private produce stalls and thriving black market, she told him, citizens in the big centers like Moscow would starve. Then she asked him, "Where are you from, Karl?"

Bolan tugged the papers from his inside pocket just far enough to show her he had the right documents. "I've got a permit to travel as a consulting engineer."

Zara suppressed a wry grin. Both of them knew it wasn't the answer to her question.

"And what are you really here for?"

"Oh, to trade," he replied. "Buying, selling—that sort of thing."

"Blue jeans...music tapes...transistor radios?"

"Whatever people really want," Bolan said, "whatever turns a profit."

"Now *that* I understand. I've got a lot of contacts in the city. Maybe there's some business there for you. Do you have a place to stay?"

"Not yet."

"You do now. I stay with friends, and they'll let you stay there, too."

Bolan returned her smile. Perhaps he wished it could be that way; perhaps in his need he was beginning to like this pretty young rebel.

But. . . . He fingered the ring on his chain.

33

Strakhov switched on the desk lamp and tried to focus his attention on the chart spread out before him. In two days he had to submit his summarized report to the chairman. He was trying to ensure that the typewritten synopsis matched the details of the organizational diagram. There were bound to be searching questions. Strakhov also wanted to be certain he had such a firm grasp of the complex worldwide operations of the KGB that he could react to any suggestions the chairman might put forward, perhaps even to counter them if necessary.

He pushed aside the saucer of lemon rinds he'd been using to weigh down the edge of the paper and studied his work. They still had no confirmation of a kill. . . .

Strakhov sat back in the leather chair. Phoenix could run, but he couldn't hide. Nowhere was safe. Every field agent on both sides was against him. So where had he gone to earth?

It was possible the chairman himself might

ask an awkward question about the killing in Zubrovna.

The story was already old news; it had been replaced on the front pages of the world's newspapers by an earthquake in Turkey and the latest airliner crash. And the major general had advance knowledge of a coming flare-up in Central America that would push the Macek assassination to the back of the foreign-news sections.

But what was he to do with Boldin? Until Phoenix had his wings clipped, there still might be a use for his double.... Yet Boldin's continued existence was a potential threat. They couldn't keep him at Akinova much longer. The risk was no less within the KGB itself than from without. How long would it be before other Chekists, those rivals outside the Thirteenth Section, knew of Boldin and the Janus Plan? Someone with ambition might seek to use it against him....

Damn Phoenix!

The shrill jangling of the phone irritated him even further. He picked it up.

"What is it?" he growled.

"I have Comrade Niktov on the line," the operator told him. "Do you wish to speak to him?"

"Yes, put him on. Hello, Niktov, what have you got this time?"

"Just some news that I thought you should hear, General. It's about a burglary in Paris...."

THE AIR WAS THICK with the smoke of Russian tobacco. In one corner of the room a pale young man dodging compulsory military service was chatting with a blond "actress" whose talents were in truth confined to faking an orgasm for her elderly clients.

Earlier, Zara had introduced Bolan to the group. Now she was listening closely to a business proposition from Yan the Fixer, while an escapee from internal exile in Siberia was being brought up to date on the local gossip by Quickfingers, the head of a pickpocket gang that worked the Moscow subway system. The man Zara had pointed out as Gregor Panov, and his companion, a well-known surgeon, were in animated discussion.

Bolan nursed his vodka. So this was the heartland of the socialist workers' paradise, the hidden face of the Soviet Union.

They were in a cavernous apartment over the restaurant run by Masha Shukina. The size of the place alone was sufficient testimony to the Widow Shukina's criminal connections. No one on the straight and narrow could have ever acquired a private apartment this large. As Bolan was learning, everything in Russia required a bribe.

The currency was always negotiable: it could be anything from a pair of imported boots or Levi's to sex or a seat at the Bolshoi. But no matter what, the wheels had to be greased. In a country where leverage was required just to get on the waiting list for a telephone, Zara's friend Masha must have called in a lot of favors.

Antonov, Bolan's drinking partner, pushed the vodka bottle toward the foreign guest. Bolan declined. He was keeping the drinking ratio at about one to five with the sad-eyed Antonov. He'd already found out that the other man was a special guide for Intourist. He made his own profit from fingering the weaknesses of foreign visitors for many of the specialists who were in the room tonight. Bolan had arranged for Antonov to give him a private guided tour of some selected areas of the city the next day.

"You're from Germany, right?" slurred Antonov. It was the third time he'd tried that question.

"Nein," Bolan replied, only adding to Antonov's befuddlement.

"Nyet? Austria, then?"

Bolan shrugged.

"No matter. You are a friend of Zara's, and that is good enough," announced Antonov as he poured himself another shot. "You're all right."

Bolan lifted his half-empty glass in reply to

Antonov's toast with an unspoken wish of his own.

This was the shadow world, the dirty underside of the Communist dream; a twilight realm where a man like Greb Strakhov could never afford to venture. To have survived this long, to have risen to his powerful position, the KGB boss must have kept his hands very clean of any civil corruption all these years.

He could never have allowed anyone, not even a close friend, if he had any, to get hold of anything that could one day be used against him.

Bolan had the private satisfaction of knowing he was just about to tempt the major general to stray over the line.

The American warrior looked across at Zara, who was still listening to the burly Yan. Her eyes were alive with laughter. It had taken him a while to figure her out. Zara's friendship was not based simply on Romany loyalty, though that was part of it. Nor was it just sexual attraction. And it certainly wasn't a question of money. Bolan had offered her none.

It was that she recognized part of herself in him. They were both loners. Outsiders. Survivors. She defined her own personality, the very worth of her own being, only in constant opposition to the malignant, murderous state.

Yan was suggesting she could make a handsome profit if only Zara would drive a truckload of handcrafted Estonian furniture down to a minister's dacha. Yan had all the paperwork. The minister couldn't keep the goods in a Moscow warehouse any longer. Zara caught Bolan's glance and shook her head. No, she wanted to stay in the city for a few more days.

Antonov staggered off to the toilet. Gregor Panov slipped into the seat he'd vacated.

"I deal with all these gentlemen at one time or another," he explained to Bolan, nodding toward the men in the room. "I'm a sort of clearing house...."

"A fence," Bolan stated baldly.

Panov ignored the directness of the remark. "Zara tells me you're in, er, trade. What do you trade in, my friend?"

"Eggs," said Bolan. "Rare eggs."

"Then I'm sure we can do business," replied Panov. He understood precisely what was required. "I take it you wish to purchase a Fabergé fake for an unwitting client in the West."

"No, I have an original for sale here."

Panov licked his lips. This was out of his league, but he wanted to stay in the game.

"I have a customer in mind," Bolan continued quietly. "I just have to get in touch with him."

"Of course." Panov smiled agreeably. The

role of middleman was something he could play. "I'm sure I can make any connections you want."

"I think Major General Strakhov will be most interested in the egg."

Panov winced. "Greb Strakhov?"

Bolan nodded. "You know him?"

"No. I'm glad to say that I don't; at least not personally. But I am in contact with someone who does know him. Leave it to me."

THE LIMPID BLUE SKIES of morning gave way to a gray afternoon. Bolan found Moscow a depressingly colorless city, probably because it lacked the familiar distractions of even a small American town.

Antonov did not appear to be suffering from any ill effects after his drinking bout of the night before. He knew the capital intimately— and people even better. He did not ask why the big foreigner wanted to be taken to the Kazan railway station, then the International Post Office and on to the Botanical Gardens, rather than seeing Red Square or Gorky Park.

The guide openly admired the digital chronometer that Bolan glanced at throughout their tour. "Got to watch the time," explained Bolan. "Said I'd meet Zara when she's finished at the *rynok*." The Romany woman had gone to make arrangements for selling off her produce at the peasant market. Actually, Bolan was making exact timings between each of a series of mental checkpoints.

Antonov explained that he, too, had to go on to another appointment. Bolan thanked the Muscovite for his help and bade him farewell outside the grandiose Exhibition of Economic Achievement.

He reviewed the events he had set in motion. The only way to clear his name was to find his own double, the man he had seen in the window at Zubrovna. The KGB could have hidden him anywhere in the vast area of the Soviet Union— if indeed he was still alive. And that was something Bolan doubted.

But if Professor Farson was right, then Strakhov was the one man who would certainly know the whereabouts or the fate of the Phoenix impostor.

And if he was dead, then Bolan would make Strakhov provide a signed confession.

That morning Zara had driven him past the KGB headquarters in Dzerzhinsky Square and Strakhov's apartment on Petushka Street. It was no use simply getting close enough to put a gun to his head and demanding the information. Greb Strakhov wouldn't scare that easy.

No, he had to be looking down the barrel of a real threat; such as being stripped of his power and privileges, of interrogation in the Lubyanka at the hands of his erstwhile colleagues, of a show trial for corruption, and a life sentence in the Gulag with all those other prisoners he'd helped send there himself. Then, maybe then, he'd talk.

Bolan was mulling over the possibilities as he strolled toward Mira Prospekt, keeping his face hidden by his collar.

He was so engrossed in his thoughts he did not see the black car that cruised quietly to the curb behind him.

34

Two men got out and fell in on either side of the foreigner.

They weren't the talkative type. The guy in the brown hat nodded at the car. Bolan was to get in. Quickly. The fellow in the leather coat shoved him through the door in case he didn't understand.

"I thought you guys would never show up," said Bolan.

They weren't cops. They did not exude that overconfident immunity afforded by the backing of the law. These were two hardmen who made the play stick with their muscles and the weapons concealed beneath their ill-fitting coats. Despite his offhand comment, Bolan was impressed at the speed with which word of his mission had spread through the underworld network.

The driver, in a chauffeur's peaked cap, did not look in the mirror as the two men frisked the foreigner in the back seat. The one in the leather coat relieved Bolan of the Beretta and examined it covetously.

They sped around the wide inner circle of the Sadovoye Ring, over the river, down Valivov Street and cut across into the Lenin Hills. The driver honked his horn at a couple of students running toward the ornate complex of the university, then pulled into the parking lot of a small chapel at the back of the bluffs.

The car that was waiting for them there would have drawn admiring glances anywhere in the world, but in Moscow the vintage Rolls-Royce must have been the object of envy. Leathercoat prodded Bolan with the Beretta to indicate he should walk over to the other vehicle.

The man in the back seat of the Rolls sat with two clawlike hands resting on a silver-topped walking cane. His pronounced forehead was framed with swooping waves of thinning hair, rather obviously dyed raven black. A pair of rimless glasses were balanced on his beaky nose. And despite the fact that he wore a dark green bow tie, he had the air of an elderly schoolteacher.

"Mr. Kelsen. . . my name is Niktov."

It was like shaking hands with water. Ice-cold water.

The Russian art expert gave not the slightest sign of recognizing Bolan. Niktov's rheumy eyes simply stared right through him. He was a man who existed exclusively in a world of beautiful objects and the fancy dealing that surrounded them.

"I understand you have something you wish to dispose of . . . privately."

"Yes. Are you speaking on behalf of a client?"

Niktov nodded sharply. Once. "In a manner of speaking. It has been suggested, Mr. Kelsen, that you might have two items that are of interest."

"An egg and a book."

"So you have the diary, then?"

"It's a package deal. I'd say the Fabergé is worth two hundred thousand U.S. dollars. Large bills will do."

"That's a great deal of hard currency."

"I'm sure your client has access to, what shall we call them, 'special funds'?" Bolan looked at the collector. "Or a friend who could lend him the difference."

Niktov had to play his hand very carefully. So far he had told Strakhov little of what he knew of Karl Kelsen. The art dealer did not want to be frozen out of the deal. "And what are you asking for the duchess's diary?"

"Oh, that's not for sale," Bolan replied flippantly. "Anyone who buys the egg gets the diary for nothing."

Those were the terms. Niktov had been in the game long enough to know that the arrangement offered was beyond haggling.

"I'll only deal with the purchaser on a face-to-face basis,'' added Bolan. ''He brings the cash, and I'll deliver the goods. Tell your client to be next to the public telephones at the Sverdlova metro station. Eleven-thirty. Tonight. And he'd better bring the money.''

''That's not very long to raise. . . .''

''It's all the time he's got.''

The man's bones shone white through the translucent skin of his knuckles as he gripped the cane tightly. He beckoned for Leathercoat to come over, and with a flick of his eyelids indicated that his henchman should hand back the Beretta.

''Take Mr. Kelsen wherever he wishes to go,'' Niktov instructed. For a fleeting moment his eyes focused on the tall Westerner. ''And a word of warning: guns are against the law of this country.''

VICHINSKY COULD SCARCELY SUPPRESS a gasp of surprise. He had never seen so many American dollars before in his life. But to Strakhov they were nothing more than bits of colored paper. He was more interested in the man—this mysterious contact Niktov had made and was keeping to himself—than the money. But more than anything he wanted the diary.

The head of the Thirteenth Section counted the last bundle, laid it in the fiberglass briefcase and snapped the lid shut. ''There's a contact bringing us a valuable object and some even more valuable information. I want you to collect it personally.''

"Of course, Comrade General.'' Vichinsky nodded slowly, but his mind was racing. Was this really official business? Surely it must be, since the major general had received such immense funds from the administration department. And yet he had the nagging suspicion that there was more to it than met the eye. Strakhov seemed distracted by private concerns.

He would leave a typewritten account of his superior's instructions in his files. Vichinsky did not want to be implicated as an accessory to corruption if Strakhov should end up accused of a counterrevolutionary crime. After all, he might well be the accuser.

"You must be at the Sverdlova metro, near the phones, at eleven-thirty,'' said Strakhov, pulling out the pocket watch from his waistcoat and checking the time. "The foreigner is delivering a Fabergé egg—a real one—and a book. It's a diary, actually. Galuzin will issue you a miniature transmitter.''

"A direction finder?''

"Yes, we'll keep a constant trace on you,'' Strakhov assured him. "Take three men to cover you. I suggest Batyuk, Sharkov and Gsovski.''

Vichinsky's narrow face relaxed. He felt safer

now. All three were born killers, and they were men who enjoyed their work.

"What if he asks questions? What should I say if. . . ."

"He won't when you hand over this." Strakhov pushed the heavy case of bank notes across the desk top. "Do nothing, I repeat, do absolutely nothing that will jeopardize the trade. Once the exchange is made and you have both those objects safely in your possession, then the others can close in."

"You want him dead or alive?"

Strakhov shrugged. No, it would be interesting to talk to this man. They might even have a future use for him. Who could say? "Alive, if possible. Remember, when this is over I want to have the artwork, the information, the money and the man. You are to bring the articles to my apartment. You know where I live?"

"On Petushka Street." Of course he knew where Strakhov lived, but he had never once been invited to his superior's residence. This promised to be a most extraordinary evening.

"Batyuk and the others can take their prisoner directly to the Lubyanka for interrogation."

"Does he have a name?"

"Karl Kelsen," Strakhov grunted. "That's all Niktov would give me."

CITIES DEFINE THEMSELVES by the sounds and smells of their subway systems. Instantly transported anywhere in the world blindfolded, the experienced traveler would know if he was riding the New York system, the London Underground, or the Paris Métro. This was unmistakably Moscow. Bolan mentally filed the peculiar tang of stale tobacco, pickled sausage and heavy Russian perspiration.

Bolan was carrying a cheap shopping bag like so many of the other passengers and clutching a woolen balaclava he had purchased on Gorky Street after Niktov's goons had dropped him off. If anyone had been following him, Bolan had led them on a merry tour before returning to the garage behind Masha Shukina's restaurant, where Zara parked her truck.

The Romany woman had not returned. Bolan found a wire coat hanger and had used it to fish around in the large can of waste oil in which he'd hidden the precious packages. He hosed down the two plastic bags until they were clean enough to extract the treasures. Now they were wrapped in yesterday's *Izvestia* and sitting in the tote bag.

He skirted the edge of the university grounds, looking down at the twinkling reflection of the city lights on the great sweep of the Moskva River. Even at night barges were still on the move.

Bolan checked his watch. It was time to start Strakhov running. He waited for a bleary-eyed drunk to wobble past the phone booth. Dropping two coins into the slot, he picked up the receiver and dialed the number of a phone at the Sverdlova metro that he had noted earlier.

It was answered on the second ring.

"Proceed directly to the Kazan railway station. No cabs, no trolleys. Go to the phone booths on Novoryaz Ulitsa." Then Bolan hung up.

He walked along a rutted path through the woods and selected the spot he wanted for the trade—a ruined gazebo surrounded by a tangle of goldenrod and camomile. Bolan judged he had given Strakhov enough time. He went back to the phone.

On this occasion it rang four times before being picked up.

"Look behind the phone itself." He waited for the Russian to extract the postcard he had hidden there. It was a picture of the main entrance to the Economic Achievement Exhibition. "Go there now. Quickly!"

Each new move was pointing to the exchange taking place in Sokolniki Park. But this time he made a switch.

"Take the subway to Leninskiye Gory," Bolan instructed on the third call, imagining his contact's frustration at having to cross town to the southwestern district. It would soon be time for the last train. Strakhov was going to have to hustle to make it.

Bolan knew it was all a hollow time-wasting exercise. Even though Strakhov could never be sure if he was being observed at any point along the roundabout route, the man was probably rigged for sound, or with a location transmitter, or he was being tailed by a carload of KGB goons. Maybe all three. Bolan wasn't fooling himself. But he wanted it to look right—all the way to the end of the line.

A gang of *hippi* ran past, laughing and joking among themselves; they were far too self-absorbed to notice Bolan. With their long, greasy hair and pimply faces, he thought they looked even more unappetizing than their American counterparts.

The drunk was weaving his way back down the street, pausing every so often to take his bearings. Two *druzhiniki* crossed over and started harassing him. Bolan melted into the shadows. He didn't want those overeager auxiliary policemen to demand his identification papers.

Bolan kept watch on the glass-sided metro station from the lower tier of the bridge. An old woman in a gray shawl gave up waiting for a trolley bus and began plodding homeward. Two lovers were giggling as they walked along under the trees. One minute they were there, the next they'd vanished. He must have pulled his girl into the bushes for one last quick petting session.

The train rolled in. Several people got off. Bolan waited, giving the bagman time to reach the bank of public phones. He dialed the last number.

"You're late," Bolan snapped. "Walk up the hill, past the tourist overlook and keep on going along the ridge trail."

Bolan stayed where he was in the phone booth up the street, the receiver still held to his ear, until his quarry walked past.

Strakhov? No way! That wasn't him; Bolan was sure of it. Not unless the major general was the only seven-year-old to have fought at Stalingrad. So Strakhov had sent a substitute.

The guy was KGB all right, and an officer— probably a subordinate from the same department. Bolan had anticipated as much. At least the thin-faced man was carrying a heavy briefcase; he'd come to trade.

A light-blue taxi cruised past and a police car rolled down toward the river. The road was clear. Bolan ran across and raced up the hill to outflank Strakhov's messenger. The man was just about to seek the shadows of the carefully tended shrubbery when Bolan saw the black Volga glide to a halt. One guy got out and followed the bag carrier. There were two more men in the front of the backup car. Bolan had them pegged.

Under the trees he shed his coat, reversed his jacket to black and slipped on the balaclava. He roiled the woolen mask down over his face; lips and eyes were all that showed through the grim visage.

Bolan ran at a ground-eating pace behind the university buildings and through the thickening woods. Ahead of him the bleached broken dome of the gazebo shone in the moonlight with skeletal brightness through the trees. He paused and glanced down at the track below. The Russian was walking quickly along the path.

Bolan snaked through the rambling overgrowth of the once peaceful garden and reached the gazebo. It was about sixty yards above the broken trail. The old brick steps leading up to it were choked with shoulder-high weeds.

The courier stopped for a second and checked over his shoulder. Bolan smiled coldly at the officer's caution. The Executioner plucked the flashlight from his combat harness. The man nervously surveyed the darkly tangled slope above him.

Bolan began to signal—a three-flash twice.

Vichinsky stopped. He saw the pinpoint of light blinking between the tree trunks. Bolan signaled once more. The colonel shifted the briefcase upward, so that he actually clasped it under his arm. Then, brushing aside the first of the greenery bending over the narrow garden trail, he began to climb toward the gazebo.

Vines littered the earth, threatening to trip him with each step. In places the old brick walkway had crumbled away and the red dirt was still moist enough to be slippery. Vichinsky paused to catch his breath.

He checked his bearings. He thought he saw a movement at the garden summit, but there were no more flashing signals. Damn, but he hoped the others were moving into position. Vichinsky set off, a little more cautiously now, and yet still stumbled on a broken brick.

Bolan crouched behind a thick clump of weeds. He had moved silently down to meet his contact. The Beretta was in his hand. He heard the messenger grunt as he stubbed his toe.

The warrior rose in the darkness, reaching forward to press the cold muzzle of the silencer behind the courier's ear.

"Stop!"

Vichinsky froze.

"Put down the case.... Now open it."

The colonel did exactly as he was told.

"Okay, walk past it. Now, move...farther. No, don't turn around. On your knees, hands on your head. Kneel!"

Bolan flashed the light for a fraction of a second. His eyes were still on the Russian officer—but in his peripheral vision he caught a quick glimpse of the bills neatly wrapped and stacked inside the case.

Vichinsky was quivering—more in anger than in fear. This amateur had given away his position and the others must be close by.

"This is what you came for," said Bolan, setting down the shopping bag beside him. "Don't move a muscle. You just stay where you are!"

Bolan risked a fast look over the tops of the tall weeds. He could make out the loitering bulk of the escort on the path below. A second shape was flitting through the trees to his right.

Bolan began to step back.

"Here!" shouted Vichinsky, rolling desperately to one side. "He's over here!"

An orange-red tongue of flame split the night as the bullet crackled through the branches above Bolan's head.

35

Primeval instincts took over in the midnight woodland. Bolan padded through the undergrowth. A jungle was a jungle—most especially this peaceful park in the heart of terrorland.

Gsovski fired at a swaying branch. Vichinsky shouted, "No, over there! I think he went that way."

Bolan put down the briefcase and let the KGB hit man blunder past him. He slid the Beretta into his belt and silently extracted the wire loop from his pocket.

The Russian marksman heard something, sensed something and began to turn as the garrote cut a burning line around his throat. He couldn't force a scream out of his ruptured windpipe; his jaw worked uselessly above the cruel caress of the deathwire.

Bolan lowered the limp body behind a screen of goldenrod. He knew the other gunman was about forty feet to his right. The Executioner picked up the dead man's pistol and fired two quick shots in that direction.

"Stop shooting, Gsovski! It's me over here!"

Bolan marked his position. Brushing the ferns gently to one side, placing each step with silent precision, the nightstalker stealthily circled toward his prey. There was a third man somewhere on the slope. Bolan heard a twig snap.... Thug Three was approaching from the left flank. Okay, Gsovski's pal would go first.

The slight rustle of the Beretta being drawn from his belt gave Bolan away. He heard the faint hiss of indrawn breath. He could feel the blood heat of the killer. Sharkov called out in a hoarse whisper, "Gsovski?"

"Nope," replied Bolan as he squeezed the trigger.

The bullet plowed a white-hot furrow through Sharkov's shoulder, but still he managed to fire back. The blinding roar of the Russian's cannon sent bullets shredding through the greenery.

Batyuk, seeking the enemy's trail, had his eyes fixed on the flickering flashes of gunfire under the birch trees. The abandoned briefcase tripped him headlong.

Bolan fired a burst in the direction of the sound, taking a quick pace sideways between shots, slowly moving toward the higher ground.

Sharkov suddenly appeared out of the darkness. He'd dropped his gun as he tried to reload it; it was slippery from the blood gushing down his arm. Now he held a dead branch in his good hand and swung it haymaker-style at Bolan's head.

The American swayed beneath the rushing arc of the crude weapon, and from the crouch position stitched three shots through Sharkov's side. The KGB goon fell to his knees, lingered a moment as if in silent prayer then crumpled forward on his face.

Bolan released the expended magazine from the Beretta and took a fresh clip from his pocket.

A flurry of snapping and crackling sounded below, as Batyuk used the briefcase as a shield to beat his way through the bushes. He broke into the open nearly sixty yards along the trail. The courier himself was less than five paces behind. They raced each other toward the soft yellow safety of the university floodlights. There was no point in wasting another shot.

Bolan squatted, balancing on his heels, catching his breath as the Russian agents fled for their lives. A whistle sounded on the far side of campus, and its shrill alarm was echoed by a siren. Time for him to get out, too.

He'd lost the precious Fabergé egg, Marijana's diary and the money. The scheme was working.

STRAKHOV WAS ALONE in his apartment. It was a rambling old place, large by Soviet standards but commensurate with his privileged rank. He had never noticed how much space he really had, not since those first few weeks following Anna's death, but tonight it seemed as if the very emptiness of his quarters made him nervous. He closed the heavy living-room curtains and carried a bottle of vodka into the study.

He could no longer pretend to be concentrating on his overview report. He was as ready as he was ever going to be to present it to the chairman. He straightened the papers in their file folder and put them away in the wall safe.

It was well after midnight. Had Vichinsky made contact? He poured himself another tot of the pale brown vodka. Did they have this Kelsen character in custody? What was taking Vichinsky so long? Perhaps he should have gone himself.

The buzzer sounded.

Strakhov waited at the open door.

He'd never seen Vichinsky look so bedraggled. His shoes were badly scuffed; the bottoms of both trouser legs were smeared with patches of dried mud, and his hair, usually so carefully combed, fell down the side of his face in unkempt strands. Strakhov was an expert at reading faces and what he saw in the colonel's rigid expression was failure.

"The diary?" Strakhov grated.

Vichinsky nodded, holding up the bag. "I

have the things he brought. And Batyuk recovered the money. But the man escaped."

"Well, don't stand there. . . come in."

Strakhov led the way through to his study. Vichinsky put down both the bags he was carrying and crouched to open the briefcase, showing his boss that at least the department funds were still intact.

"Yes, yes, but give me that other bag!"

The man would not get far. They could hand over the matter at any time to the Moscow police. Anyway, one of his key informers might still call with a lead they could act on. What was important now was the diary.

He'd have to humor Vichinsky for a few moments, just as long as courtesy demanded and no more. "I expect you'll want to get off home quickly. But pour yourself a drink first."

Vichinsky was in no hurry. He'd been led on a wild-goose chase around Moscow, confronted a foreign gangster and very nearly been killed for his pains. He drained the glass in one gulp and poured himself another.

Strakhov screwed up the newspaper wrapping and swept it to one side. He looked at the locked journal; in fact, his eyes never left it. "No need to make your report until the morning."

Vichinsky nodded but made no move to leave.

Strakhov touched the smooth leather binding,

as if, like a blind man, he could discern the book's secrets through his fingertips.

He felt his throat constrict; there was a fast, fluttering disturbance dancing somewhere between his stomach and his lungs. He reached for the letter opener—a czarist dagger with the imperial eagles on its hilt. He slid the polished blade through the hasp and snapped open the tiny lock.

He took a deep breath; he was determined that Vichinsky should not see how shaken he was. Strakhov opened the thin volume at random.

From where he sat, Vichinsky could see that the pages were crowded with a fastidiously cramped script.

Strakhov tilted the book closer. "What the...!"

The phone had started to ring. Vichinsky swung around. Perhaps it was someone with information on Kelsen.

It continued to ring as Strakhov sat there mute, enraged. Then he slammed down the diary and stomped to the phone.

"Yes, yes...of course...as soon as possible. I understand.... No, in a matter of minutes."

He put down the receiver and stood there a moment, chewing his lower lip as he stared at the wall.

"There's been a call from Washington. On the hotline. They don't like what we're doing in Central America, and they're prepared to push back. An emergency meeting has been convened to review the options."

Strakhov scooped up the diary and the unopened case containing the Fabergé egg and locked them in his safe. He straightened the framed photograph of Lenin, then turned to his assistant with a curt nod. "I think you should come with me, Colonel. You can tell me everything that happened to you tonight on our way to the Kremlin."

"Certainly, Comrade General, I am more than willing."

"These meetings can be difficult. Blame may be apportioned, diversionary subjects can be raised.... There's no way of knowing what might come up," Strakhov explained. "But if there are any questions at all about the Janus Plan, you will be there to explain it."

Vichinsky suddenly felt sick. Very sick indeed. He wished he had gone home sooner.

BOLAN WAS ANGRY.

He was angry with Strakhov. Angry with himself. He knew he had been playing percentages all the way along. What other choice did a man have when he was that far out on a limb? But he'd felt so certain he was going to catch

Strakhov red-handed. He even had the tiny camera ready to take some fatally embarrassing shots of the man. But the musty apartment was deserted.

Getting inside had proved easier than he'd allowed for—maybe that should have warned him.

Zara had found out the address the same evening she'd introduced him to Panov. The cousin of a friend knew the woman who was Greb Strakhov's part-time housekeeper. A sour bitch, he'd said, but he knew where she worked on Petushka Street. The Romany woman had then driven Bolan past the place on his way to meet Antonov.

The mansion, built by a wealthy merchant in the twilight years of czarist rule, was a sprawling Gothic monstrosity surrounded by a wall. Strakhov had the third floor of the three-storied house to himself.

A KGB snoop, in fur hat and upturned collar, was lurking at the front entrance. Bolan walked along the side streets and made his final approach from the rear. He scaled the wall with no trouble. From there it was a short jump to a ledge that ran around the building. Police cruisers drove slowly past at twenty-minute intervals. Bolan watched one go by from his vantage point, keeping check of the time as he inspected each of the windows in turn.

The side windows of the two main rooms facing west were wired to an alarm system. Bolan wouldn't trust the skylight with its frosted glass; it was probably wired, too. But there was a small window that he decided to risk. Within moments, he'd forced his way inside.

Strakhov, ever vigilant of the security of the state and the Soviet leaders, lived with the assurance that no one would break into his apartment. It wasn't extravagantly stuffed with Western consumer goods like so many of the ruling elite. Bolan was surprised at how ordinary a place it was; almost as surprised as he was to find it empty.

He prowled from room to room. At this late hour he'd felt it doubtful that Strakhov wanted to attract attention to his questionable operation by having a lot of activity at headquarters. Surely the man would have wanted to sit down with the rest of his private collection of Romanov material to read Duchess Marijana's conclusions.

Bolan checked out the study. Standing on the floor by the desk was the dark brown briefcase. A daub of red mud was still caked on the side. Strakhov must have left in a real hurry; and, to be so careless, he must have had his mind fully occupied with other problems. Something big must have come up!

He made another sweep of the apartment, searching even more thoroughly for the Fabergé egg and the journal. Bolan made periodic checks of the street outside, taking care that the movement of the floor-length draperies could not be spotted from below. He had worked his way back to the study when he noticed that the Brezhnev photograph was in a far larger frame than it needed.

It concealed a Victorian safe.

He had to stop twice when the phone rang but within nine minutes, using a sonar device that registered and calculated the tumbling numbers of the combination—ironically of Russian manufacture though supplied by the Stony Man organization—he had cracked the wall safe. The first thing he saw was the familiar leather case of the turquoise egg. He unclasped the doors. The imperial toy was safely cocooned in the velvet.

The diary was lying underneath it. So Strakhov had found time to break the lock before he was called away. Bolan took a rubber band from the glass dish on the desk and wrapped it around the book. He put both objects in the small cloth sack he'd brought and pulled the drawstring tight.

Bolan lifted out the folder from the bottom of the safe. He left the study door ajar and kept one ear cocked for the sound of anyone approaching as he flipped open the file.

He couldn't translate the typewritten copy perfectly, but his fundamental grasp of the language explained its significance. And he understood the diagram. The left-hand side represented the United States. Bolan glanced down the list next to it. It was the eastern net that riveted his attention.

Bolan wanted to light a cigarette; he did not dare to. He needed time to think; he didn't have it. He knew this wasn't a complete listing of every Soviet field agent and KGB operation, but the explanatory chart gave a concise summary of the entire infrastructure of the Reds' subversive army. This wasn't the moment to consider the implications of his find—he had time only to photograph it.

He placed each sheet under the desk lamp and took the shots. The big diagram had to be photographed in two parts. He used up a roll, reloaded and finished the task.

The phone started ringing again as he replaced the papers in the exact order he'd found them. At that moment, in between the repetitive rings, he caught the whirring sound of the elevator cables. Bolan had been concentrating so hard on photographing the KGB plans he did not hear the car draw up outside.

Strakhov was coming back.

36

Bolan replaced the file, closed the safe door and spun the recessed dial of the combination lock.

The phone stopped ringing.

He replaced the Lenin picture.

The elevator door clanked open.

Bolan looked around the study. There was no sign of his visit. There wouldn't be until Strakhov discovered the stolen treasures were now missing.

The key was rattling in the front door lock.

He was too late to cross the hall to the kitchen area and the pantry window. Bolan had no other choice.... He picked up the cloth bag and stepped behind the thick draperies. The bay window they covered had been painted shut long ago, but it was still attached to the alarm wiring.

He remained motionless.

"This matter must be brought to a head. We have to finish it." Strakhov was lecturing his subordinate as he ushered Vichinsky down the hallway. "We have to come to a decision now."

Vichinsky felt absurdly grateful for the way Strakhov had backed him. Questions regarding the recent events in Zubrovna and the pursuit of the American agent had come up in the course of the meeting. Vichinsky had been summoned into the planning room, feeling that his whole career was about to be dashed on the rocks. But to his surprise, Strakhov had not thrown him to the wolves; of course, the major general was ultimately covering himself and protecting the reputation of his department, but Vichinsky was no less thankful for that.

"Drink?"

Vichinsky nodded. He needed one.

Strakhov poured out two stiff measures of vodka.

"The question is how we can best use—" began Strakhov, but the phone started ringing again. He sounded tired when he grumbled, "What do they want this time?"

Strakhov picked up the phone. "Yes...yes, anything you know about him!"

Vichinsky watched his commandant's face as he listened intently to the news from his *stukach*, his stoolie. "At Masha Shukina's? Yes, I know the place.... You're absolutely certain?... No, stay right where you are.... Not long."

He put down the instrument and growled, "He's here, Vichinsky. In Moscow!"

"Who?" Vichinsky was still thinking of his narrow escape at the meeting.

"Phoenix! Karl Kelsen *is* Colonel John Phoenix. You were standing a foot away from him in the park tonight!"

Vichinsky felt giddy. It was all closing in on him with a rush. Things were moving too fast, too dangerously: the gun to his head; the Kremlin briefing; his whole plot unraveling.... Everything was spinning out of control. He managed to force out little more than a plaintive whisper. "But why...why has he come here?"

"For the truth, you fool!" Strakhov had run out of patience. "Or can't you recognize that much anymore?"

Strakhov took a gulp of vodka and gestured to the phone. "That was Yura. He had a few drinks with a young draft dodger tonight. The youth says he knows the foreigner, Karl Kelsen. He met him at Masha Shukina's. The boy's willing to testify if we give him a clean slate. Well, he can miss out on his army service in Siberia! I'm going to pick him up now."

"What shall I do?"

"Phoenix is here searching for the truth about his double. He mustn't find him. You're to go straight to Akinova. Pick up Stefan Boldin and drive him down to my dacha near Dnestropol. We'll hide him there."

"I'll take Lednev, too."

"Take as many men as you need," Strakhov urged. "And kill him at the first sign of any trouble. Now, come, we've no time to waste. Phoenix is so close I can almost smell him."

The two men drained their glasses, then marched down the passage. The front door slammed shut behind them.

Bolan took a deep breath. He'd just made the hardest decision of his life: he knew the information he had photographed was more important than anything else.

He had sacrificed an opportunity to even the score with Strakhov directly. He had avoided executing his enemy. Because the gains to be had from the list were too great to alert the KGB machine that it might have been found. It was the blueprint for his new war against the global terrormasters.

People spoke of the KGB with awe and fear, as if whispering its very name would contaminate the soul. They thought of the Soviet terror machine as some virulent and unbeatable scourge. And it was—to those unfortunates who dared speak out.

But Bolan felt differently. He had fought the Mafia in thirty-eight campaigns, weakening their infrastructure with each thrust, bewildering the enemy with his brazenness and persistence. He would do the same with the KGB; in fact, it was time to abandon the idea that the

Mafia and the KGB were geographically and philosophically separate. They were not.

Intrinsically they represented the same thing. Evil—cancerous and insidious evil.

Bolan knew he would never eradicate the menace. Like the Mob, the sheer manpower of the Soviet secret police was formidable. Amorphous and pervasive, it multiplied like cancer cells over the entire globe. But he would fight them—not only for what they had done to him, but because he felt that the goodness of man must and will prevail over its nemesis.

Bolan had a primordial instinct that man was inherently good, indeed, great. And every ounce of his soldier's strength was devoted to achieving the best that a man could achieve.

Was he a fool? A victim of delusion? Did one man really have a chance of making a difference?

The tentacles of the KGB wrapped themselves around the soul of a fatigued world. But that octopus functioned more like a rodent, or even a seething mass of germs.

The KGB agents were not soldiers, not commandos, not men responsible to themselves. They represented only the boundlessness of Death. They thrived only on the corpses of their victims. The Soviet empire itself was threatened with suffocation by the KGB slime.

Well, they could condemn Bolan to living hell in Siberia.

But first they would have to catch him.

BOLAN HAD TO TAKE ZARA into his confidence. How else could he persuade her to drive him south?

"Tell me about it on the way," she had said. "It is a long journey to Odessa."

She was right.

Yan the Fixer felt so relieved that Zara was ready to take the furniture to the minister's holiday retreat that he never asked her why she had so suddenly changed her mind.

Bolan warned her of the treachery of Masha's nephew. Sometimes you had to take a chance with someone; Zara's eyebrows indicated she'd never taken more of a risk than with "Karl Kelsen"—but for the most part she was careful.

The crates of handcrafted furniture were quickly loaded and within two hours they were on their way.

They stayed with some Romany friends on the first night. After that, the two of them rigged a makeshift tent next to the truck, or napped in the cab on the side of the road. The papers Yan had supplied were examined at intervals, but they were accepted without any awkward questions. No petty official wanted to receive an irate call from a minister in Moscow.

Zara detoured around a forbidden-entry zone. The forests thinned out, the air grew warmer and the sandy yellow soil gave way to the rich dark earth of the heartland steppes. Bolan had always thought the prairies were impressive, but their distances shriveled in comparison with the almost incomprehensible vastness of the Russian landscape.

Imposing whitewashed gates marked the dusty side roads leading to collective farms somewhere far beyond the horizon. Tree-planting schemes withered before the winds. Irrigation schemes seemed abandoned before they were completed.

Only the small plots that villagers were allowed to tend for themselves were already sprouting green with the new crops. What a land this could be if the people were allowed to work it for themselves!

It was midmorning on the third day when Zara pulled the truck over to the embankment of a gurgling stream. She climbed out and stretched under the huge shimmering vault of the azure sky.

"It's in the air," she said.

"What?" Bolan asked her, puzzled.

"Can't you smell the sea?"

"WILL HE HELP YOU?" asked Zara, when she picked up Bolan on the beach outside Orekovo.

"Yes, for a price Zakop will risk it. It's going to be an expensive trip, especially when I told him there would be two of us. Zakop doesn't know the other man is going to be my identical twin." Bolan closed his hand over Zara's. "Are you sure you won't come with me?"

The Gypsy driver shook her head. "I have learned to survive here. I could not do that all over again in another land."

"What did you find out?"

"The minister's gardener helped me unload the furniture. I told him I had to make a delivery at Strakhov's place. He gave me the directions." Zara grinned. "Dnestropol is thirty minutes on the other side of Odessa. The dacha is about two miles farther on along the coast road."

It took them an hour and a half to reach the seashore village of Dnestropol, because Zara drove them along a narrow country road around the back of the mineral lakes. "I want to make sure we can get back to Orekovo after dark. If we use the main road we'll be stopped for sure."

They came out onto the coastal highway near a summer home that had been converted into a sanatorium. They turned right and followed the sweeping curve of the bay. The Black Sea had earned its name. Bolan watched the dark inky waters splashing the shingle on the far side of the road.

"I think it's coming up on the right, behind that row of poplars."

Zara drove past so that Bolan could get a good look at the dacha. The place was worthy of the major general. It was a huge wooden chalet, painted green and brown, set back from the road on its own exclusive estate. Apart from a dilapidated boat house farther on the beach side of the road, there were no other buildings along this stretch. The privacy must have suited Strakhov fine.

"Can we get up into those hills?" Bolan asked, pointing to behind the estate.

"Let's find out," said Zara.

About a mile beyond the dacha, on the shore of the next secluded cove, was a small ice-cream kiosk. Zara bought two scoops of the confection and jumped back into the cab. "There's a gravel track we can follow. Used to be a vineyard up there. It's abandoned now."

She drove them as far as she could, then they left the truck and walked along heath-covered hillside. The path brought them to a stand of stunted pine trees. The overlook gave them a good view of Strakhov's property; it was almost directly below them.

The estate was a wedge-shaped acreage on the narrow strip between the shoreline and the coastal hills. To the left, the stately row of poplars formed its eastern boundary, dividing the garden from the open cabbage fields of a neighboring collective. Strakhov's grounds were mostly grass, and much of that unmowed, with a stagnant pond and rambling orchard bordering the stream that marked the back of it.

On the right-hand side of the house was a large wooden shed that served as a garage and behind it a greenhouse.

Bolan calculated the approximate distance across the brick-lined patio from the garage to the side door of the house.

One of Vichinsky's sentries was washing down the black sedan parked in the driveway. A second guard came out from the kitchen to join them.

The two men were too far away for their voices to carry up the hillside. Bolan watched as the newcomer said something to the man cleaning the car. He dropped the soapy rag and reluctantly offered his partner one of his own cigarettes.

"They look bored," said Zara.

"Yeah, and that just might make them careless."

"How many do you think are there?"

"Four, I'd say," replied Bolan. He pointed to the big Volga. "There's only one car. Strakhov's second-in-command must be inside with the prisoner."

The smoker wandered down the garden path, tossed a pebble in the pond and turned to slowly survey the wild slopes on the other side of the stream. Bolan and the woman shrank into the shadows beneath the trees.

"Look.... Who's that?" whispered Zara. She poked her finger toward a small window set high under the carved eaves at the rear of the dacha. The pale oval of a man's face stared out at the fleece-lined sky.

The distance that separated them now was greater than in Revolution Square, but Bolan had no doubt who it was who gazed longingly from the confines of the top room. It was the guy he'd come to find; the man he was going to take back.

He would give his double the opportunity to cooperate. Despite the danger he was in, the prisoner might not come quietly. Still, Bolan would give him that chance. It was better odds than Strakhov had allowed.

His callous threat echoed in Bolan's mind: *"Kill him at the first sign of trouble!"*

37

So it came down to this....

Bolan was alone.

A friend of the night.

And that's the way it would always be.

Bolan watched, and waited.

Then he moved as silent as a wraith of mist, gliding over the stony bed of the stream bordering the back of the lawns. The dark wall of poplars loomed like sentinels ahead of him, blocking out the starry spangle above the horizon and the dim glow from the far-off lights of Odessa. A crow uttered a muted caw as it performed a restless dance on a nearby birch. A cricket chirped in the grass.

Bolan's pulse throb matched the flicking digits of his chronometer as the seconds flew by.

He was in a race against time.

Zara was waiting in the truck behind the boat house near the beach. "We must leave within forty minutes," she had warned him, "if I'm to get you back to Orekovo by two o'clock."

That was the deadline Zakop had given him

when they made the deal. They had to put out to sea no later than two in the morning. And Bolan knew if he showed up with the other man over his shoulder, then Zakop would know for sure that they weren't Bible-thumping evangelists. The fisherman might want to raise his price, or he might not risk taking them across at all.

Bolan cautiously raised his head above the level of the bank and watched the house. There should have been at least one man circling the grounds.

Light from the kitchen window threw a pale yellow square on the patio bricks. It lit up the sentry as he strolled by outside. They were getting careless, thought Bolan, but he refused to feel overconfident.

It was still several top KGB guns against his solitary Beretta.

He withdrew the pistol from its holster and climbed up into the long grass. The reflection of the moon shimmered on the surface of the pond to his left. A frog croaked in the weeds as the deathshadow stalked along the edge of the orchard toward the greenhouse.

A light showed through the window of the room where they were keeping his double captive. There was probably one soldier in there with him, or else on guard outside the bedroom door. Whichever, Bolan had to reach his target before the others could put a bullet through his brain.

Bolan crouched behind a withered apple tree, waiting for the lookout to complete another circuit of the garden. In the ghostly moonlight the guy looked like the squat hardman who had been washing the sedan that afternoon. The sound of the sentry's footsteps diminished as he wandered up the front drive.

A small door led into the back of the wooden shed. Bolan eased it open and slipped inside. The big black limo was parked squarely in the center of the floor. It took a few moments for Bolan to accustom himself to the deeper gloom within the garage.

He carefully skirted the cleaning pail and moved to the far end of the workbench, where he found a pile of old rags. Bolan tucked the gun in his belt.

He picked up several cloths, slit them into strips with his knife and quickly knotted them together. Then he went to the car and unscrewed the gas cap. He took one end of the rag rope and fed it into the tank, then drew it back out until the other end touched the floor. He checked again through the grimy panes of the side window facing the house. Nothing. No one out there.

Retreating to the farthest corner, Bolan took a pack of cigarettes from his pocket. He extracted one and located a book of matches. Cupping his hands, and further shielding the brief flame with his body, he lit the cigarette and took one deep drag. Then he jammed it sideways through the back of the matchbook and shut it tight.

Crouching, knife in hand again, he gently positioned this crude time-fuse so that it just touched the end of the gasoline-soaked rags. If the fumes didn't ignite prematurely, it should give him about . . . .

The main door creaked open. "Uksov? What the hell are you. . . uhh!"

A silver flash was all the sentry saw before the blade buried itself in the hollow of his throat. He swallowed against the cold steel and felt the warm rush of his lifeblood gushing from the severed pipe. The Executioner caught him before he hit the ground.

Bolan propped the body against the rear fender, pulled out the knife and wiped it on the shoulder of the dead man's jacket.

One down.

Bolan had guessed right from his earlier reconnaissance. It was a good twenty yards from the garage to the kitchen door, vaguely illuminated by the light from the side window.

He stepped outside and was poised to make his move when the patrolling guard came strolling around from the back garden. Bolan realized the man he'd killed must have come directly from the house. He turned to greet the guard.

"Cigarette?" he growled.

"You're always smoking mine," Uksov complained. But he shifted the submachine gun to the crook of his left arm and reached for his cigarettes anyway. "Here...."

The rest of his offer was slurred into the grunting explosion of his last breath, as The Executioner rammed the point of the knife hard up under Uksov's rib cage. The wicked blade sliced straight through his heart.

Two down.

Bolan ran to the back door. The fuse was still smoldering. He had to move fast. Time, like the fuse, was running out!

The kitchen was empty. A kettle boiled on the stove. Evidently the first soldier had been making some tea when he decided to investigate the garage.

A short passage led from the kitchen to the main room. The door was half open; a single table lamp was still switched on in there. With the silenced Beretta ready, Bolan peered around the corner.

Lednev was stretched out full length on a comfortable leather couch. His shoelaces were undone, and a black-market imported skin magazine had fallen down across his chest; his sweaty fingers still had hold of it. There was a smirk on his face as he slept.

Bolan picked up the plump pillow from the

other armchair and padded across the room to stand over the KGB marksman.

He clamped the cushion over the man's face, pushed the muzzle of the silencer toward it and pulled the trigger twice.

Lednev twitched once.

Three gone.

Tendrils of smoke were still curling upward from the blackened holes in the cushion as Bolan swiftly mounted the stairs.

He automatically oriented himself to the layout of the dacha's interior. The room he was seeking should be on the left, opposite the top of the stairs. An empty chair stood outside the door, marking it as the temporary cell.

Bolan gently tried the handle.

Locked.

He took two paces backward and smashed it open with one well-placed kick. He executed a sideways tumble into the room, coming rapidly to his feet, the Beretta sweeping the room.

Stefan Boldin had been sitting on the edge of the bed, reading by candlelight. He jumped to his feet in surprise as the big apparition rushed in.

They stood staring at each other for a second—a mirror image in flesh.

There was compassion in Bolan's eyes. He, too, knew what it was like to be trapped in a false identity.

At that instant, the impostor really didn't look like him at all. Brothers against the system maybe, but not the same man.... Boldin had bewilderment and fear written across his face, and that made him quite different from Mack Bolan.

The impersonator grabbed the candlestick, fearful that he was going to be executed on the spot. It was the only weapon he had to defend himself. He took a wary pace to the left.

Bolan circled counterclockwise. He lowered the muzzle of his gun, then dropped his hand completely to his side. This man had fired a blank in Zubrovna. Bolan meant the man no harm....

A floorboard creaked behind him. Bolan spun around to see Vichinsky standing in the doorway behind them. A checkered gown hung open over his pajamas. He held a Tokarev automatic in his hand.

His startled eyes flashed white in that narrow pockmarked face. There were two of them in front of him! And he had them both!

The gas tank exploded with a roar, blowing out the side of the garage wall. The incinerating blast showered glass fragments and flaming wood over the side of the chalet.

In the momentary confusion, Boldin drew back his arm to throw the heavy candlestick.

Instinctively, Vichinsky twisted in his direction and fired. The Polish prisoner was thrown back onto the bed.

It was a split-second decision that cost Vichinsky his life.

"You bastard!" Bolan snarled, as he squeezed the trigger. "You've cheated me!"

Vichinsky staggered back across the landing, clutching his dressing gown about him as if it would protect him from the deadly hail of hot lead. Bolan kept shooting until the final hit spun the KGB colonel around and he tumbled head first down the stairs.

The faded paintwork had caught fire outside, and a burning plank had been hurled through the kitchen window. The whole west side of the dacha was going up in flames.

It was too late to do anything for the pretender. Vichinsky's one shot had smashed through his face. No one would recognize him now.

Bolan started to tug down the top of the sheet. It was eerie—it was like covering himself with a shroud.

He paused, even though he could hear the flames crackling fiercely below. If Strakhov was confused and frustrated and angry by the burglary of his apartment, then he'd be really upset when he got the report on the charred carnage at his dacha!

Bolan slipped off the chain he wore, removed

only the Gypsy amulet, and draped the chain around the impostor's neck. He looked down at April's ring lying there against the stranger's skin.

It was his past he was leaving behind.

Phoenix could return to the ashes from which he had sprung.

EPILOGUE

Kirov poured the brandy.

Bolan swirled the Rémy Martin in his glass.

The duchess had wine. She lifted the crystal goblet, softly glinting in the candlelight. "To victory, Mr. Bolan."

The Fabergé egg and the diary were displayed upon the fourth placemat at their dinner table.

"I knew you would come back," she said, sipping the last of the Pouilly-Fuissé. It was not so much an affirmation of her trust in Bolan's strength and his will to endure, as it was a hint of her mystical insight into his destiny. "You have made an old woman very happy, Mr. Bolan. He has given us fresh hope, hasn't he, Alexei?"

Her companion nodded gravely.

"But tell me, ma'am, what was in the diary that so intrigued Strakhov he'd kill to get his hands on it?"

The duchess brought the wineglass to her lips before she spoke. "The man is consumed by the mystery surrounding the fate of the Romanovs," she said. "He thought the contents of the journal would reveal the whereabouts of some surviving members of that ill-fated family. Perhaps he had the idea he could use them for his own venal puposes within the Soviet socialist republic."

"So what was in the book?" Bolan repeated.

The duchess lifted her hand at the interruption. Her aged features became animated as she continued her explanation.

"Please bear with me," Bolan's benefactress said. "I would never let the information Strakhov seeks fall into his hands. The diary he got from you was not a diary at all, just the bindings from the original."

"But what did it say?" Bolan persisted.

"You've met my friend, Professor Farson. He sent me a package before your first arrival here. It amused me, being handwritten in Russian Cyrillic script. Excellent piece of work," said the duchess, warming to her tale as she realized she'd now thoroughly aroused Bolan's curiosity. She would play the game a bit longer.

"Please, Duchess Marijana, you must tell me what was in the—"

The duchess chuckled at her performance. But it was time for the denouement.

"Why, Mr. Bolan," said the diminutive noblewoman, "it was the story of one man's war against the Mafia. It listed every mobster killed, every battle fought. Two thousand homicides documented in detail. Mr. Farson has superb intelligence access and he told me that together with a colleague of his, a certain Mr. McCarter, they were able to compile this extraordinary record. I thought it would be amusing to declare war on the KGB. Your history, such as we know it, is just such a declaration. A calling card, you might say. An Ace of Spades. I hope you have no objections. . . ."

Bolan's ice-cold eyes bored into her, riveting her with his gaze.

"No," he said at last. "I have no objections whatever." Then he smiled slightly and stood up. "It's time for me to go. I have a rendezvous with yet another fast boat."

"It was a cunning thing that you did," concluded the duchess. "The ring you left around the neck of your dead impersonator—undoubtedly it helped your escape, convincing those who found it in the ashes that it was John Phoenix who died there. You said that the ring was uniquely yours. It must have been very special. What did it mean to you?"

They lingered in the doorway for a long, silent moment. Bolan, standing erect in his dark clothes, towered over the diminutive duchess. He might have been a Cossack officer reporting to the patroness of his regiment.

"I'm proud to have served you, ma'am."

It was a permissible lie. Who had served whom? But Marijana enjoyed his compliment nonetheless; she decided not to press her questions. She kissed him on both cheeks.

Bolan signaled for Kirov to stay. He did not require the car. Tonight he would walk.

Bolan strode along the Paris pavement knowing that he was taking the first few steps down another long road that he had to walk alone.

The microfilm of Strakhov's plans for the KGB's terror network was in his pocket. Bolan knew where he was going. He knew what he had to do.

And nothing was going to stop him now.

The man in the Scotland Yard-type raincoat had been following him for three blocks. Was he KGB? An enemy of the duchess? The Sûreté? CIA? They would always be out there in the shadows—lying in wait for him, or else snapping at his heels. Well, he'd fight them as they came.

A mist was blowing up from the Seine. He was confident he would lose the man behind him in the fog rolling across the boulevard.

It would always be this game of cat and mouse; the test of the hunter and the hunted. But who was the cat, and who was the mouse?

Bolan vanished into the drifting, silvery cloud with an easy catlike grace.

DON PENDLETON'S EXECUTIONER
MACK BOLAN

Sergeant Mercy in Nam...The Executioner in the Mafia
Wars...Colonel John Phoenix in the Terrorist Wars....
Now Mack Bolan fights his loneliest war! You've never
read writing like this before. Faceless dogsoldiers have
killed April Rose. The Executioner's one link with com-
passion is broken. His path is clear: by fire and maneuver, he will rack up hell in a world shock-tilted by terror.
Bolan wages unsanctioned war—everywhere!

GOLD
EAGLE

Available wherever paperbacks are sold.

Mack Bolan's
ABLE TEAM
by Dick Stivers

Action writhes in the reader's own street as Able Team's Carl "Mr. Ironman" Lyons, Pol Blancanales and Gadgets Schwarz make triple trouble in blazing war. To these superspecialists, justice is as sharp as a knife. Join the guys who began it all—Dick Stivers's Able Team!

"This guy has a fertile mind and a great eye for detail. Dick Stivers is brilliant!"

—*Don Pendleton*

Able Team titles are available wherever paperbacks are sold.

GOLD EAGLE

Mack Bolan's

PHOENIX FORCE

by Gar Wilson

Schooled in guerilla warfare, equipped with all the latest lethal hardware, Phoenix Force battles the powers of darkness in an endless crusade for freedom, justice and the rights of the individual. Follow the adventures of one of the legends of the genre. Phoenix Force is the free world's foreign legion!

"Gar Wilson is excellent! Raw action attacks the reader on every page."

—Don Pendleton

#1 Argentine Deadline   #6 White Hell
#2 Guerilla Games   #7 Dragon's Kill
#3 Atlantic Scramble   #8 Aswan Hellbox
#4 Tigers of Justice   #9 Ultimate Terror
#5 The Fury Bombs   #10 Korean Killground

GOLD EAGLE

Phoenix Force titles are available wherever paperbacks are sold.

BOLAN FIGHTS AGAINST ALL ODDS TO DEFEND FREEDOM!

Mail this coupon today!